Moon Dance

The Blood Pack Book One

Kay Zempel

Black Valentine Press

eBook ASIN: B0FGW1DQWV
eBook ISBN: 979-8-9995062-0-7
Amazon Paperback ISBN: 979-8-9995062-2-1
Ingram Spark ISBN: 979-8-9995062-1-4

Book Cover by The Red Fox Creative.
Scene Break Illustration by mgs.designs.
This book is typeset in Riesling and
Fraunces 9pt.

For the depressed, the anxious, and the introverted.

Author's Note

The world of the Blood Pack books is similar to our own, and as such, contains many of the issues, bigotry, and cruelty we find in our own. While I would like to think I handled these topics with as much grace and nuance as possible, I understand there are topics some readers would wish to avoid.

Content that readers may find triggering are domestic violence and stalking; discussion and depiction of depression; suicidal ideation and attempted suicide (in the past); infertility and miscarriage; references to child abuse; and on-page blood and gore. Content that may not be triggering but may still not be for every reader are language and explicit sexual content. No dogs or children are harmed in this novel.

If you suspect you are experiencing intimate partner abuse or violence, contact the National Domestic Violence Hotline in the United States by calling 1.800.799.SAFE (7233) or by texting "START" to 88788.

If you are in the United States and experiencing a mental health crisis, help is available. Call or text 988 to reach the 24/7 suicide prevention hotline. You are not alone.

Chapter One: Christi

I hated waiting, but I really needed a job. I could always dip into my savings, but I wouldn't unless I absolutely had to. You never knew when you would have to start over. I definitely didn't anticipate it the first time, so I was going to make damn sure I had a safety net for the next.

The South Bay Bureau outpost, like any government department office, had long wait times and an even longer line of patrons. There were faeries with fluttering gossamer wings, holding their documentation tightly. One missed document could mean rejection today, and they would have to come back again to repeat the whole process. Vampires with red eyes and sunglasses yawned at what was an early hour for them, though it was near closing time. Most patrons passed as human, and they blended in just like I did.

"Now serving guest number 150," the automated voice rang out, as the screens around the office changed from 149 to 150. I checked the strip of paper with my number on it and groaned. 160. I should have brought a book to help pass the time, but instead, I was stuck watching the news streaming on the screens along the walls.

"—news for this hour: riots break out in Wyoming today as protesters rally against the Plains Plateau proposal. Pilgrams enter the Kingdom for the annual Veneration of Our Lady. Banditry is on the rise for train travel along the

Wilderness. More on what you need to know before you go, at seven. And now, we continue our exclusive news coverage of the anniversary of the Reveal. It has been eleven years since a magical virus caused a global pandemic and forced the supernatural to reveal their existence. We tune in now as President Ciarán delivers a message of hope and cooperation from the Oval Office."

I rolled my eyes. We still hadn't elected a woman as president, but were perfectly fine putting one of the fair folk in office. He literally had to obey the whims of the Tuatha Dé Danann, but that was fine compared to a competent woman.

"Now serving guest number 160," the automated voice stated.

Finally. I had waited over half an hour, and not patiently. I gathered my things and walked up to the window. My heart sank when I got there. *Just my fucking luck.*

The agent was a middle-aged woman with a face heavily frozen with Botox. A bad bleach job covered any gray hair she may have had. Her body looked toned in the way that only several hours of daily exercise could produce. In an age where you could buy a glamor from any hedge witch, it seemed excessive. She smirked when she saw me, smug that she could hold a modicum of power over me. Jessica Ashton was my least favorite agent to work with at the Bureau. She started in the office about four years ago, and I went out of my way to avoid her if I could. She thought she was better than me, even when she'd bullied me in high school. She

8

figured that her life was so superior to mine because she married shortly after high school and immediately started breeding equally nasty children.

As though I would want to ever step into her life. The thought churned my stomach.

I swallowed my pride and plastered on my most pleasant smile.

"Driver's license and bureau ID," Jessica demanded, even though we've known each other for over 20 years. I rifled through my bag to find my identification.

"It's Christi Owens," I told her. "I'm a licensed and registered witch, you know that."

I should have had my cards ready before I came up to the window. The news had distracted me, or maybe it was the date.

"I know of a Christiana Bianchi," she said unkindly. What I wouldn't give to ask the Goddess to hex her right now. I finally got hold of my IDs, and one of my bracelets got stuck on the closure of my bag. *This fucking day*. I yanked it free. Thankfully, it didn't break. It was a good luck charm, which I sorely needed right now.

I slammed my cards on the counter. "Christiana Owens," I told her through my teeth. "Bureau ID is 284190558004."

She slid my license back to me through the slot in the window separating her from the riffraff of the office. Her fake nails clicked loudly on the keyboard as she ignored me, her gaze on her computer. Goddess, we were too old for this kind of passive aggressive bullshit.

When she looked back at me, she asked with a yawn, "And what brings you into the Bureau of Magical Affairs today?"

I sighed heavily. She knew why I was here. I tapped my foot restlessly. "I was hoping," I said, digging my nails into my hands, "to see if there are any job openings for a witch."

More clicks on the keyboard sounded, and Jessica looked at me. "I'm sorry, but there doesn't seem to be any openings that meet your profile. The Bureau would have contacted you via email should a job opening been available."

Like hell, there weren't any jobs open. After the Reveal, magic bars, magic shops, even magic brothels had sprung up out of nowhere. They'd quickly become regulated under the new Bureau of Magical Affairs. The government had tried referring to it as BOMA, but we all just called it the Bureau. If you had magic and wanted to make some money, you had three options: work for the Bureau on one of their many requests, work for the magitech industry, or work for the local alchemy. As a witch, I had an additional option to work for the coven.

As someone who had been raised in the old magics, I wouldn't trade hard-won secrets to the corporate magitech trash for all the money in the world, unlike some people I knew. I could always ask Rachel for a shift or two at the alchemy, but I knew her answer already. That left the Bureau or the coven, and my relationship with the coven was strained at the moment. I needed a job, not just to make money, but to keep me from sitting in my house alone with my thoughts. This was a hard time of year for a lot of people. Magic's reveal came at a huge cost and most of us, human or no, had been changed forever. Alone in my head—well, the darkness lurked there, and I have pulled myself out of it enough times to know that I was the best version of myself with a project.

"Please, Jessica," I begged, softening my face and my voice. "I need a job."

Jessica frowned, only her lips moving as the rest of her plastic face stayed in place. Her voice was harsh and shrill when she responded, "That's not my problem, Christi! Maybe if you were nicer to the other organizations, you wouldn't have to come crawling to me. I don't have anything for you, I mean it!"

I exhaled through my nose, biting my lips to keep tears from falling. My stomach clenched, and I knew if I opened my mouth, a sob would escape and it wouldn't go back in. I nodded silently. "Okay. Thanks anyway," I said, staring at the floor as I grabbed my license and stuffed it into my pocket.

When I turned away, she sighed and whispered loudly, "How desperate are you?"

I turned back to her and raised an eyebrow. "What do you mean?"

"I mean that I need a favor, and if you help me, maybe I could pull a few strings, get you on some of the big projects coming our way."

On one hand, that sounded like risky business. On the other hand, I needed to pay my bills and buy dog food. *You have your savings*. I could practically see the angel on my shoulder. But the devil sat on the other shoulder and responded, *but you never know when you'll need to run.*

"I'm listening."

Jessica leaned in conspiratorially.

"The coven needs a book. *Hysop's Bestiary*. Apparently, *Harold's* on Main Street has a copy, but you didn't hear it from me."

"Why can't they just buy it?"

"It's not my job to know. Bring the book to me next week," Jessica responded. She slid a small envelope across the counter to me. "And more importantly, plant this in the shop."

This sounded fishier by the minute. I bit the inside of my lip. Sensing my indecision, Jessica started to pull the envelope back.

I trapped it with my fingers. "I'll do it," I told her. "But the next job I get better be big."

She smirked at me. "Oh, it'll be a big one alright."

Weird, but okay.

I should have felt a weight lifting. There would be a job. There would be money. I was still free. Instead, I felt the walls closing in on me. My eyes flitted to the exits. The darkness pooled around my feet, threatening to pull me under. I hurriedly pushed the envelope into my bag. I could feel it radiating out, like a beacon. I held my bag in my hands, as though the envelope within would contaminate me if I held it too close to my body. I shouldn't be this tied up in knots over a slip of paper. Sure, this was under the table, but it was Bureau business. It had come from Jessica, though, and that left a sour taste in my mouth.

"Thanks, Jessica," I said with a fake grin.

She rolled her eyes at me. "Yeah, whatever. Bye."

Ines sat elegantly on one of the booths in bar of the Crimson Dahlia. Moody, otherworldly jazz played in the background. The Dahlia had been one of the first supernatural bars to open after the pandemic. Since the coven owned and operated it, the Bureau couldn't touch it. It had sprung up in the industrial part of town—a large warehouse converted into a high-end lounge, complete with a bar, a nightclub, a gambling hall, a fighting ring, hotel rooms, and apartments. It was designed as an Art Deco bordello with lots of draped crimson velvet, plush black carpet, gold fixtures with crystal chandeliers, and plenty of mirrored surfaces. Many creatures of the night hung around the Dahlia, Ines included, which catered to them as much as possible. The club was exclusive, members only. Since Ines rented rooms here, we could come and go as we pleased.

I plopped in the booth next to her. She picked up the magazine she had been reading, swinging it in my direction.

"Have you seen this shit?" she asked, tossing it on the table. The words *Nothing Is Impossible* were emblazoned in red across a sharp photograph of a woman. She looked powerful, arms folded across her chest, head held high. Her blue eyes pierced through you, and her black hair, pinned up, was just messy enough to look like it was on purpose. She wore dramatic eyeliner and red lips to complete an all-black outfit. In smaller print were the words: *Alice O'Shea, Apex Predator of the Wilderness.*

"They mention nothing about her terrorizing the Aviary," Ines ranted, "just how wonderful she is for giving lost shifters a refuge. Give me a break."

"That's where your friends are, yeah?" I asked, still looking at the cover.

Ines nodded. "They really need help. Not only did the she-wolf buy out the land from under them, but children have started to go missing," she said, reclining back to cross her legs. "Last time we spoke, they wanted me to visit."

Getting reliable cell service in the Wilderness was difficult. The situation at the Aviary could have gotten better—or worse—in the meantime.

"When was that?"

"A month or so. There's a reason the postal service is called snail mail."

"They haven't upgraded to magitech yet?" I asked,

absently flipping through the magazine until I paused on the two-page spread of Alice O'Shea. Something about her stare bothered me. I shivered. Alice had taken control of the pack a couple years ago, and since then, had made her pack famous. Whenever shifters were mentioned, so was the O'Shea pack.

"It's hard to upgrade when your tech gets stolen before it even makes it on the train," Ines scoffed. "Besides there's not much tech left after the pack takes their cut."

I shook my head. Unless you had a satellite phone or magitech in the Wilderness, you had to rely on good, old-fashioned letters.

"Where's Rach?" I asked, and Ines gave a little shrug. Her baby face made the movement adorable and sweet instead of the actual, impatient gesture I knew it was.

Ines picked up the magazine again, gazing that the woman on the cover. "If only she wasn't such a sexy bitch. Then we wouldn't have to see her *stupid* face everywhere."

A human thrall came up to our table, offering her arms to Ines. She looked at the poor girl with disdain, giving her a tight-lipped frown and a quick shake of her head. Thralls circulated the club. They made a little money off their blood, but most were hoping to be turned. That was how Ines and I had met, but I had been looking for something a bit more permanent than undeath. That seemed like a long time ago now.

"Who's ready for some drinks?" Rachel exclaimed with a shimmy that almost spilled the three glasses she somehow fit in her hands. I grabbed my Manhattan quickly before she could spill it all. She slid in on Ines' other side, sliding a goblet of synthetic blood her way. Ines preferred it to the human stuff, though I had never thought to ask her why. Rachel's drink bubbled and smoked like someone had dropped dry ice into it. It was showy and fun, but I doubted that made the drink taste any different.

I sipped my drink slowly, relaxing for the first time all day. We made quite a trio. There was me, a witch rocking the latest bohemian trends that came in plus sizes and inevitably had dog hair on them. Ines didn't even look like a typical vampire. She instead had dyed her long waves cotton candy pink and wore ruffled, puffy gowns in the same shade. Only her red eyes marked her as a vampire, and the round, rose-tinted glasses that covered them. Rachel, on the other hand, wore all black. She was tiny, both extremely short and thin. Her baggy black tee contrasted her skintight black jeans. She tied up her black hair—with teal money pieces—into space buns. The style showed off her undercut and the various jewelry sticking out and dangling from her ears and eyebrows. Ines wore white gloves with pearl buttons, and Rachel had a septum ring.

"What'd I miss?" Rachel asked excitedly. Ines pointed to the magazine. Rachel laughed. "Hot! Next question."

I laughed, but Ines pursed her lips. "Really? I didn't think she would be your type."

"I mean, I love me a doe-eyed, innocent-looking angel

baby," Rachel winked at Ines. "But I don't think there's a soul on earth who doesn't find the O'Shea alpha sexy."

"Striking, yes," I disagreed, "but I wouldn't say *sexy*. There's something *off* about her."

Both Rachel and Ines leaned in to look, each making a *hm* noise.

"I don't think so," Rachel said, as Ines expressively questioned, "You think so?"

I laughed, "Never mind then. Oh, I went to the Bureau today. That was a big old waste of time."

"Do we have a job or not?" Ines asked impatiently. I didn't know how old she actually was, but she looked somewhere in her late 20s. Her face still had baby fat. It wasn't until she smiled with bloody fangs that I was reminded of her predatory nature. Still, she made our jobs easier—except when she didn't.

"No job," I huffed, "but I did get a tip. It's likely nothing. Any shifts coming up at the alchemy, Rach?"

She pointed at me with all the menace she could muster, which wasn't much, "You are not allowed in *my* alchemy! The last time I let you take a shift, I nearly had a strike over personal protective equipment and worker safety. It's not a chemistry lab and you can't treat it like one."

Before the Reveal and the following pandemic, I had been a pharmacist. I had worked in chemistry labs through undergraduate and graduate school, so working in an alchemy came easily. But I made sure to follow the protocols and use proper technique, which most self-taught alchemists didn't know how to do. I may have worked slowly, but my potions were excellent and Rachel knew that.

I sighed, but raised my hands up in surrender. "Well, just the tip then."

Rachel giggled as Ines smiled, fangs gleaming. Her voice purred like a cat, "When do we start?"

"There's no *we* this time. The coven's the client, and we are already on their shit list thanks to the rat incident."

"They should have been more specific," she growled. Her accent had always seemed broadly European to me, but what did I know? She could have been living here for a hundred years. We didn't talk about her past, and that seemed to work for us.

The 'rat incident' had been our last job for the coven. Sometimes being a magical problem-solver involved pest control. Ines and I had vanquished a talking rat infestation that was taking over the natural rat population. Just put that on my resume: *Exterminator. Ecologist. Non-magical species conservationist.* However, Ines had taken the extermination to the extreme and wiped out all traces of the talking rats. They'd apparently been the only colony of talking rats on the coast, and the rats were on the endangered magical species list. The coven looked on it as a giant fuck-up and put us in timeout. No new jobs for us.

That happened six months ago.

Since then, I'd done odd jobs when I got them, so I could

pay my bills. It didn't keep me from feeling blocked and stuck. It wasn't all Ines's fault, but that made me feel even worse.

"There's always the Aviary," Ines suggested, and I made a noncommittal sound. Going through the Wilderness wasn't easy, and I couldn't just pick up and leave for a job with no expiration date. I had Sadie to take care of and my family to consider.

"Just forget it," I told her. "Hopefully, this tip will put us back in the coven's good graces."

Ines laughed, throwing her head back. "As though the coven has good graces."

"You know what I mean."

"Yes, yes, we scratch their backs, they scratch ours. Stupid witches."

"You mispronounced it," Rachel joked with a grin. "And I did not come here for happy hour to talk about work."

"You missed happy hour, little mouse," Ines teased. "Late as usual."

"Some of us have real jobs! You try coming in from downtown on a Friday!"

My heart warmed as they bickered. After my day, I had needed this. I needed to be reminded of what I *do* have, instead of what I *don't*. But the day still needed to be celebrated, like it or not.

"Can we get it over with?"

Rachel pointed at me. "No tears! Drinks after work are

supposed to be fun. Don't make me get shots."

"Don't encourage her," Ines quipped, gently nudging me. "She doesn't need an excuse." Ines turned pointedly to Rachel. "Remember the last time you ordered a round of shots."

"*No!* That's the fun of it. You get drunk, you argue, you wake up in a stranger's bed, and you take a pick-me-up potion so you can go to work."

"And then crash when the pick-me-up potion wears off," I added, shaking my head. "Seriously, though, I need to do this before I can truly enjoy the night."

Rachel bowed her head and Ines leaned back. She motioned for me to start.

I raised my glass. "To Troy," I said shakily. "I wish we had had more time together. May the Goddess continue to protect and guide you while I cannot."

Rachel lifted her glass, adding, "To Troy, the best friend a girl could have asked for. I still wish you were actually my brother instead of the loser I'm stuck with. Thank you for all the times I stayed on your couch. If you are looking down on us now, I hope you know that I was the best at annoying you." She paused before adding, "Amen."

Ines sighed reluctantly, and I waved her on.

"To Troy. We may have never met, but your loss is still deeply felt."

The three of us clinked our glasses together, "To Troy!"

I took a sip, then wiped my face with the palm of my

hands. I didn't want to cry here. I could grieve later. This was a celebration.

I touched the rings that I kept on a chain around my neck. I whispered, once more, just for me. "Happy anniversary."

Chapter Two: Derrick

I knew the vote would happen, but I had assumed it would take more time. We'd barely had time to mourn. For six months, I had been fucked up and strung out. Not once did my useless beta or my equally useless hunters challenge me. I rescued or trained them, and they couldn't do the decent thing. They should have given me a fucking chance. Instead, the omega had woken me up gently and given me the notice of a vote of no confidence. They forced me to watch as the pack I had rebuilt, the pack that I sacrificed everything for, voted to dissolve.

The fucking cowards left before the morning. They had planned for their exit before the vote even happened. Not one of them stayed with me. I couldn't even blame them. I knew what they were thinking: Sarah was the leader and Nate was the brains. Without either of them, there was no point in challenging me.

Sarah was gone. We had been their alpha pair. Sarah had been an alpha worth fighting for. But if she was worth it in life, wouldn't she be worth it in death? My wife had died. I would go to war with every goddamn werewolf pack that stood in my way if that could bring her back. The pack knew that I was no Sarah. Still, *I* was their fucking alpha by right. They could have at least *challenged* me! Cowards, the lot of them. When I met the bitch responsible for this, I would kill her.

After the vote, I stared at the check the treasurer handed me. I should have known then, when he showed up to the vote with checks for everyone, that voting to dissolve was just a formality. As part of the alpha pair, I knew how much money the pack had. I had helped manage it. Fuck, I majored in finance. Yet, after distributing it to the pack as they moved on, it wasn't enough. Either I was shit with money, or the pack was larger than I thought it was. Sarah would have known how large the pack was. She was good at that sort of thing.

There was nothing keeping me here anyway. The pack had made its money in tourism. That decision had been all me, by the way. Leading tours through the desert helped take us from my father's dinky cult to a legitimate shifter pack. *I* did that. Not Sarah. Not Nate. *Me!*

As I handed the keys for the fleet of utility vehicles to the new owners at our storefront, I wanted to scream, yank the keys away, and force them to fight me for it. I deserved to fight someone if I was going to lose all that I built, all that I survived. The new owners were out-of-towners in clean dress shoes. They would make the money while they hired guys like me to get dirty. Typical.

There wasn't much else to do after that. Money was tight, but it'd get me to California. I had called up every alpha I knew. All of them were equally useless. I had moved on to calling the brokers. Finally, one knew of a lone wolf renting from a bookwyrm near Los Angeles. If that wasn't who I was looking for, then I was stupider—stupider? More stupid? No, definitely stupider—than I thought.

I packed up the remnants of my life into Big Bertha and slapped her side. The old van better hold up on the drive. She had been a birthday present for Sarah. I had spent weeks restoring her and painted her powder blue, Sarah's favorite color. The paint had started to chip now, and I couldn't remember the last time I serviced the van.

We'd never used it. I had thought that we had time.

I rolled the windows down, letting the breeze in. I wished I had a dog beside me for the drive, but I'd never heard of a shifter having a pet. The lack of companion didn't keep me from sticking my head out the window. I scream-sang along with the radio.

I had done enough wallowing, and now I had to give someone else the news. He would know what to do.

Chapter Three: Nate

My bed called to me in a siren song I could not ignore. Only one more block and I would be home, where I could pass out immediately. Last night's full moon had left me feeling like my bones had broken and knitted themselves together again, which they had. *Twice.*

I considered myself unlucky. Wolf shifters, those born with the wolf inside them, controlled their change and shifted with an elegance I could never master. I'd had the unfortunate fate of getting attacked by a wolf shifter and thus turned into a werewolf, ruled by the whims of the moon rather than my wants. The cold goddess did not care if I lived or died, as long as I obeyed her call.

My body ached, and I was exhausted in a way that even coffee wouldn't fix. After the exertion of the change, my joints ached, radiating out into my muscles. My muscles, not to be ignored, burned from the sheer violence of the shift. I limped, hiding myself behind a large garbage container in a public parking lot. I had stored some clothes in a neat pile there. It didn't matter if they smelled slightly, I was only going to wear them up the stairs and into my bed. Each motion was agony until I was finally dressed.

It was early morning, and few people were out, with even fewer cars driving home from the night shift. Even the vampires were heading home to sleep. I preferred being out this early myself, hating the throng of people that usually patronized Main Street. I liked being alone. It meant fewer smells and sounds for the wolf to experience, less of an assault on my sense. Apart from being a werewolf, I led a rather quiet life.

I'd never planned to move to California, but I'd needed a change of pace. Luckily, after the Reveal, brokers started matching beings like me with the right homes. I couldn't exactly give work history or a bank statement when I'd been a pack beta for much of my adult life. Most human landlords didn't want to be paid in cash.

Let the witches deal with the Bureau. I used the free agents and I got lucky. A literal bookwyrm had needed someone to protect his bookshop hoard while he went on his once-in-a-century mating journey. It paid well. For all their hoarding, I'd never say a dragon was miserly; their generosity might have to be earned, but it was vast. It included an apartment above the shop. There had been some issues to negotiate, like how attached he was to his hardwood floors, and if he'd mind wolf dander. But somehow, the broker had managed to convince him to trust me.

I didn't remember a lot of that year. I referred to it as *the year of the wolf.* My wolf had been so close to the surface that I lost swaths of time to it. Sometimes it would be hours. Or days. When it was bad, I lost weeks and months to the wolf. That year had been the worst.

After that, I stayed to myself mostly. Of course, I

engaged in small talk with the folks who came into the shop, but I didn't leave the apartment unless I needed to. The smells outside made my stomach ache and the sounds gave me a headache. My wolf was constantly on guard in unfamiliar settings, so I stuck to places I knew. Since the bookshop catered to the more magical clientele who could afford the expense, it was pretty quiet unless I had a showing. I had access to all the books I could ever want. Harold's hoard consisted not only of the books in the shop, but his personal collection on the third floor. He kept the real interesting items up there—the books that weren't for sale.

Harold obsessively collected arcana and the occult. Even after the Reveal, wolves were pretty insular. My pack had only concerned themselves with their safety and their strength compared to other packs. I'd struggled with the resources we had, and now I had a whole library to work with. But for all my research, I still hadn't found what I was looking for.

I paused at the door to the stairs that led to my apartment, keys in hand. I smelled salt, and herbs. Maybe rosemary? *Fuck.* I kept my blades upstairs. This was what happened when you got too comfortable. You made mistakes. I should have known better. My shoulders pulled up and I held my back against the wall. My heart raced. *Not again.* I couldn't run away again. Slowly, and as stealthily as I could be, I slid along the wall. It would be much easier if I hadn't put my shoes on, but the scents from the city would really overwhelm me then. My wolf growled in my mind, readying me to fight for its territory. This would be easier if I weren't dealing with the post-shift hangover. My head throbbed as I peeked out behind the wall.

I breathed a sigh of relief. I could handle this threat.

The woman embodied chaos. I had seen her around town, walking her dog or running past the store. I'd wanted an excuse to speak to her, but I couldn't risk it. And here she was, crouched at the entrance of my store, muttering to herself. If she was trying to be inconspicuous, she failed, *badly*. With every move, she jingled. She wore tons of jewelry—bangles and charms on her wrists, jeweled rings on her fingers, chains around her neck. Each move caused them to clatter against each other. Each jingle made my ears hurt, reverberating to my forehead.

Then there was her outfit. She could have at least *tried* to blend in. She wore a billowy, sage green linen skirt that flowed over her body with every movement. It looked like real linen too, so it was expensive. Her crop top was brown, cotton maybe, and it clung to her body. It wasn't exactly out of place for a beach town in Los Angeles, but she looked expertly styled. Thought went into this outfit, an intention most people didn't give their daily wardrobe. Dog hair immediately ruined the effect.

I admired people who dressed well. That alone caught my attention. But her actions intrigued me. Even the wolf in me agreed, content to wait and watch her next move. It had been a long time since I had noticed someone like this. While I was staring, she was *trying* to rob me.

She wasn't a typical thief, though. A stupid thief would have just thrown a brick through the window. She was trying to get in undetected. *Why?*

I strolled over as quietly as I could manage. She didn't even notice me when I stood over her. She ran a hand through her thick, curly black hair, swearing under her breath.

"Hey, can I help you?" I asked gently.

Now that I stood next to her, I could smell the slightly sulfurous odor of magic. I fought the urge to gag as it filled my nose. Just my luck if she was a witch. I did not want to fight this woman, but I kept up my guard in case this got ugly. I didn't know who she was or who she worked for.

She jumped at the sound of my voice and turned to me, her large green eyes going wide as a flush graced her round cheeks. She stood slightly shorter than me, about average height for a woman. Her eyes betrayed an intelligence that did not match her actions.

"Hi," she said stretching it out into two syllables. Her voice was naturally low, but I could tell that she raised it higher. "I don't think you could help. I'm friends with the owner of the shop. He wanted me to open up for him and set aside a book while I waited for him, but he forgot to give me his keys."

She put the heel of her hand to her forehead and pushed

it out in a gesture of forgetfulness. I saw a couple of holes in her story. First, I owned the shop and I would remember if I had a friend like her. Second, the sign clearly stated that the store was closed today. She was a bad liar, but I could play along.

"I live just upstairs," I explained, pointing up. "There's an access to the store through my apartment. I could open it up for you."

Her face lit up, and I struggled not to fall for her act.

"Perfect," she said, in a sharp voice that was clearly her own, before returning to her higher register. "Lead the way!"

"What book did you say you needed set aside?" I asked as she hunted along the bookshelves.

"I didn't," she stated, no-nonsense this time. "But if you wouldn't mind looking, it's *Hysop's Bestiary*."

I could laugh at how easy she made this for me. A tome of that importance would be held on the third floor, only accessible from my bedroom. She had no clue what she looked for. I sauntered over to her and leaned on the bookshelf that she searched.

"Now, that's funny," I said, my voice measured and my arms crossed over my chest, "considering I sold that volume to the coven last week."

The woman stopped her rummaging before turning very

slowly to me.

"You own the bookstore," she said, her face paling.

"I own the bookstore," I confirmed.

"Shit fuck," she swore. I finally laughed at that. She scrambled backwards. "Please don't report me. This has been a big misunderstanding."

"It seems to me that you were trying to break into my store and steal a rather expensive volume. What did you plan to do with it? You must know a tome like that would be impossible to fence."

She had the gall to huff at me. If this woman hadn't been trying to steal from me, it would have been charming.

"I was going to sell it to the coven," she exclaimed, throwing her hands out for emphasis. She brought her hands back to her forehead. "Fucking Jessica set me up, that bitch. Look, a Bureau agent gave me a bad tip. She told me the coven wanted the *Bestiary* and they'd pay well for it. She did *not* tell me that the coven had already bought it. I am so sorry."

She looked sincere and she smelled truthful, unlike the sweat and anxiety from earlier. I remained suspicious, though the wolf in the back of my mind lazily dozed. When had that happened? Even if my wolf wasn't on guard, I still was.

"You work for the Bureau?" My guess that she could use magic seemed correct.

She shook her head frantically, causing her curls to go

everywhere. "Sometimes. I usually work for the coven. I was trying to get back into their good graces with the book. Goddess, I'm stupid." She pressed the heels of her hand into her eyes. I wanted to touch her, to comfort her—a ridiculous urge, considering she tried to rob me. Even the wolf eyed me curiously. What was the *matter* with me? "Can you just forget this ever happened?"

"Can't you *make* me forget?" I challenged. I could practically feel my wolf jump up, bouncing in my head. I rolled my head on my shoulders to get rid of the sensation. The shift had already caused tension in my neck.

She huffed at me again, and I got the impression that she did that a lot. "Of course I could, but that requires preparation. I don't just keep curse tablets on me, and do you know how long it would need to be buried in grave dust? It's not like I can just dig up a cemetery whenever I feel like it."

She finished her rant with her hands on her very generous hips, and I realized that her eyes weren't lying: this strange woman was intelligent and bold. Despite her bungling the robbery, her mind could probably run circles around mine. I wanted to dive inside it and dissect it. Remove all the gears and cogs until I could figure out how it ticked.

Immediately ashamed for thinking that, I stepped away from her. A safer distance. This full moon must have made me wolfier than usual. That must be it. I reached out for the wolf to fight for control, but it had fallen back to sleep peacefully in the back of my mind. *Strange.*

"Here's my card," she said, flipping her wrist and producing a card-sized piece of metal out of thin air. She handed it to me, adding, "Again, I am so sorry."

She rushed out the front door before I could even figure out what was happening. She escaped while I gaped at her. Shameful.

"Some guard dog you are," I addressed the wolf in my head. I could hear the whimpering.

I took a look at the card. Embossed on the metal—definitely not silver, or it would have burned—was her name, a phone number, and an office address. "Christiana Owens, sorceress, huh?"

I placed the card behind the register and decided to finally drag myself to bed. I could worry about this woman later. Her scent still lingered in my nose and mind long after she had left.

Chapter Four: Christi

Shit fuck! Jessica set me up. I knew I shouldn't have taken her up on her offer. Stupid. Impulsive. *Typical.* I probably shouldn't have left the envelope with him either. I don't even know what it was, and I just slipped it under some papers at the register. Leaving the envelope lifted some of the darkness, and I felt incredibly guilty about that. Fucking Jessica.

Ringing came from my pocket and continued to get louder. I pulled my phone out. "What!" I snapped.

Giana's voice came through on the other side of the line. What was it this time? She usually only called if she needed something. Or to complain about Dustin. Or to complain about our mom. Or to complain about our father. Or even to complain about me.

"Jeez, Cece! Can't I just call you?" she complained. I rolled my eyes, even if she couldn't see. "Look, I know it's a rough time of year for you and your anniversary was yesterday, and I just wanted to check in—"

I cut her off. "I'm fine."

I had been walking pretty quickly from the bookstore. I finally took a pause and a breath. A coffee shop was right ahead of me, so I ducked in before starting again. "I'm fine, Gigi. I mean it."

"Sure, okay," she said, in the voice that meant *she* didn't mean it. "What about your birthday?"

"What about it?" I snapped. I didn't like celebrating it and Giana had already begun to annoy me.

"Do you want anything? We could go to dinner or something."

"Let me think about it," I answered as noncommittally as I could. If I gave her an inch, she would take a mile.

"Okay, just don't take too long. Anyway, are you coming on Sunday?"

Sunday dinners were mandatory in our house growing up. Giana had carried on that tradition after our parents split up. Once I moved back home, I came over to her house pretty much every Sunday.

"Yeah, of course. Why? Do you need me to bring something?" I stepped into the line to order. I needed an excuse to stop talking to her right now. I needed a second to think, not more emotional upheaval. Why would Jessica even set me up? I felt the darkness wrap its tendrils around me, clutching my chest and making it difficult to breathe.

"Yeah, you know the wine that Mom likes? We ran out."

I knew she needed something. I closed my eyes and took a deep breath. *In for four, out for seven.* And repeated. "Sure thing. Look, this isn't the best time, okay? See you Sunday."

"Alright, Cece. See you."

I hung up the phone and looked up at the menu above the register. It was still really early, and I could use some caffeine. What was going to keep me up the most? I hated coffee, but today was looking like a coffee day, so I tried to figure out what combination of milks and syrups would make it palatable.

I wasn't paying attention as I bumped into the male in front of me.

Rich, mahogany fur covered him from head to toe, further highlighted by the pale gray sweatsuit he wore. Turning to me, he said in a soft voice, "Excuse me."

"Matt!" I exclaimed, recognizing the seven-foot-tall sasquatch wearing dark-framed glasses. I had done some warding for him a few years ago. Some teenagers harassed his family. It had been an easy job, but Matt paid me my usual rate and then some. He and his family had simply been grateful someone was willing to help them out. I grinned. "How are you? How's the family? Are you still working for that magitech firm on Aviation?"

He shook his head. "Layoffs. You know how it is."

My face fell. Magitech jobs were competitive and companies had high turnover. Firms went on a hiring frenzy when a new project started, only to lay off employees when the project fell through.

Matt ordered a drip coffee, and I insisted on paying for it. He waited with me as the barista grabbed it for him.

"Tough luck. What are you going to do now?"

He shrugged. "Look for another job." Coffee in hand, Matt held it up in a toast to me. "It's good to see you. Don't be a stranger."

"See you around." I watched as the sasquatch left the coffee shop. I worried about his fate. The Reveal meant that beings like Matt could come out of hiding. It didn't protect them from the troubles that came with integrating into human society.

I continued to think about Matt as I ordered. Hopefully another magitech firm would hire him. Distracted, I stepped to the side to wait. As I stared into space, I noticed a very handsome, well-dressed man in line. *Hello, there.* I ogled him for a moment longer before realizing that he looked a little too familiar. He cleaned up nicely, but it was definitely him. Mr. Bookstore. *Shit fuck.*

I hid behind other people waiting for their orders, averting my gaze in hopes that he wouldn't see me. What was he *doing* here? The lack of stubble emphasized his already sharp jawline. He must have had a shower and a shave. His rich brown skin seemed to glow from the inside out. It reminded me of a sable coat of my grandmother's that hung in my closet. Growing up, I loved to nuzzle my face into that coat, just to feel how soft it was.

Stop being weird. I looked down at the floor again.

I'd barely walked from his store to here. He didn't look undead or fae, so that left shifter. *So, what kind of shifter are you?* He had changed out of the workout clothes that looked like they had been ironed and into simple khaki slacks with a lavender sweater. Goddess, I loved a man who could wear a pastel.

My heart twinged at that thought. I bit my lip to keep from crying. That would only draw more attention to myself. These baristas were taking forever, and I was going to *cry* in a coffee shop in front of the really hot guy that I just tried to rob. Sometimes I wished that the earth would open up a gaping hole and put me out of my misery.

"I've got an order up for Christi!" the ethereal faery barista called out. Her skin sparkled in the dim light of the coffee shop. What would it be like to be so beautiful?

I collected my coffee and thanked the baristas. Crisis averted. Until I looked up and right in front of me, holding a travel mug of coffee, stood Mr. Bookstore.

"So, this is awkward," I said, when he didn't just look away and pretend he didn't know me, like a normal person would. He laughed, and I could see all of his very white teeth. Did all predators have the same dental plan? Not once have I seen any staining or buildup, always pearly white. "I would love to pretend that we've never met, if that's okay with you."

He smirked and shook his head. "And miss out on having coffee with you?" He leaned in, and my heart thumped a bit faster. I froze in place, staring into his eyes. Classic prey response. But those eyes, I could drown in, like two black pools with no bottom in sight. "It's not every day that someone tries to rob me. Care to join me, Christi?"

"It's the least I could do—" I paused, and when he didn't say anything, I prodded, "This is when you tell me your name."

"Oh, yeah. Sorry, Nathaniel, uh, Nate."

I motioned to a corner table near the big window that looked onto the street. If he was a major asshole, I would at least be by the door and in view of the passersby. He held an arm for me to lead the way. I took the seat with my back to the window, and he surprised me by sitting at the wall, next to me instead of across from me. How *intimate*, Mr. Bookstore. I arched an eyebrow at him, but he didn't notice. He slumped against the wall, closing his eyes and leaning his head back. He seemed distracted, so I started up the conversation.

"Again, I am so sorry about earlier. I am absolutely mortified."

He shrugged, eyes still closed. "Who'd you say the Bureau agent was?"

"Oh my Goddess, her name's Jessica and we went to high school together. Honestly, it was probably her idea of a mean joke." Where was the giant hole to swallow me again?

Something changed, and Nate relaxed, leaning forward with his eyes alight and smiling at me warmly. "I don't think you're one of those blended frothy coffee drink kind of women. I'll go out on a limb and say tea. London Fog, maybe."

That came so far from left field that I just gaped at him for a moment before asking, "I'm sorry, what?"

39

"I was thinking about what you could have ordered. You're going to have to tell me now. I'm dying to know."

He looked at me so earnestly that I had to wonder, *who is this weirdo? And* why *haven't we met before?*

I smiled through closed lips. "I got a London Fog," I said, but I didn't let him win entirely. "With an espresso shot, so you weren't completely correct."

He smirked and *mm-hmm*-ed into his coffee. Oh Goddess, was he flirting with me? It was one thing to have coffee with a sexy mystery man with arms that could probably bench press *me*, but flirting? *With me*? He was just being nice. There was no way. Men like him didn't flirt with women like me. They tended to sniff out the sadness and steer clear.

"Okay, you can't drop that you're a mind reader without explaining."

"Oh?"

He was spot on, and I was curious. "Why a London Fog?"

"It's complex with the Earl Grey, while still being warming with the vanilla and milk." He shrugged. "It seems like it would go well with reading a good book."

On the outside, I smiled and quipped, "Says the bookseller."

On the inside, I liquefied, died, and was reincarnated. I didn't care whether or not he was flirting, I just wanted him to do it more. Briefly recovering, I reached over and took a sip of his drink. The bitterness hit my tongue, and I forced

40

myself to swallow. I winced and made a big show of gagging.

"Oh Goddess, I knew you would drink black coffee."

"Black coffee?" He faked offense. "I will have you know that this is pour-over coffee, freshly ground and individually prepared."

I laughed, at ease now that he was more open and chattier. "You're really into coffee, huh?"

"I don't sleep much," he said, shrugging. No wonder his arms looked so good, his shoulders worked overtime. I wanted to reach out and push down. Maybe massage them, if he'd let me. "Insomnia."

"You don't have to do that, you know," I said, seriously. I knew the Reveal didn't rid all of us from the fear of discovery or the shame at who or what we are.

"Do what?"

"I figured out pretty quickly that you're a shifter. You don't have to hide it," I said with a half-smile. "Besides, you already know I'm a witch."

His jaw dropped, but his smile stayed. "Your card says *sorceress*. That is some false advertisement."

I doubted that he knew the difference.

"I'm surprised you didn't just toss it," I told him, my cheeks burning as I looked down in embarrassment. He must have found the envelope already. I felt a twinge of guilt. When I looked back up, he was staring at me.

"I thought I might need your number. Looks like I didn't."

His gaze sent shivers up my spine. He *was* flirting. *Oh no.* I liked it, but this poor man did not realize just how terrible his timing was. *You can just leave now*, I told myself. But I didn't, and he kept talking. "So, are you new to town?"

"Not really. More of a prodigal daughter. I grew up here."

His face fell for a moment, and he sipped his coffee. His smile returned when he set his mug down. "Ah, so you came back with your spouse to raise a family then?"

"You cut straight to the point, don't you?" I laughed, taking a big swallow. I couldn't seem to get down the lump in my throat. We had to move on from this topic, or I really *would* cry in front of this man who was flirting with me. It wasn't his fault he had shitty timing. I ran my fingers through my hair, probably messing it up even more. "No spouse. No plans for a family, either."

Nate leaned back casually. "What a coincidence, same here," he said. "Then tell me, why'd you come back home?"

"Next question," I teased.

But he shook his head. "No pressure, Christi. We're just having coffee."

It didn't feel like *just* having coffee. I steered the conversation elsewhere. "So, Nate, you have a steady job, you like books. Things are looking pretty good for you," I joked. "You must have some flaws. Skeletons in the closet?"

"I used to drink a lot. Not anymore. I'm sober now." He yawned and stretched. Once again, he distracted me with just how great his arms looked. I couldn't figure out how he managed that with two layers of clothes over them. He made an almost imperceptible wince, but smiled quickly to cover it.

Maybe I was reading into it too much, given how close we were to my anniversary. But it was a face Troy had made often when he was uncomfortable or in pain while he was sick. I had to remind myself this was a stranger whose facial expressions I didn't know and couldn't interpret.

Nate lifted his mug to me. "Thank god for coffee."

"Ah, there's the dealbreaker," I teased. "You like coffee, I like tea. It'll never work."

"You'd be surprised what I'd be willing to overlook. Like if you cook, I may have to marry you right now."

I flinched at the word *marry*, but tried to shrug it off. *Nothing is holding you here. You can always run.* I felt the cold caress of the darkness and shuddered.

"I hate to disappoint you, but my sister is the cook of the family. I do order a pretty good takeout."

"I like takeout."

Our hands had inched closer as we'd talked. Neither of us was going to make the first move. I started to feel a little giddy, but that could be my rising panic.

Nate pulled away first. "Sorry," he said, placing one hand behind his head. I knew that he meant it sheepishly, but it showed off his muscles. I started to think that this man did not realize how hot he was. "I don't get out much."

"Says the man who is indeed *out*," I said, motioning around to the coffee shop around us.

He laughed warmly, holding up his mug. "Exceptions are made for coffee."

"And takeout!" I reminded. "What does a bookseller read, anyway?"

He snorted. "I know I'm not supposed to say eighteenth-century treatises on why werewolf fur harvested on a full moon is more effective in shape-shifting spells. Hezekiah George knew nothing about werewolves, but damn, he was an excellent scholar. Completely wrong, by the way. No such thing as a shape-shifting spell, but you should know that. Anyway, other than that, I'm not picky."

This fucking *weirdo*. I had to be his friend, and not just so I could look at him.

"Oh, good," I joked, "for a second, I thought you were going to be one of those pretentious literary fiction guys."

"I should take offense on behalf of all pretentious literary fiction *men*," he laughed. "If you must know, I mostly enjoy thrillers and mysteries, if I'm not reading to learn."

"Reading to learn," I breathed. I tossed my hair back mischievously. "Say more sexy things." His cheeks went purple, and I bit my lip. I made my eyes as large as possible and pouted innocently. "Am I making you squirm?"

He shook his head. "Not a bit. Just wondering what you read."

I took a long sip of my tea. "I feel like this is a make-or-break moment. What would you say if I said I didn't read?"

"I would shake your hand and tell you it was nice to meet

you, but this is obviously not going to work."

I laughed, still looking to rile him up. "I read the usual things—shifter fated mates, faery porn."

"I believe you just said you read faery porn," he repeated. It used to be a huge genre prior to the Reveal, and the only good fantasy romance out there was now vintage or out of print.

"Mm-hmm." I sipped my drink.

"Which is what, exactly?"

"Your typical romance novel, but instead of marrying a Highland lord, the young, vulnerable woman marries the 500-year-old fae king, who has a penchant for tying her up and having his way with her," I explained, completely unfazed. "The genre kind of plummeted with the Reveal. You sell books, shouldn't you know this?" I winked. "I'm teasing, but there are some books that are really good, even if the premise seems ridiculous."

"I'd be interested in your recommendations, then. I'm always looking for something new to read."

I was never, *ever* going to admit the worst filth I read. But he didn't know that. *Always keep them wanting more.*

This was as good of a place as any to cut this conversation. I lit up.

"Okay, sure! Look, I should probably go, but I'm glad I ran into you. Let me give you my personal number. I'll text you. Maybe we can do this again."

I typed my number into his phone and handed it back to

him. I stood up, but didn't leave the table. He shook his absolutely ancient flip phone at me.

"We will definitely do this again."

"Yeah, okay. Good."

"Good."

I gave him an awkward little wave. "Good. Okay, well, I guess I'll see you around."

Chapter Five: Nate

The next day at work, I couldn't stop thinking about Christi.
My anxiety had sunk in. What was I thinking? Christi was
nice, more than nice. But I hadn't been on a date in fifteen
years. Longer, if you considered my engagement to Alice.
Maybe it was better *not* to think about Alice. If I thought of
her, I might manifest her appearance. My stomach churned.
Any chance at love and romance died when I was turned.
That sort of thing only existed in the novels Christi read.

A woman shouldn't be able to get under my skin like this.
I barely even knew her. Stupid wolf. Besides, it was safer if I
stayed away. For the both of us.

I dusted the shelves and put any unshelved books back
in their proper place. The store needed to look neat and clean
for tomorrow. I hated a messy store. The bookstore might
sell priceless magic tomes, but it didn't need to look the part.
There were no wizards waiting to appear from behind the
stacks and hand you a quest. There was just me. If the store
was going to be run by me, then it would reflect that. It made
me think of my father drilling into my head that I was a
reflection of my parents and should act accordingly. I felt a
twinge of guilt.

As I completed my locking-up routine, I organized the
paperwork at the register. It was one of the few tasks I could
do seated. Considering my body still felt the effects of the

change, I could use a moment off my feet. My muscles, fatigued to the point of pain, threatened to seize up and never move again.

Most of the loose paper just needed to be filed. A receipt here. An order there. I felt a calm wash over me as I placed each piece in its proper file. I paused at Christi's card and smiled. I should have filed it away like everything else, but instead, I took the thin metal card and tucked it into my wallet.

Underneath the card was a crisp white envelope. Strange, since I didn't leave mail at the register. It smelled of magic, but gave off an insidious aura. It was as though I could see the cloud of malice around it. Only the worst of the worst magical items in Harold's hoard gave off this noxious air. I put on my archival gloves just in case. I picked up the envelope and nearly dropped it, the scent of magic so thick it burned my nose. Carefully, I sliced it open with a letter opener.

Inside was a white postcard. I would know the handwriting anywhere. My hands trembled as I dropped the postcard. Three words knocked me off my axis. *I found you.*

I threw open the door, running down the block. No one looked suspicious. I couldn't remember what any of my customers that day looked like. I remembered what books they purchased, how much they bought them for, but not their faces. *Fuck.* A cool sweat dripped down between my shoulder blades. I wiped my face with my hands. I needed to calm down. Once I calmed down, I could think. I leaned forward, hands on my knees, forcing myself to breathe. *She found me.*

A fortifying breath later, I stood up and walked calmly down Main Street. I had systems in place for just this reason. My blades and a go-bag waited underneath my bed. I felt a little ashamed that I would have to abandon the bookstore and let Harold down. But someone else would take my place. I needed to do just one more thing before I disappeared. A ringing in my back pocket distracted me. I stopped and answered it, my heart pounding.

"Hello, Nathaniel," an all-too-familiar voice cooed. A voice that haunted my dreams and ruined my life. "Missed me?"

I snapped the phone in half. As I walked, I tossed it in the trash. Cheap flip phones were easy to get rid of. I walked deliberately back to my apartment. The less attention I could draw to myself, the better.

With the bookstore locked up, I had to use the back entrance to my apartment. Cautiously, I entered the alley. The usual human scents—piss, sweat, perfume—flooded my nose and made me nauseous. One scent lingered above the rest, raising the hairs on the back of my neck. I growled. Another wolf had been here. Recently, too, if the smell was this fresh. I bared my teeth instinctively. It pushed me to the edge of my limits. This wolf didn't have permission to be on my turf. No one wanted to be up against another wolf or an enemy pack on their own. This wolf was either very stupid or very cocky.

If it was who it smelled like, maybe both. Either way, this wolf wasn't supposed to *be* here. Especially not now, when I was about to make a break for it.

The door to the stairs didn't lock, so I opened it slowly to make sure I wasn't walking into an ambush. Despite wanting to, I didn't run up the stairs, but took each step confidently, naturally. The stairs left me breathless anyway, my body still weak from the change. My wolf, on the other hand, excitedly circled in my mind. It gleefully prepared for a fight.

If there was another wolf upstairs, I didn't want to tip him off. His smell grew stronger the closer I got to my door. My hands shook as I fumbled with the keys. I wanted to sleep more than anything and forget about life for a little while, but that wasn't in the cards. I needed to grab my bag and run, not have a standoff with a strange wolf. Finally, I got the right key into the lock and opened the door.

I didn't bother turning the light on; I could see pretty well in the dark, thanks to my wolf. It snarled at the back of my mind, hackles raised. It sent a jolt of adrenaline, flooding my body and tensing my muscles, to make me ready for a fight. I tossed the keys on the side table and kicked off my shoes. I debated taking off my sweater, but didn't bother. Either I would get jumped, or we would try to settle this like men, and I could forcibly remove him from my apartment. I just wanted to get to the bed and grab the bag.

A man sat casually in my leather wingback chair. He held both of my blades, Hope and Strength, inspecting them. A bottle of vodka sat on the floor. The scent of it stung my nose, and I reflexively took a step back, gagging. I turned on the light and he grinned, his canines like fangs ready to bite. I knew that smile. I used to see that smile and know I'd have to keep him from doing something stupid. Except he had already done the stupid thing by coming here.

"Hello, Nathaniel," Derrick said. "Missed me?"

My hands were on his shoulders before I really thought about what I was doing. *Stick to the plan.* The plan would keep us safe.

"You need to leave. Now."

He dropped the blades. Leave it to Derrick to dull my blades and try to take a toe in the process. I could almost laugh at the predictability, if I wasn't so concerned about getting him out of here.

Pushing me off, he stood up. *Fine.* I set my jaw and started to move around my apartment, collecting my own books and some additional clothes. The record player and all my vinyl would have to stay here. Maybe I could come back and get them, but I doubted it. I'd have to start over. I collected my blades from the floor and laid them on the bed. Pulling my go-bag out from underneath the bed, I tossed it next to the weapons. Grabbing a leather holster out of the bag, I fastened it and sheathed the blades. Everything else got stuffed into the duffel.

I snarled at Derrick, still keeping my distance. I hadn't seen him since I left the pack. The last words I'd spoken to him had not been kind. I never expected to see him again, let alone have him track me here. He wasn't supposed to try to find me, he knew that. My anger at him built. Not only did I have to run, but now he would have to start over too. *The idiot.*

"Get. The Fuck. Out," I growled, swinging my duffel over my shoulder. I tried to push past him. Wolf shifters were bigger than werewolves. If he shifted, I was dead. In a fistfight, I might be able to take him. Derrick was bigger than me, stronger than me. I was faster and smarter. But I was also out of shape, barely practicing with my blades, and fresh off the change, so there were trade-offs. I could only hope that baring my teeth was menacing enough.

We circled each other. Neither one of us struck and neither backed down. I would not back down. I needed to leave. This chapter of my life was over now. This was my home, my town. He'd invaded *my* space even as I was leaving it.

Finally, he stepped back.

"I have to go," I said sadly, opening the door. "If you know what's good for you, you'd leave too."

Derrick reached out for my shoulder, but I shrugged him off.

"Brother," he said gravely. Derrick rarely lowered his voice like this. I used to call it his battle command voice. *Shit.* "That's why I'm here."

Realization shook me. *Please, no.*

"Derrick, go home. Back to the pack. Back to Sarah," I told him, ignoring the pit in my stomach. "You can't be here."

"Nate, I'm serious," he said, his hands raised in surrender. "We need to talk. Sarah's been murdered."

No. *Fuck, fuck, fuck, fuck, fuck.* Once again, I found myself with my hands on my knees, struggling to breathe. It would have been easier if he had just punched me in the gut. I panted. I couldn't get sick here. I'd have to clean it up before I left. The thought made me laugh cynically. I shouldn't care about how tidy my place was when I was leaving it. I dropped to my knees and Derrick followed me to the floor.

"We're in this together. She finally caught up to us."

Well, shit.

I brewed a pot of coffee, and we settled downstairs in the bookstore, where I had more than the one chair. Derrick drank vodka out of the bottle. He must have brought it with him. Hopefully, the coffee would sober him up. I didn't need a drunk Derrick to deal with. I needed my alpha.

"Hunters. It was a day or two before we found her. Well, what was left of her." His voice broke. He held it together better than I expected for losing his mate. Wolves mated for life. It would be rare if he ever found a love like that again. My heart hurt for him, but I found myself unable to shed a tear for Sarah. Sarah and I hadn't always gotten along. She was a hard woman and an even harder alpha. He shook a bit, trying to contain his fury.

"Jesus," I muttered as he downed half the bottle of vodka in one go. I bit the inside of my mouth and let him grieve. I wanted, no, needed to leave. I failed to understand how this connected to *her*.

"That was six months ago."

"It sounds like an accident. You said she was murdered."

"Nothing gets past you," he said bitterly. "For fuck's sake, Nate, you're the smart one." I laughed. We were in a sorry state if I was considered the smart one of the bunch just because I bothered to read. "Think about it. You see a gray wolf, you can't fucking shoot it. Not in shifter territory." His voice wavered. He pulled up his too-tight shirt and blew his nose into it. I winced and grabbed a box of tissues. "We fought and she went out. That was the last time I saw her alive." That broke him, and he started to cry. "She was such a beautiful gray wolf."

I gave him a minute to control himself. "You should have been able to get the pack through it. It's still yours."

He laughed bitterly, taking another swig. "Mine? You'd think so, huh? No one even bothered to challenge me, brother. They took a vote and just left. Without Sarah, they didn't even bother to fucking stick around."

I wasn't surprised. Derrick was pure brawn, with his too-big muscles and his too-tall size, and his barrel chest. He'd had a militant buzz cut when I met him, but his blond hair hung past his shoulders now, and a scraggly beard replaced his five-o'clock shadow. Derrick might have been the largest and the strongest, but he could never be Sarah, and the pack knew it.

He shook violently, leaning over so his elbows rested on his knees. He handed me a white postcard with the same insidious feeling as the one I found today. I didn't want to take it. My wolf growled, baring its teeth at the threat. The card was empty except for one handwritten line and a bloodstain. *You can run, but you can't hide.* Fuck me. It was message, but not for the pack.

When will it end?

"She found you." It was a hoarse whisper, as though saying the words aloud could summon Alice out of the notecard.

"There wasn't a body, Nate. They skinned her and left her pelt with a fucking note. I'm going to kill that bitch, and you are going to help me."

I was sick of running, of looking out for trouble and never relaxing. Why now? It had been quiet for so long. Would I be looking over my shoulder and waiting for the other shoe to drop for the rest of my life?

When it hit me, I swore. I couldn't leave. I needed

Harold's hoard.

I leapt out of my chair and began pulling books out of the stacks.

"What are you doing?" Derrick asked, confused.

"Why do you think I was getting ready to run? She found me too. I got a similar postcard and worse, a phone call. I didn't put the timing together until now. Think about it," I urged him. He frowned and shook his head. "Why'd I leave the pack, Der?"

"You and Sarah got in a huge fight." Derrick paused, realization dawning on him. "Over her heat. Then Alice got close and you ran without saying goodbye."

My feelings for Derrick were *complicated*. I had been coming to terms with who I was, *what* I was. Derrick had made me feel seen, made me realize I shouldn't be ashamed. Not just of being a werewolf, but of being bisexual. He hadn't grown up with the stigma like I had. Eventually, though, we'd grown closer as friends rather than lovers. It was difficult to love someone whose bad qualities smothered the good ones.

"The timing lines up. Alice is looking for me because she's preparing for her heat."

Derrick exhaled through his teeth. "Your dick isn't a magic wand, man. I don't get why she is *so* obsessed."

How did one untangle twenty years of history into a single response? The most obvious answer was that she wanted what she couldn't have. I was the only person who had ever told her no.

I just shrugged, pulling more books off the shelves. I hadn't spent my time at the bookstore idle. I focused on a singular goal. I knew which volumes to pull and what tomes I needed from upstairs. After all, what did a bookseller do with his free time? I'd been reading and researching nonstop for five years.

"Slow down," Derrick shouted, standing up and striding over to me. "What's with all the books?"

"There's only one way Alice will leave me alone for good." I groaned in frustration. I really needed him to stop with the vodka and start with the coffee. Most of all, I needed him to follow my train of thought. "A cure, man!"

Derrick glared at me. My wolf did the same. It hated when I went down this rabbit hole. Like it or not, it was part of me, and it didn't *want* to be removed. I tried to ignore it.

Alice had forced the wolf on me. Suddenly. Violently. It had taken my life from me, my career, my family. I constantly mourned the loss of what I had and who I was, even when I had been *this* for almost as long as I had been him. The wolf was the one thing I had no control over; it controlled me.

Even right now, the wolf's anxiety at being removed made my own heart beat faster and a cold sweat start at the nape of my neck.

"You've been searching for one for years. Don't you think you would have found one already?"

I handed him a stack of books. "Sure, but now I have you to help me."

He dropped the stack, and I winced, bending over to pick them up. Stack in hand, I gave him a look, affronted.

"What, then? She *murdered* Sarah!"

We couldn't take down the most powerful shifter in the country, not without a plan. I didn't have one yet, but I'd get there. I just needed a clue.

I chuckled to myself, shaking my head in disbelief. I thought I didn't have a clue, but I might know someone who did.

Chapter Six: Nate

I wished that I had been joking when I told Christi I had insomnia. The truth was more complicated than that. When you think werewolf, you think full moons. While a full moon caused the change, any moon awakened the wolf. My wolf howled in the back of my mind all night, making it impossible to sleep. I hadn't had a good night's sleep since before the Reveal. The bookstore had such odd hours because of it. I slept during the day when I could. I used to drink myself to sleep at night. Now, I used a better coping mechanism— copious amounts of coffee.

I had brewed my third pot of coffee and paced around my apartment. Even my wolf screamed at me to run. The noise it made in my head wouldn't let me sit and rest. I tried to remind myself that I didn't have all the information I needed to make a plan. Where would I run to? What would I do there? How would I keep Alice from finding me then?

Would she ever stop?

Alice loved mind games. Even while we'd dated, she'd make up excuses to break up and force me to win her back. Once I left for good, the letters, phone calls, and text messages had started. I'd get a new phone and she'd find my number again. I had tried going to the police, but they couldn't believe she had threatened someone like me. I didn't try again after that. There had to be more to it this time, if she was willing to kill just to send me a message.

I grew tired of her games. I might have come to her willingly if she had collected me after the Reveal. Once the existence of shifters was out in the open, part of me had hoped that I could create a new normal, even after years of her stalking me. But she hadn't come, and my love for her finally extinguished.

I drew the curtains to look out at the night. The wolf made my life feel so empty without a pack, without an alpha to serve. I looked at Derrick, curled up on my bed in wolf form, sleeping off the vodka. The pack bond lightly tugged at my heart and mind. This was all my fault. I knew how to fix it, but I couldn't bring myself to do it.

I finally gave up on my pacing after tracing my apartment a hundred times. The wolf whined in the back of my mind. *Not now. Go to sleep!* I read until my eyes hurt. As usual, the tome held no great secret to curing my lycanthropy. With Harold's hoard, I had access to a large collection of magic books and documents that existed. Still, I couldn't find what I was looking for. Anger tightened in the pit of my stomach. I threw the book across the room.

Derrick raised his head at the crash of it against the wall. When he confirmed that I had made the noise and not some kind of threat, he settled back into sleep. *The bastard.* He didn't understand. He had been a wolf all his life. He shifted instinctually. Nothing separated the man and the wolf. There was only the shifter. He was always going to be a wolf, an alpha. There was no line in his life marking the *before* and the *after*. His wolf hadn't taken his life away from him like mine. I'd had potential!

I was so tired. This wasn't the first time I sought out a cure. After my wolf-led stupor, I would be immensely motivated to find an end to it. It felt like I had tried everything. The return of my clothes. Wolfsbane. Opium. Antidotes to shapeshifting spells. The touch of a king—that had been particularly difficult to obtain.

I'd once tried an ancient Greek curative that nearly killed me. Derrick had bled me until I had passed out. Afterwards, I bathed in water sweetened with flowers and honey. Then for three days, I rubbed myself with milk, adding canned pumpkin on the second and third days. I had a feeling that one wouldn't work, but I had tried it anyway.

The process always ended the same way. I'd come down from losing days and weeks to the wolf. I'd throw myself into finding a cure. I'd try everything I could find, only to be disappointed after nothing worked. Eventually, the wolf would either calm or I would be so exhausted that I'd resign myself to the fact that I'd never be cured. Lather. Rinse. Repeat.

It had been easier in the pack. In the pack, the wolf didn't fight me for control. The pack bond and the dominance of my alpha pair soothed the wolf. My wolf only became a problem at the full moon. I'd lost fewer days and felt more like myself. After I had lost my pack, my wolf easily grabbed control.

I had very few memories from *the year of the wolf*. The memories I had were unpleasant—lying in agony on my bathroom floor, breaking plates and glasses in anger, waking covered in blood after the wolf ate some poor coyote.

I didn't know what to do with myself. I stood up again before sitting down. Even as my fatigued muscles screamed at me, the vibration I felt in my body forced me to stand. I grabbed my blades from underneath the bed and practiced my positions. Derrick used to say that I needed two blades so I could slice *and* dice. A short sword with a wicked blade could slice at limbs and strike at throats. A dagger for stabbing. Both with wolf heads on the hilts. Derrick thought he was being funny with that. My muscles burned with the exertion, but at least my mind quieted.

A clatter wrenched me out of my brief moment of peace. I dashed to the window again. The trash bin had been knocked over. That must have been the noise. My wolf growled in my mind. Its hackles raised at something out there. Derrick agreed. He had jumped off the bed and prowled towards the door. I took a deep sniff. I couldn't smell anything out of the ordinary, but the overwhelming scent of Derrick's alpha wolf masked the scent of anything new.

Something scratched the glass. It sounded like nails on a chalkboard. I closed my eyes and grimaced. I could feel my heart pulse in my ears with each scrape. Holding my breath, I tried to listen for where the noise came from. It went from one window to the next, making its way to my door. My wolf sprang into action, sending me flying down stairs. I held my blades, ready for any threat. When the howling started, Derrick pushed past me down the stairs.

Dammit! By the time we made it down the stairs, the source of the racket was long gone. Derrick ran ahead to scout, but returned shaking his head. He'd found nothing. I cursed, anger settling as a hard ball in my stomach. I howled in frustration, a low mournful cry. Disappointed, I shook my head, trying to ignore how similar I sounded to the howling we investigated. Derrick shifted back into a human and clapped me on the shoulder. I winced, inhaling sharply; even the faintest brush against my skin burned like fire. I still ached from the full moon nights ago. Yet, here Derrick stood, freshly shifted without breaking a sweat.

"Must have been coyotes," he shrugged, with his cock out like he was on spring break.

I knew what coyotes sounded like, but I nodded. "Yeah, coyotes." My wolf bowed in submission to Derrick's. I hated it. "Let's get back inside before you get us arrested."

"My only crime is looking this good." Derrick grinned cheekily, opening his arms to display his nakedness further.

I rolled my eyes and ushered him into the stairwell. I paused at the door, listening for something, anything. But nothing was out there except for me and the moon.

Chapter Seven: Christi

I worked in my office, which was the guest house of my
grandparents' home. Though I technically owned the home, I
still couldn't consider it anything but theirs. They had lived in
a small beach bungalow with a detached garage and a large
yard; a tiny back house next to the garage sat across the yard
from the main house. I preferred working here because it had
a separate entrance on the street so clients—if I had any—
didn't have to come to the house. I could also leave the back
door open so that Sadie could come and go as she pleased.

My lack of clients didn't prevent me from being
prepared, so I crafted amulets and curse tablets that I
anointed or buried. It paid to be prepared. I worked on two
matching amulets in smokey quartz. For some reason, I
etched little wolves onto the cabochons. It veered from my
usual style, but the stone seemed to call for it. Just as I
considered whether to charge the amulets for healing or
protection, someone knocked on the door.

"Just a minute," I called out, taking off my gloves and
jeweler's loupe. Another knock sounded. "Coming!"

The interruption annoyed me, but I couldn't let a client
see it, so I opened the door with my brightest smile. I almost
shut the door again when I saw who had done the knocking.

"Shit fuck," I exclaimed. "It's you."

Nate stood in my doorway. He wasn't much taller than

me, but he was leaner. Even though he wore a pale blue sweater—who wore a sweater in Los Angeles in the spring? — I saw the cords of muscle along his arms underneath. Goddess, he sure was pretty. He smiled softly, not showing his teeth, and his black eyes looked so kind. I assumed he was close to my age, given that his close fade was salt and pepper. But his face showed little signs of age, his skin the rich, dark color of the smoky quartz I had been working with. There was something lupine about him, as though if he smiled, it would reveal rows of very sharp teeth. He moved gracefully as he held his hands up in surrender.

He hadn't texted me. Not that I expected a text the next day, or the day after, but it had cooled me down a bit. *See?* I'd told myself. *He wasn't flirting with me.* He had been nice, that was all. What a sad state I must have been in to mix up the two. It was better this way. It would have made it harder to run if I wanted to. *Besides*, the darkness whispered, *who would want you anyway?*

"I come in peace," he said. Even his voice sounded kind, and I realized how stupid it had been to read into things.

I stared at him in stunned silence, and then I opened the door wider. "Do you want to come in?" I asked. He hesitantly stepped into my office. I put on my best customer service voice. "Can I get you anything? Water? I think I might have some instant coffee stashed away in the house."

He wrinkled his nose at that. "Water's fine, thanks." His voice was warm and husky, even though he spoke softly. I worried at how much it put me at ease.

I poured him a glass of water from a carafe I kept in the office and placed it in front of him.

"Thank you."

He sat down in the chair in front of my desk, so I sat across from him. I tried not to be nervous. I always felt a little weird talking to genuinely attractive people. I was not conventionally attractive; though I considered myself a catch, I knew what people thought when they saw me. Too fat, too frizzy, too emotional, too smart, too outgoing. Too much. Always too much. I'd cried after we had coffee, upset that not only had Jessica set me up, but that I had been so thoroughly embarrassed in the process.

I plastered on a smile, but my stomach clenched. I tried to remind myself of what an absolute *weirdo* he had been at coffee. He probably thought I was some kind of criminal. Or worse, someone desperate. "How can I help you?" I asked, my voice measured and positive. I folded my hands on the desk to hide how they shook.

The man from the bookstore took a long sip from the water glass, and then set it down gently on my desk. "I'm in trouble, and I think only you can help me," he said, every word thoughtful and planned. Had he rehearsed this?

My heart pounded, and I had to swallow hard to contain myself. This was it, the other shoe was going to drop and he was going to turn out to be an asshole. Just my luck. "What do you mean?" I questioned.

"Who are you working for?"

"Excuse me?"

He swallowed once and repeated coolly, "Who do you work for?"

I paused as I tried to understand his interrogation. "Myself?"

He stood up, his hands on the desk, and he leaned over. Suddenly very nauseous, I realized that I was very much alone with a strange man.

"The Bureau," he said, his voice even. He didn't raise it, but somehow that made it more threatening. "What was the job? Was it just to steal the book, or did they want you to plant something?"

Oh no. I knew I shouldn't have left that envelope. Stupid. Impulsive. *Typical.* I swallowed hard before answering, "Yes, I was given an envelope. I am so sorry. I knew I shouldn't have left it. I'll tell you anything you need to know." I hated how small my voice sounded. I was a fucking sorceress. I could handle him.

He collapsed into the chair, every muscle relaxing. I'd seen him do that twice now. One moment his body tensed, on guard and looking for threats, and the next, it melted, liquid and at ease. It unnerved me. Now that I thought clearly, I could see the bags under his eyes. He looked like he hadn't slept in days. A heavy stubble replaced the clean-shaven face of a few days ago. Even his sweater looked wrinkled and the shirt underneath was untucked.

"Well, shit," he said, and I couldn't do anything but laugh. He laughed with me, and I just stared at him.

"Care to fill me in on what's going on here?"

"It's a long story," he sighed. "But it would really help if you told me who gave you the envelope."

"Jessica Ashton," I replied, having no problem throwing her under the bus. "She works at the South Bay branch of the Bureau."

I had gone back to the Bureau to confront Jessica, but she wasn't there. She hadn't been back since.

"It'd be easier if I didn't have to involve the Bureau," he frowned. "But what can you do? Thanks, Christi. I'm sorry if I've come across as intense. There's a lot on my plate right now."

No shit. Take a number, man, I had a lot on my plate too. I bit my lip to keep my mouth shut.

"Thanks anyway. I'll, uh, see you around." He stood back up.

"Wait!" I stood up. He paused. For some reason, I didn't want him to leave. "Let me help you. I promise not to steal any more books."

He laughed, finally showing his bright white teeth. No fangs, I noted. "You sure? Because I think that book, the *Bestiary*, might be important. I wouldn't say *no* if you offered to steal it back for me."

"I can't," I confessed, guiltily. Though I couldn't understand why I felt guilty one, for not wanting to steal something, and two, for disappointing a stranger. A very handsome stranger, but a stranger nonetheless. "I'm already on the coven's shit list and I can't afford to anger them further."

"Is that a theme for you? Just how many shit lists are you on?"

Ouch. That hurt, but it was fair. I disappointed a lot of people.

"Just the one big one. Are you sure you don't need any help that doesn't involve stealing from the coven?" I smiled, wishing I could control the tears welling in my eyes.

"Unless you are willing to read esoteric texts about werewolves, I don't think there's anything you can do."

I could totally do that.

"I can read," I said softly, with a shy smile. That had to work on him. "I can also translate several of the old and new world languages used for magic."

Even if I couldn't do it directly, I definitely had reference books that could. His face lit up. *Yes!*

"Are you sure? We could really use another set of eyes that know what they're looking for."

And what are *you looking for, Mr. Bookstore?* He didn't want to go to the Bureau. He'd all but confirmed that he was a shifter at coffee. The Bureau would be pretty hands-off if this was pack business. Shifters existed outside of most modern strictures, so law enforcement usually let them take care of meting out their own punishments.

"You found the right woman," I told him. "That's right up my alley. Why don't you come by the house tomorrow? Bring your books and we can tag-team it. The more, the merrier."

He asked for my number again. *Weird.* But once we exchanged information and goodbyes, I sat back down in disbelief. It looked like I would be seeing a lot more of him.

"Hey, everyone," I called out into the house after I let myself in. "I'm here."

Giana's house was oddly quiet for family dinner, so I dropped off the cupcakes I'd brought and the bag of wine for Mom in the kitchen. I poured myself a glass of Shiraz. As I savored the first sip and the silence, I looked out into the living room. Sophia sat on the couch, hunched over a notebook and writing furiously. I hoped that it wasn't her dream journal.

"Hey, Soph," I called out to her. "Is that any way to greet your aunt?"

She huffed, disdain thick in the sound. *Ugh, teenagers.*

She finally looked up. "Hi," she said, and then returned to her writing.

"Whatcha working on?"

"Stuff."

Sophia was thirteen. I worried about her. She was super smart, but sullen and closed off. I knew more than most how mental illness ran in our family. But worse than that, I knew that her gift plagued her more than my sister would admit. Sophia dreamed of the future, a clairvoyant like our grandmother. I wished that I had paid more attention to what Grandma Ida taught me about divination. I had a pale imitation of her gift, having to go to great lengths to produce a vision. Grandma Ida was already dying when Sophia was born, which meant that Sophia had only my guidance. And she didn't want it.

"You wanna talk about it?"

"Nope," she said curtly, hiding behind her long black hair. "Why waste time talking about it? Everything breaks. You'll see."

Okay, then. "Well, I'm here if you do." I walked over to the sliding glass door. My mother played soccer with Liam as Giana and Dustin looked on from their seats on the retaining wall. Dustin whispered into Giana's ear, and her face went tomato red. He nuzzled into her neck. My heart ached. I looked away, feeling like I wasn't supposed to see it.

Giana and Dustin had met on my first day of high school. Dustin was Rachel's older brother. She was in my class, and he was a few years older than we were. He and Giana had reconnected once she graduated, and they've been madly in love ever since. I envied what they had and how quickly they found it. I wanted someone to come home to, to love and care for. Every time I seemed to find it, it slipped through my grasp. I neared forty and I felt so very alone. *But wasn't the freedom worth it?*

The door opened, and a new flurry of activity spilled out.

"Zia!" Liam wrapped his arms around my legs. Four years younger than Sophia, Liam had yet to outgrow hugs and kisses from his aunt. "Where's Sadie?" he asked in a yell.

"Sorry, bud," I told him. "She's at home today."

"Ah, man!" Liam, distracted by the lack of dogs, ran back outside.

"You know the rules," Gigi reminded him, stepping through the door while he ran out. I heard his wicked laughter. "Be gentle with your grandmother!" She motioned for the wine. "Ooh, are we drinking? Gimme!"

I handed her my glass and poured myself a new one.

My sister Gianina got the good genes. She had Mom's height with Dad's looks. Her long dark hair has a hint of a wave so it looked perpetually blown out even when air-dried, and her eyes resembled hot cocoa rather than muddy brown. I, on the other hand, looked like my Italian grandmother: fat, with supple hips and ample boobs. I inherited one thing from my mom's side: her green eyes. Gigi specialized in illusion magic, so all she had to do to touch up her flawlessness was a bit of magic.

"Zia, you're getting married, right?" Sophia asked, looking up.

"Goddess only knows, Soph. It's close to my anniversary, though. Maybe you're thinking of that," I explained, knowing that things were never quite as they seemed with Sophia's questions.

She scoffed with teenage disgust. "I don't mean your first wedding. I meant your second," she corrected, clearly annoyed with me.

"Well, I would have to find someone to marry me first," I joked, a twinge of grief squeezing my heart. Despite my asking her not to, Mom still had my wedding portraits up on the wall. I found them difficult to look at, even now.

"You already have," she sourly exclaimed. "God, adults don't know anything." She got off the couch and stormed into her room.

"Was that a premonition or just her imagination?" I asked carefully.

Giana gulped her wine, shaking her head. "We never know anymore. She has these dreams, Cece." The color drained from her face. "She can't sleep. They scare her. I hear her puttering around in the middle of the night. She says it's better to be awake and exhausted than asleep and not getting any rest."

"Do you want my help?" I asked her. It wasn't the first time I'd offered.

Giana chewed the inside of her cheek, a bad habit she never grew out of. It was the only thing that screwed up her face unattractively. "Not yet," she said thoughtfully. "Soon, but not yet." She filled her wine glass up again before pointing at me seriously. "If you start giving my child psychedelics, I'll kill you and make it look like an accident."

I laughed. It was one of the ways I could get into a trance state. It was also something I would never try with Sophia without a lot of training first. "Noted."

"But if I were you," Giana laughed, "I might take note of any handsome strangers that walked into my life."

I briefly thought of Nate, but shook my head. "Handsome strangers?" I joked. "Can I get one delivered?"

Giana and I erupted into giggles that we couldn't stop, even though what I said really wasn't that funny. We started giggling harder when everyone came inside and asked us what was so hilarious. I took a moment to look around. I might not have a life partner, but I had my family, and that was enough.

That night, though, I dreamed of a magical forest filled with fairy lights and evergreen trees. People sat silently in the seats in front of me, and I walked down the aisle in a black dress that dripped with blood.

Chapter Eight: Derrick

At first, I thought Nate had taken me to a brothel. I didn't think he had it in him, but he quickly disappointed me with his explanation that it was actually the seat of the coven. Still, the place *looked* like a brothel, with its mirrored surfaces and red velvet everywhere. Even the music screamed brothel, jazz-adjacent with a deep bass beat. Nate scowled at me as I paused to mimic slapping an ass as the beat dropped.

"This is serious, Der," he scolded me.

Yeah, duh. I knew it was serious. My wife had been murdered, but I just wanted to forget for a while. Which was why I had wished he had taken me to a brothel and not this pale imitation.

Nate walked me through his plan again. "Are you sure you can behave while I haggle?"

I scoffed. *Behave? Me?* I was an alpha wolf. I should be asking if *he* could behave! Someone needed to remind him that I should be in charge. Sure, I had no idea what we were doing here, but that was beside the point.

"Heard," I muttered, not entirely listening. "Stealth mission, behave myself, *blah, blah, blah.*"

He gave me a look. Shaking his head, he disappeared into the crowded bar. I prowled the perimeter. Behave myself. *Behave.* How was I supposed to do that when there were so many tempting vices in one place?

I did one more lap around the perimeter before locking on my target. *Bullseye.* She had a goblet of blood in one delicately gloved hand. I had never been with a vampire before, and the thought thrilled me. Her hair had been dyed a pretty pastel pink and she wore round, rose-colored sunglasses over her red eyes. She wore a giant dress shaped like a pastry, all ruffles and ribbons and bows. It too was cotton candy pink. She drank alone.

"Hello, princess," I said, sliding into the booth next to her.

She slid over, glaring at me pointedly. "Leave."

"What, no *please?*"

She pulled out a baton from somewhere within the folds of her skirt. In a flash of hot pink, the baton lengthened out into one of those curved spears carried by the grim reaper. Warm desire flooded through me. I loved playing *fight or fuck.* She raised an eyebrow, and smiled with blood red fangs. Without spilling a drop of blood, she pointed the weapon at me. "Please."

I smirked, leaning in. I was an alpha wolf. I could play dominance games.

But the reptilian bartender slithered forward, interrupting us. "Godsssssdammit, Inesssss!" the reptile shouted in a female voice, shoving a scaled green finger at the vampire. "How many timesssss do I have to tell you? No weaponsssss!"

76

The vampire—Ines—actually pouted. I imagined that pout underneath me, pink hair splayed out on white sheets. In this dream sequence, we weren't crammed in the back of Big Bertha.

"He started it," she hissed.

I couldn't stop myself from smiling, which seemed to incense the vampire further. *Game on.*

The reptile groaned. "I don't care who sssssstarted it. Thisssss issssssn't pressssschool! Put that away."

Without a word, *Ines* returned the baton to its place in her skirts.

"Thank you," the reptile stated as though this was a nightly occurrence. She turned to me, poking my chest. "And you, you leave her alone or I will let her ssssskewer you!"

I stood, backing away from the two of them, hands raised in surrender. "Fine by me!"

I sulked now that playtime was over. Without anything better to do, I returned to my prowling. When would Nate be finished? This was turning into a giant bust. I needed him here with me. Alone, I started to think too much. Thinking too much led me to think of Sarah. Thinking of Sarah led me to thinking about her death. Then my chest would ache and my eyes would sting. I hated that feeling. Nate needed to give me something to do.

The elevator gave a cheery *ding*, opening on a dejected Nate. He ushered me out of the club and into the parking lot.

"I take it that didn't go well," I said when we settled into Big Bertha.

"I don't have anything of value," he sighed. I didn't quite understand what he meant by that, but I nodded. He wiped his face with his hand. "And they won't sell the *Bestiary* back to me. I mean they will, but I don't have the money."

"How much?"

"One and a half million dollars."

I whistled through my teeth. That was a lot of zeros. Even at the height of the pack's success, we never had that much. "How much did they pay?"

"Half that," he groaned. "But that money doesn't go to me. Most of it goes to Harold's hoard. I'm just the broker." He slammed a fist on the dash. It made me jump, and we both stared at the spot in disbelief. Nate didn't lash out. He was a strong, silent type. He shook his head. "Sorry, the wolf is more active than usual. I wish I could just figure out what was in there that was so important. Why do both Alice and the coven want it?"

"Brother, it could just be a coincidence."

"I don't believe in coincidences. Not anymore." He scowled.

I might be catching his paranoia, but I also knew my friend. Nate was rarely wrong. He had been my second for a reason. Sarah hadn't picked him. I had.

Our coup had been a quick one. Once we killed my father, the rest of the wolves fell in line. Sarah and I had been teenagers, barely adults when we took over as the alpha pair.

Nate was a proper adult in my eyes then, with his fancy college degrees from the big city. We had needed him. Sarah had hated that Nate asked questions and wouldn't make a decision unless he had all the information he needed. Sarah was hard-headed. She had wanted to do things her way and only her way. I was impulsive. I still dove into problems head-first without a plan. We had needed Nate's influence.

Everything I had done, I had done in service of Sarah and the pack. Nate had been the only one to look out for me. He had helped me get my GED and enrolled me in night classes. He had encouraged me to grow the fuck up and become a man. I loved him—as a mentor, as a brother, as a friend, as a lover. I used to mix up admiration and desire then. Hell, I still did.

The only time I had ever seen Nate look dejected was when a cure hadn't worked. He looked so much older now than he had five years ago.

"We could write her back," I suggested. It was a stupid idea, but it was the only one I had besides storming the O'Shea pack in a blaze of glory.

"What do you mean?" He looked up finally.

"I mean, we know where she lives. That was never a secret. We could give her a taste of her own medicine."

I imagined thousands of little white cards embossed with *fuck off, bitch* and smiled.

"I can't imagine that taunting her is the right move," he said thoughtfully. He threw his head back. "It might force her to act earlier than she wants. It's not a bad idea." I preened a little at that. "But!" I deflated. "We have to time it right. We don't want to provoke her unnecessarily."

Oh, but I really did. I wanted to provoke the shit out of that bitch. And then, I wanted to kill her. Just as I had to every other threat that had stood in my way.

Chapter Nine: Christi

The next morning, the darkness settled over me in a cloud. I couldn't shake off the dream, and frankly, it gave me an excuse. I drew all the curtains. Pulling my blankets over my head, I fell back asleep, not emerging from my cave until noon.

As much as I didn't want to, I knew I had to get ahead of this, or I would miss out on days of work, or even weeks. Every step felt like I wore lead shoes, but I eventually got on some workout clothes. I sat on the edge of the bed, staring into the void, before lacing up my shoes. I pulled my hair into a messy bun and left my room. Sadie lay by her food bowl, obviously perishing because I hadn't fed her yet. I knelt and gave her a pat.

"Where would I be without you?" I asked her, kissing her black nose and hugging her neck. She wiggled free and placed an impatient paw in her bowl. "Okay, okay, I get it. Here's your breakfast."

She chowed down happily, her tail wagging in lazy circles. I sunk to the floor next to her, petting her absentmindedly. I stared into my space, unable to shake the heavy cloud off me. The dream of me in a bloody, black gown unnerved me. I could go into a trance to examine the dream further, but I knew I shouldn't get high right now. I could take Sadie on a walk, but that meant getting off the floor, and that felt impossible at the moment. So, I just sat there in my nothingness.

The doorbell sounded, and I lifted my head. *Shit fuck*. I had told Nate to stop by today.

"Come in," I called from the floor. Thankfully, Ines and Rachel stepped through my front door.

"It's the middle of the day," Ines complained. "This better be good." She stopped when she saw me. "What are you doing on the floor?"

The question irritated me. Why did she think? Why else would I be on the floor in the middle of the day on a Monday?

"Up! Up, up, up!" Rachel said, grabbing my hands and pulling me up. "Sexy shifter guy will be here any moment and no offense, dude, but you look like shit."

"Thanks," I muttered. Sadie excitedly circled around us, warbling softly for attention. "Yes, obviously everyone is here to see you, Sadie."

Ines bent down and buried her head in Sadie's fur.

"Speak for yourself," she said. "I will take care of the beast while you shower. Rachel, can you find something edible? Maybe some takeout in the fridge. I doubt she's eaten."

"On it!" Rachel saluted and ran into the kitchen.

"You don't have to talk about me like I'm not here."

"Are you here, mouse? Really here?" Ines asked. My heart ached. "Or are you somewhere else?"

When I didn't answer, Ines ushered me into the bathroom.

I barely had time for a breath after I showered. Immediately, Rachel handed me a plate of leftovers from Sunday dinner, which they'd both missed. I couldn't even bring it up, because after a few mouthfuls of spaghetti, the doorbell rang.

"I'll get it," Rachel volunteered, running to the front door. Sadie pranced at her heels.

I heard muffled hellos as she opened the door and brought them inside. Nate and his friend, a man with a barrel chest trapped in a black tee and a blond man bun, entered the kitchen. He looked like one of those Scottish men who participated in the Highland games, huge and solid. On the other hand, his clothes were too tight, as though he was going to be called on to model at any moment. His scraggly blond beard made him seem like a guy who lived in his van at the beach, like he only drank microbrews, and knew the best dispensaries for organic weed. It was so unlike Nate's clean-cut appearance that it was comical seeing them together.

Behind them, Rachel jumped up and down, giving me two thumbs up.

I waved her off. "Hey," I said, setting my plate down. I hugged Nate, which caused him to tense up. I didn't even mean anything by it. I just hug people. I could at least *try* not be silly around him.

I held out my hand to the other man. "I'm Christi."

"Derrick," he said, bypassing the handshake and hugging me. Cool. I wasn't the only touchy person here.

"You met Rachel, and this is Ines."

Ines didn't say anything, just lifted her chin up at them.

"Hello, princess," greeted Derrick. He went to hug Ines and she hissed. He backed away with a snarl.

"We've met," Ines said with a frown.

I looked between the two of them, confused.

Rachel grabbed Ines' arm and gave a little wave. "And we will be going!" As they retreated, Rachel continued to give me a silly grin and two thumbs up.

Nate knelt down to pet Sadie, who had been nudging his leg. Sadie immediately jumped up and put both front paws in his lap, licking his face.

Mortified, I knelt to pull her off him. "I am so sorry."

He waved me off, scratching Sadie's neck and chest. She softly sang her pleasure.

"Not a problem. I love dogs. What's her name?"

"Sadie. She's a Samoyed and very much a people dog. You are her best friend right now."

"And I'm okay with that," he said to Sadie in that scrunched, goofy voice everyone used when they talked to pets. "You are such a pretty girl, but you know that, don't you?"

Something stirred in me as I watched him with Sadie. A

flush of heat ran through me. I ignored it the best I could. "Well, don't blame me for the dog hair," I joked, before moving everyone into the living room.

I thanked Ines in my mind for ensuring I had showered. She'd gotten me into brown, wide-legged linen pants and a tan shirt that was ruched in the middle at my cleavage and had long bell sleeves. It was comfortable, but looked amazing on me. It also meant that I smelled good, which was a plus, since I sat next to Nate on the floor. Sadie had wormed her way into his lap, and he happily scratched her fur.

Derrick awkwardly sat on my chaise, clearly uncertain on how to sit on a chaise to begin with.

"Nate, why don't you start with what you need help with?"

"I'm trying to figure out why the *Bestiary* was so important. I think it might have something to do with lycanthropy."

So, he *was* a wolf shifter. Unless...

"Wait," I said, leaning forward on my hands. When all eyes went to my chest, I leaned back. *Shit fuck.* I took a deep breath to refocus. "Do you mean werewolf or wolf shifter?"

"He's a werewolf. I'm a wolf shifter." Derrick looked at Nate pointedly. "Are you sure we have time for this?"

Nate shrugged at him. At least I wasn't the only one who got that reaction from Nate.

"Derrick's not wrong," he confessed. "We need a cure and fast. I'm being hunted by the most powerful shifter in the country, and if I don't have a cure soon, she's going to collect me."

Derrick groaned impatiently. "I don't know why we're tiptoeing around it. Look, Alice O'Shea has been stalking Nate for over a decade, and she's desperate to have his puppies. She already knows where he is, and she's already killed for him."

Nate hung his head. "She killed Derrick's mate."

My stomach clenched as I saw Derrick's face. I had been there. It was different, but I knew that grief. "I am so sorry." Derrick turned his head away. I changed the subject. "What about Jessica? Do we know how she got involved?"

"She's gone. Picked up and left, according to the officer I spoke to," Derrick said. "That lead has dried up. It's either the cure or storming the O'Shea compound."

I looked to Nate. He wiped his face with his hands. There had to be more that we could do besides wait.

"You mentioned books. Do you think the cure might have been in the *Bestiary*?"

"It doesn't matter. It's with the coven now. All we know is that Alice wanted it."

"Shit fuck." I muttered. "Still, I'll take any texts you have on magic."

"Thank you," Nate said. "I'll take any help I can get."

I reached out and took Nate's hand. I squeezed it and gave him a smile.

He squeezed it back, stood up abruptly, and apologized.

"You don't know me and you don't have to do this. I really appreciate it."

We started to file out to the car to pick up the books, but Derrick stopped me. He handed me a white postcard with one large bloodstain. It had the same foreboding feeling as the envelope I left with Nate. I didn't want to take it, and I felt dirty immediately after I did. I read the words scrawled on it. *You can run, but you can't hide.*

"This was found where my wife was killed. It reeks of magic," he said. "I need you to trace it back to whatever sick fuck did this. Alice has other people to do her dirty work. I'll kill them first before I get to her."

A shiver ran down my spine. I looked down at the postcard.

"If it gets destroyed in the process—" I started, but he held up a hand to stop me.

"Burn it, bury it, eat it if you want. I don't fucking care. I just want to know who did this to her."

I placed one hand on his very large bicep. It was all muscle. How did a person *get* this large? I rubbed his arm comfortingly. He purred.

"We'll find them." I couldn't promise that, but I would try as hard as I could. I placed two amulets into the palm of his hand, one for him and one for Nate. I *knew* something had guided me to make them. Without realizing the significance, I had etched wolves into the stones. "These should help keep you safe for now."

He nodded before heading out the door. The darkness didn't leave with them.

By the time I checked my phone later, I had dozens of voicemails and text messages from Giana. Liam had fallen off their retaining wall and broken his arm. I thought of Sophia. Everything breaks, doesn't it?

Chapter Ten: Derrick

I sat on the floor, petting Christi's big, white floof of a dog. Sadie climbed into my lap, her head back, tongue lolling out. Petting Sadie gave me something to do besides looming over Christi as she worked.

"You know that this might not work," Christi repeated. She'd reminded me of this like a thousand times already, and I groaned. I didn't care if it was useless. I owed it to Sarah to try. Still, Christi spoke to me as gently as she would a toddler.

"Yeah, yeah, I get it, babygirl. Magic is unpredictable."

She turned to me, holding the note, a bowl, and a compact mirror. She set them before me and sat down on the pink rug next to me. "Mirrors have always been portals." She placed the mirror into the bowl, which was full of water. "We can't go through the looking glass, but we can use it to see the other side."

"Enough exposition, Christi," I said impatiently. "Let's do this shit."

She gave me a look before continuing. "Fine. I'm going to place the note in the water, and hopefully that will ground the spell."

The moment the note hit the water, it hissed and boiled. A green smoke enveloped it. Both Christi and I coughed at the smell. It smelled of hot garbage and rotten eggs. Sadie ran away to hide unsuccessfully under the couch, but she only got her head under it. Her giant fluffy butt stuck out like a dandelion in a pavement crack. I laughed loudly, waving a hand in front of my face to disperse the smoke. Christi's face paled, but I was getting excited. This looked like it was working. *Let's go! Show me the money!*

She nudged me. "This is your part. Put your hand in the water and focus on Sarah. Then say *Magic mirror, show me what I seek.*"

"That's it?" I questioned. "Why'd I need *you* for this?"

"If you don't want my help, you can go," she said, exasperated. When I didn't move, she added, "Magic is mostly intention. It's instinctual for me because I was taught how to use it. But how do you think I was taught? Even if I told you what to do, you'd still need supervision."

Like a child. *Stupid Derrick.* I thrust my hand into the water and muttered, "Magic mirror, show me what I seek."

Nothing happened, and I almost pulled my hand away. The green smoke spiraled up my arm and I flinched. It didn't hurt, but it made me feel dirty somehow. Slowly, the water rippled and swirled around my fingers. I looked to Christi with a grin. She nodded hopefully. The vortex continued to spin until the reflection on the mirror distorted, shifting in circles with it. *Come on. Come on.*

"Please work," I murmured to myself. It seemed like the mirror was searching and couldn't find anything. I didn't know how it worked. Was it looking for a signal or something? The image distorted on the mirror. Butterflies built up in my stomach. I rocked back and forth in excitement. *I'm a fucking wizard!* I laughed nervously. The swirling vortex slowed and the water started to clear.

My hope died quickly when the mirror showed the spot where we found Sarah's pelt. In slow motion, I watched Sarah's wolf racing through the desert. The mirror showed my Sarah being cornered, growling and snapping at her hunters. It showed the glint of a knife and a puddle of blood.

I gasped, recoiling from the bowl. The water sloshed as I hit the bowl with my legs. My jeans darkened with the wetness. The image in the mirror disappeared as the mirror slid out on the floor.

My chest ached. I clutched it, contracting in on myself. I felt Christi rub my back, but I couldn't see her. All I could see was the patch of blood and a gray wolf's pelt. I held my breath.

"I'm sorry, Derrick," Christi said uselessly. I shrugged her off. Sadie licked at my face, and I came back to myself. I scratched behind her ears as I buried my face into her fur.

"You were right. It didn't work," I said with a bite.

She shook her head at me. "I understand," she said simply.

Well, I didn't. I didn't understand any of this. I stood up, dusting the dog hair off my jeans.

"For what it's worth, I'm sorry for your loss." Christi said softly.

I was about to shrug her off, but something made me

pause. "Do you hear that?"

Christi stood and looked around. Looking wasn't going to help her hear better, but whatever.

"I hear howling," she said. In the distance, somewhere, a wolf howled. We both stepped to the sliding glass door that led to her backyard. Nothing. Silence. Christi rubbed her arms as though she had a chill. I couldn't shake the feeling. Something was out there. Something was watching.

I wanted to tell Nate about the howling, but he was out when I returned to his apartment. I slunk back to Big Bertha and stewed. Wolves have a voice, just like humans do. I'm not very smart, but even I can tell the difference between voices. I knew that voice.

Chapter Eleven: Nate

Every good Plan A deserved a Plan B. In this case, I needed a Plan C. Plans A and B weren't even that good. I knew I couldn't research my way out of this. I had one final idea, and it wasn't that great either. Still, I had to try again. Maybe this time, I had something valuable enough. I clutched the little wolf on a string that was supposed to keep me safe.

I stood at the doorway of the Crimson Dahlia. Working up the courage to go inside, I could already hear the music and smell the patrons. I scrunched up one eye to stave off the impending migraine. My stomach tightened, and I swallowed hard. I could do this. I needed to do this.

The bouncer stood inside the doorway, so he couldn't be seen from the street. He was enormous in the way a giant boulder was enormous—rotund, solid, and stocky. It might be a trick of the dim light, but his rough skin had a gray pallor to it, like he was made of gravel. He waved me into the hallway with a giant hand. The doorway flashed once as I entered. Magic stung my nose and I gagged. The rock-solid bouncer nodded.

"Free the first time," he warned me. "Next time, you either need a membership or know someone who does."

He said that every time. But each time, he hadn't asked for payment or my membership card. I don't know if he knew how desperate I was or if he just didn't care. With that, I gained entrance to the Crimson Dahlia. The interior looked like an old movie. Art Deco goldwork on the walls lined the walls. Red velvet draped on walls and couches, and a giant gold bar with a mirror underneath it served imbibing patrons. It looked old-fashioned, but didn't settle on one architectural or design style. It was meant to look old when it really wasn't. It was like synthetic fabric—you could always tell that it just wasn't quite right.

Beings of all kinds lounged on plush black velvet couches and drank out of real crystal glasses. It felt opulent but private—each couch was recessed, creating personal lounges within the bar. Music played, something jazz-like but definitely not made by humans. It wasn't too loud, so I could still hear the chatter of conversation around me. The patrons dressed well, like coming here was an event and not just a stop after work.

I had been here so many times with the same request, only to be rejected before I could even ask it. I don't know why I expected tonight to be different. The elevator down opened. I tapped my foot impatiently as I plunged into the depths of the coven's domain. I stepped out onto the bottom floor of the Dahlia and into the Proprietor's office. When the coven wanted something out of Harold's hoard, they summoned me here. When I wanted more information about a cure, I stopped here first.

No matter how many times I requested an audience, I never had something valuable enough to barter with.

The Proprietor, always bathed in shadow, didn't look out at me from under his top hat. White gloves stood out against a backdrop of black, as though he only existed when the light touched him. He already knew it was me when he spoke in the grave tones of true dark and moonless night. "We have told you our price, wolf."

I cleared my voice, holding out the little carved wolf. "I have come to request an audience."

The Proprietor scoffed. "And you think that is a sufficient enough sacrifice? Begone with you."

I struggled to breath and my wolf whimpered in my mind. Trapped. It felt trapped. So did I. I ignored the nudge from my wolf to run. Slamming my hands down on the desk, I stood my ground.

"Please!"

The Proprietor loomed above me, looking larger than a person should. He reminded me of things you find in the middle of the night. Tricks of shadow making you think the branches of a tree were a threat lying in wait. I breathed heavy as I looked up.

"You have nothing of value, wolf. The value that you do have is borrowed." His voice was an indigo midnight. I shivered in its cold. "I said, *begone!*"

My wolf knew an order when it heard one. I ran out of the office without another thought.

Hesitantly, I approached the bar, still trying to catch my breath. A reptilian female with scales and a green pallor gave me a bored look as she wiped glasses with a white cloth.

"Can I help you?" she asked. I took a seat on one of the barstools. It squeaked, betraying the upholstery as plastic, not leather.

"I don't think so." I said, sadly. In that moment, I realized I could have asked Christi. She would know how to properly request an audience with the coven. Maybe for the first time, I could have brought something of real value. But I needed to do this on my own. The fewer involved, the better. I had already involved too many people, and those people were winding up dead.

If a reptile could laugh, the bartender did. "What do you want? Healing for boilsssssss? Blood bargainssssss? Children to eat? Maybe even love potionssssss." She scoffed with a flick of her forked tongue. "No need for the coven for that."

"I need a cure for lycanthropy," I said, mostly to myself.

She ignored me and busied herself by making a drink. She set it down in front of me. It smoked from the top. "What you really need isssss a drink."

I pushed it away. "I don't drink."

"Sssssleeping draught," she responded. "Putsssss werewolvesssss to ssssssleep. It'sssss on the houssssse." She slithered away, addressing the other patrons.

Defeated, I rested my head on the bar. What was I going to do now? How many times must I try and fail?

I couldn't shake the feeling that this wasn't the life I was supposed to have. I had done everything right. I got into the right schools. I majored in the right subject. I got the prestigious internship. I was going places. I had a career that I loved. I was going to publish books that meant something, so that some other lonely kid could lose themselves in them. I had meaning and purpose and a life worth living. I had a family, a fiancée.

Alice took that all away from me. Worse, the wolf took that from me. Everyone had someone in their past who broke them. Mine just left a reminder that I could never get rid of.

It was more than just Alice. It was more than just Derrick. The night was a reminder. The moon was a reminder. The pack was a reminder. The wolf was a constant reminder of what I had lost. I was a different man now than the man I had been. I could never get back to that man with the wolf in me.

Sure, Alice pushed me to this. But I needed the wolf gone. I had to do this to feel whole again.

I heard a squeak and I looked up. An older man sat on the barstool next to me. He dressed in a white tee shirt, dark jeans, a linen blazer, and Italian leather loafers. Chic.

Expensive. He adjusted his wire-rimmed glasses to take a better look at me. His dark hair was gelled back and glamoured not to show his age. He reeked of magic, masked with copious spritzes of cologne. It burned the hairs in my nose, and I could barely sit next to him. Something about him looked familiar, but I couldn't place it.

"I couldn't help but overhear your predicament," he said in a voice reserved for advertising and used car salesmen.

"Leave me alone," I grumbled. I didn't want to deal with some hedge witch selling cheap spells and garbage potions.

"Come now, son," he admonished. "I'm only offering to help. Stevie's right. You don't need the coven. You need a real witch. Those biddies only care about maintaining the status quo. They don't care about innovation." He clapped me on the shoulder. "And you need an innovative solution."

I shrugged him off with a sigh. If I left now, restaurants would still be open. I could get a pizza on my way home and change into sweatpants. I shifted my weight on the bar stool, already growing uncomfortable sitting for so long. My wolf snarled at this threat. Still, I took the man's bait. "Let me guess, you have just the solution I need."

"That is correct," he answered, just like I knew he would.

Maybe I was wrong. Maybe he smelled of magic because he was a faery wearing a glamor. He could be trying to lure me into a fae bargain. But I was desperate. I forced the wolf further from the surface, so I could ignore the obvious warning signs. The growling in my head didn't stop, but at least I felt less shaky with adrenaline. "I'm listening."

"I knew you were a smart man." He spit snake oil out so easily, he could lubricate an engine. "I'm working on something experimental. Top secret. For a very wealthy patron. I could use a volunteer."

My wolf growled at that, but I blocked it out. "What do you mean?"

"I'm talking a cure, son," he said, leaning in conspiratorially. "I mean, it's still experimental, but results are promising."

I should have listened to my wolf, I should have paid more attention to the red flags waving, I should have asked more questions. But this man dangled in front of me the one thing I wanted most in the world. How many times had I found myself here, only to be disappointed? But it couldn't hurt to try.

"I'm in."

The man grinned before reaching out a hand. I took it. We shook on the agreement.

"Joseph Bianchi, warlock, at your service," he said. "But you can call me Joe."

"Nate," I responded. He handed me a metal card, stamped with his information. I slid it into my wallet next to a similar card.

"Let me buy you a drink."

I knew temptation when it stared me in the eyes. I shook my head, holding up the smoking drink in front of me. "I'm all set."

Joe gave me a wink. "Bottom's up!"

That night, I slept better than I had in years.

Chapter Twelve: Christi

"Take a shot!" Rachel chanted as I relaxed into the couch. "Shots, shots, shots!"

Rachel made a drink in the kitchen. Ines, on the couch with me, drank blood out of a self-warming mug with a straw.

"No shots!" I called out. "Goddess, Rach, it's a Wednesday night." Rachel scoffed and I gave in. "Fine, I won't say no to a glass of wine. Whatever's open. Please, and thank you."

"That's never stopped you before," Ines complained. She'd dressed for a pajama party, in baby pink silk pajamas, a fancy robe that would fit in an old Hollywood movie, and an eye mask resting on her perfectly imperfect messy bun. Rachel too had dressed for the occasion, in a white tank top and boxers. I had thrown on some soft leggings and a sweatshirt that read *Bad Witch* after my run.

"I don't want to be hungover tomorrow."

"Because of the wolves?" Ines arched an eyebrow in my direction.

I glared at her, but was answered with a glass of wine in my hand by an already tipsy Rachel. The glass was filled almost to the top. "Goddess, Rach, this is a *fuck the bartender* pour, and I am not fucking anyone tonight."

"Can't hurt a gal for tryin'," she said, winking at me before she collapsed onto the couch. "That werewolf was a lot of man meat. If you were to fuck anyone, it should be him."

Ines cocked her head, considering the two shifters for a moment. I wondered what went through her head, but I had to get this conversation under control.

"Rachel, what would you know about man meat?" I quipped. Ines snorted in agreement, a coy smile on her face.

Rachel stuck her tongue out at us. "I don't, but I know you! That bookstore dude is every single one of your types. Even down to the shifter! I've seen your books!"

"The blond one?" Ines asked as I tried to hide my blushing face with my sleeve.

"Ew, the other one." Rachel made a face. "But the real question is not which flavor of shifter Christi should boink. *Mean Girls* or *27 Dresses*?"

"*Mean Girls*, obviously," Ines decided.

"Why not *Magic Revealed*?"

Both Ines and Rachel groaned.

"A documentary?" Ines snapped, as Rachel exclaimed, "That's not remotely romantic!"

I rolled my eyes and flung my head back in frustration. "It's up for tons of awards." Rachel and Ines started to argue with me again. "Fine, I give up. *Mean Girls*, it is."

The doorbell interrupted our disagreement. Rachel and Ines happily put the movie of their choice on as I answered the door. My easy smile disappeared when I opened the door.

"What are you doing here?" I asked, closing the door behind me as I stepped out. The night was still warm, but I shivered in anticipation of conflict.

Dad stood in front of me, hands in his pockets. His pose suggested nothing of the fights we'd had or the times I've told him to stay away. "Can't your dad just drop by?" he said, all smiles. "I was in the neighborhood."

I crossed my arms, frowning. Ignoring the speed of my heartbeat, I focused on staying as impassive as possible. It wouldn't help me to get upset or overly emotional. He'd only use it against me later. There was nothing he did better than emotional manipulation.

"I'm serious, Dad. We talked about this. No more unannounced visits. When I said I don't want to see you, I meant it." I tried to remember how I practiced this in therapy years ago. My voice shook, but I stood firm.

"Honey, you make it sound like wanting to see my daughter is a crime." He laughed softly, but I knew that tone of his voice. Anger lurked underneath that surface-level charm. His smile never quite reached his eyes.

He didn't respect me or my boundaries. He wasn't here to visit, as much as he might feign to be. I bit the inside of my lip, worrying my tongue against it. If I met him on his level, I'd get upset, which he would use as another arrow in his quiver to wound me. If I ignored him, he always managed to show his true intentions.

He stepped forward. I didn't move, preventing him from entering my house. I wished that he were a vampire and required permission to step through the threshold. Not for the first time, I wondered if my wards would hold against him. Technically, I set the wards against any being or thing threatening my person, my dog, or my possessions. He certainly fell into that category, but how much would he have to hurt me to register as a threat? I didn't want to perform that particular experiment tonight.

"How can you *be in the neighborhood* when you live on the other side of town?" I asked, forcing a smile into my voice. If I smiled, I wouldn't cry. If I smiled, I could act like this was just an unpleasant interruption to my night and not a devastating reminder that I continued to disappoint my family. If I smiled, I could keep the darkness from taking root. Reflexively, I tapped a foot onto the step. If only it were that easy to stomp out the darkness, to keep it from pulling me down.

"Well, honey, I have a business proposal for you—"

I scoffed. *There it was!* Typical Dad, always trying to sell something.

"Funny," I said. "Last time you spoke to me about my job, it was to berate me for being a no-good, goddess-damned witch. You called *the coven* on me! I spent months straightening it out with the Bureau to prove that I was properly registered." I looked at him incredulously. "I fail to understand how you could possibly want my help."

I panted with anger. Dad held up his hands and stepped back. I got a big whiff of his cologne and shuddered. I used to love that smell growing up, now it made my whole body tense up.

"I think you are making a big mistake, Christiana," he chided me, like I was a child. I would always be a child to him. There was no getting through to him that I was very much an adult now and could make my own decisions.

I sighed, shaking my head. "No, Dad. The only mistake I made tonight was answering the door." I stepped across the threshold into the house. "Go home, Dad. I'm sure your new family's missing you."

My head touched the door as I leaned back. Squeezing my eyes shut, I struggled to keep from crying. I still shook long after he left. Wiping my tears off my face, I took three steadying breaths. When I finally moved from the doorway, I didn't notice the darkness trailing behind me.

Chapter Thirteen: Derrick

I needed money. My funds were running low, and the camping fee for Big Bertha continued to drain them. Maybe I could kill two birds with one stone. The howling echoed in my ears. Sarah's wolf howled in my ears. Over. And over. And over again. I wanted to hit something. I wanted someone to hit me. I wanted the howling to stop. I ran to the Dahlia at top speed.

The reptile-thing at the bar nodded when she saw me. "Can I help you?"

"I need a fight. Like, right now."

"Level 5," she said, bored.

Fine, whatever. I didn't need her to be nice if she gave me what I needed.

I stomped through the club, pushing past anyone who got in my way. If they had a problem with it, they could fight me too. Anger balled up in my stomach, only growing as I moved. There was something sadder underneath the anger, and I wasn't about to let myself feel *that*.

I spotted the rickety elevator. It looked like it was a hundred years old. The grate resisted when I went to open it, so I forced my way through. There were no buttons for the levels, and I pounded my fist against the metal wall in frustration. "Come on!" I yelled.

Something joined me in the elevator. I looked down at

the ugly creature. It was the size of a child but built like a man, and covered in hair except for its human-looking face. It was a fucking ugly mug too, huge nose and big ears, its teeth hanging outside of its mouth. Along its back were long spikes, hundreds of them. It smelled male, if I had to guess, though really, he mostly smelled damp. I took a quick glance to see what he was packing. Definitely male—his dick hung out, just as disgusting as the rest of him. The porcupine thing smiled at me, pointing to a circular piece of machinery next to me that looked like an old school bell.

"What?" I snapped.

"It's the controls," he said, waddling over in rodent-like small, quick steps. The wolf called to me; this was prey. I snarled when he made a show of gently moving me to the side so he could take over. I could eat him in one gulp if I wanted to. But then, who would control the elevator?

See? *Smart.*

"Careful, rat," I warned him with a growl.

He hunched even lower to the ground and raised his hands in supplication. I fought the urge to bite down on his neck.

"I mean no offense. No offense at all. Please. I help you. Where do you wish to go?"

"Level 5."

"Very good, very good," he said, placing a hand on the controller. "This is where I plan to be as well."

The elevator jerked and began to descend. The rat thing

looked at me, and I growled. He withdrew back into the corner of the elevator. When I stopped growling, he smiled, and I could see all of his long, crooked teeth. Disgusting. The elevator stopped and he grabbed my hand. *Ew.*

"Come. Come."

The cheers drowned out everything as elevator doors opened. I couldn't even hear myself think. The beings of all kinds crowded into the room from wall to wall. I could barely follow this rat through the mob of beings. While some sat in bleachers along the walls, most of the humans and creatures stood on the floor, screaming for whoever their champion was. A boxing ring filled the middle of the room, where two creatures battled it out. Blood and bits showered the audience when a particularly rough hit landed. That riled the crowd more. Some booed, some cheered, but all of them made noise. My wolf and I grinned.

The rat thing scurried through the crowd, gesturing for me to follow every few steps. He guided me through a small hallway that opened up to a black room with one counter. Bars separated us from the creature at the counter: it had white antlers, an animal skull for a face, and spindly arms that looked like they were made of shadow. There was a bowl of meat next to it, raw and bloody. It stained its long fingers and white snout red. I sniffed and recoiled. The meat smelled human.

What the *actual* fuck.

The rat thing scurried right up to the counter and

pointed at me. "He wants to fight."

"Of course he does. They all do," the skeleton thing said slowly, its voice papery and ancient.

It gave me the creeps. There was something not right about a prey animal acting predatory. Maybe this thing had never been an actual deer. What wore the bones of an animal? I shuddered. Something bad.

"Human?"

"No," I said quickly, not eager to be this thing's midnight snack.

"Shame." It took a chunk of meat, dripping in its hand, and placed it in its waiting maw. It smacked on it as it chewed. I controlled the urge to retch. I never developed a taste for meat in my human form. Still, I knew how the wolf ate. Who was I to judge this human-eating skeleton-deer demon-thing?

It gestured with its clean hand and a piece of paper and quill appeared, suspended in thin air. What was it with magic and quills? This thing couldn't book fights with a computer? It looked at the paper. "You can have the next fight."

Yes!

"That's with the Big Guy, yes? The Big Guy?" the rat thing asked eagerly, and I knew it should worry me, but I didn't fucking care anymore. *Let me fight the Big Guy!*

The skeleton nodded.

"Yes, the opponent is the *Big Guy*," the skeleton said, jotting something down, and then both the paper and quill disappeared.

"How much?" I demanded. The skeleton cocked its head. "If I win, how much do I get?"

The quill and parchment reappeared. The skeleton scrawled a number on it and passed it through the bars. I exhaled through my teeth. That was a lot of zeros.

The rat started to scurry out of the room, gesturing for me.

"Wait, what about the rules?"

"Rules?" the skeleton asked, and made a hollow, rasping sound. It took me too long to realize that it was a laugh. "Survive."

The fight wasn't over when we left the skeleton deer shadow demon's hidey hole. The rat practically jumped up and down with excitement. He led me to the ring, where a troll had a centaur in a headlock. I couldn't believe my eyes as the centaur kicked two hooves right into the troll's massive balls. What *the fuck* was this place?

It wasn't long before I was caught up in the excitement, cheering the centaur on. The troll looked rough, his ear bitten off, his balls swollen, and his left eye dangling out of its socket. The centaur had big gashes in his hide where the troll had scraped the leathery hide away with his fingernails. The troll reached for the centaur's tail, but didn't manage to grab hold. The troll planted face-first into the ring. The centaur jumped up on his hind legs and brought his front hooves down on the troll's head. Again. And again. And again. It cracked open like a melon, spraying blood and brains into the audience. Only when the troll's brain was mush did the centaur stop. He was declared the winner over a loudspeaker, but I didn't see any referee or announcer. A cleanup crew began to work on the ring so it was ready for my fight.

I couldn't back out now, despite some pre-fight jitters. The risk of death made me a little nervous. Go big, or go home, am I right? Besides, with no rules, I could fight as a wolf-man, adding the wolf's strength and instinct to my own. My wolf snapped its teeth excitedly in the back of my mind, ready to come out and play.

While I waited, I transformed, skin stretching, bones breaking to accommodate my more wolfy features. In this half-wolf, half-man form, I gained height and muscle as well as large canine legs with paws and claws on my fingertips. Gray fur covered my body, my clothes were torn to pieces, and my snout grew long. My ears twitched as they listened to the new sounds around them.

The cleaning crew finished, but I could still smell blood underneath the chemicals and magic in the ring. *Good*. I could use it. Let it fuel me. Drool dripped down my muzzle and onto the floor below. Sawdust covered the ring's wooden floor to sop up the blood. When I hopped into the ring, the crowd went wild, and I threw my head back and howled. On the other side of the ring was a bipedal covered in brown fur that was over seven feet tall at least. The *Big Guy* was a fucking Bigfoot. A fucking sasquatch. He wore glasses and threw them to the side. He jumped up and down with nerves.

"Matt! Matt! Matt!" chanted the crowd. *Matt?* What a dorky fucking name for Bigfoot!

If there was a signal to start, I didn't wait for it. Once the Bigfoot started moving, I was off.

And quickly disappointed. The squatch was fucking slow. Every punch, kick, and jab, I dodged, but not before I slashed at him. I tuned out the crowd and listened to the squatch's breathing as he tried to keep up with me. *That's it, ugly. Keep running around. Come catch me.* Adrenaline coursed through me as the wolf enjoyed the chase.

I stayed low to the ground, so the squatch had to bend over to even touch me. I nipped at his heels before running through his legs and landing a kick to his chest. As the Bigfoot fell on his ass, he managed to box me on my ear. I saw stars and my ear began to ring. I shook my head to snap out of it, but I felt blood leaking from it. He might be slow, but he hit hard. It didn't matter. The Bigfoot was still flat on his back. I slid to the other end of the ring, using my claws to stop me. *Get up, you slow fuck! Stop making this so easy.*

I ran full speed at the squatch and pounced. Everything slowed down for me: the cheers, the squatch, my launch into the air. This was too easy. I landed on his chest and dug my claws into his arms. He beat at me, but he couldn't move all my weight from on top of him. I smelled his fear; I saw his helplessness. Prey. Useless.

I ripped out his throat with my bare teeth, blood spraying me. The squatch stopped fighting and I got up, spitting out the fur and skin from my mouth. I opened my arms wide and threw my head back. I howled on top of the cheers. Over the roar of the crowd, I heard a voice declare me the winner over the speakers.

People gave me a wide berth when I climbed out of the ring, and this was what I have been missing. Respect. Fear. They knew I was a fearsome predator and they shouldn't fucking cross me.

Except for the stupid rat thing, who found me right away. The blood started to dry, and I was still naked. A hand touched my shoulder, and I turned. There was a man, tall, skinny, in a suit and top hat, with a cane. A shadow obscured my view of him so I couldn't see his face, but he handed me a white towel.

I took it, covering my bits. "Thanks."

This enraged the rat and he screamed, grasping at me with his fingers. "Mine!" he screeched, digging his fingers in further.

I wanted to rip *his* throat out, but the man took his cane and poked the metal head at the rat's chest. The rat released me, and all the spikes raised on his back as he hissed.

"Now, now," the shadowy man said, firmly. Now that I could smell past the blood and gore, I smelled the air of magic on him, burning all my nose hairs off. A witch. "You've had your fun for the night. Run along before *you* end up in the ring."

He gave a final poke, and the rat reluctantly scampered away. Prey. My wolf growled underneath my skin, begging to come out again. The witch set his cane back down.

"Well, now that pest has been taken care of," he said in a deep voice that sounded like the night itself. "You should be more careful, my wolf friend. That one is notorious for luring unsuspecting humans to their deaths."

"Not a human, but that explains why he wanted me to fight the Big Guy," I muttered.

"I'm surprised the organizer let you fight him, to be perfectly frank. Sasquatches may be hulking beasts, but they certainly are not as smart or cunning as a wolf shifter. It made for a very uneventful fight."

"*That* was uneventful?"

"You could have ended it in the first minute, but you forced us all to watch you play games. I should say it was uneventful. But you made quite a bit of money. Keep coming back and you can be a very rich man indeed."

I felt the pull of the magic, hypnotic and heavy like waking up in the middle of a dream. A powerful witch. My wolf raised its hackles. I shouldn't trust this man. "Why do you care?"

"As the Proprietor, I have a vested interest in the fighting ring champions."

"That so?" I growled, unimpressed.

"Follow me," he said. "Let's get you your prize money."

"If this is when you are going to ask me to suck your dick, you're going to have to buy me dinner first," I told the Proprietor, after I'd showered in his suite at the Crimson Dahlia. I had changed into black silk pajamas that he provided, which of course, *magically* fit me.

My nose burned with the smell of magic. The room reeked of it, like standing next to a dumpster.

The Proprietor laughed as he handed me a glass of some kind of alcohol, motioning for me to take the bed. He might be a witch, but I knew better than to accept food from a stranger. Too many shady bargains were made that way. I sat on the edge of the bed.

"If I require your services in that respect, I'll be much more forward. Don't worry," he said. "Glad to know that you would be receptive to the offer."

"Man, woman, cryptid. Doesn't really matter to me." I smiled. I could play this game. I could dance this dance. I was an apex predator, after all. I still tasted blood and the triumph of a hunt ran through my veins. I was suddenly very hard. I ditched the alcohol and decided to try my luck. I lay back on the bed, my hard dick prominently displayed, with my hands behind my head. "Now, how about my dick getting sucked?"

"Oh?"

"You can't blame me for trying," I said, starting to get up. I tried to play at seduction, and I failed. That meant it was time to go home with a bag full of crisp bills.

The Proprietor deliberately stood up, strode over, and pushed me back on the bed. I loved this—the thrill of a new lover. The chase. He knelt in front of me and pushed my thighs apart. I liked where this was going, and the anticipation of it made my dick twitch.

"That wasn't a *no*."

Chapter Fourteen: Nate

I arranged a few of the more comfortable seats in the bookstore into a circle near the stacks in the back. I glared at Derrick, who sat uselessly behind the counter.

"You could at least help," I snapped at him. "Christi will be here any minute."

He grinned like an idiot, and I wanted to punch that grin right off his face. My wolf, on the other hand, rolled over and showed its belly. It pulled me back and tamped down any aggression I had wanted to display.

"Oh yes, we must make a good impression for *Christi*." He said her name like a game show host announcing his next contestant, all sunny and excited, complete with jazz hands.

"What is this, man?" I questioned, waving my hands in his direction. "You seem awfully chipper for someone who lost his mate."

I tried so hard to make this clear for him. We *should* have run. Joe may have made promises for a cure, but the clock was ticking down.

"I'm doing this for you, you know," he grumbled.

I threw my hands up in frustration. "But I'm paying for it!"

I was paying for Christi to help us. I had insisted on it, and Derrick just expected I would. Typical alpha laziness. My only plan was to find a cure, and the wolf in my head paced back and forth, unable to sit still at that thought. Every fiber of my being said to run. Yet, I waited. When the Bureau lead had dried up, I'd almost bolted. But my alpha was here, and Christi had helped him. She might be able to help me too.

"I told you I would pay you back." Derrick lived in his 1970s camper van down at the beach. It had barely gotten him to California. I didn't believe his promises. He wasn't paying me back. "But admit it, you *like* her." He sauntered out from behind the counter. "When's the last time you got laid?"

I ignored him, dragging a small table into the middle of the circle.

"Oh, brother, you can't mean that I was your last fuck," he teased. I scowled at him. "Then we will make a good impression on *Christi* and get you laid."

He patted my shoulder, and I shrugged it off.

"I don't do casual," I said through my teeth. I had to get to know the person before I could take them to bed. But Derrick knew that. I appreciated Christi's looks, but more in a beautiful-work-of-art way rather than a I-want-to-rip-your-clothes-off way. I found her mind more interesting than her body anyway.

Derrick found any and everything attractive—man, beast, woman, five-headed hydra. It didn't matter to him. I didn't necessarily need to have feelings for someone before I jumped into bed with them, but I needed to understand them—their heart, their mind—and form some kind of emotional bond before I even found them sexy. That was how

I'd ended up with Derrick in the first place. Being friends first helped. Looks didn't matter until after I had a connection.

Derrick eased into one of the chairs, crossing his leg on his knee, taking up as much space as possible. An alpha tactic, trying to prove his dominance. Gone were the tears over Sarah.

"Seriously, Derrick," I pleaded. "What is going on?"

I could barely eat and couldn't sleep. Day and night, I spent all my free time reading. The rest of my time, I waited to hear from Joe. My body still burned from the change, and the wolf stayed so close to the surface that I feared I would lose control. I felt like I was losing my mind while Derrick was having the time of his life.

"The howling has stopped. I'm getting dicked down on the regular. Nothing bad has happened yet." He produced a few notecards like a magician performing a card trick. "These babies are ready to send. I'm taking a breather, man."

"Lucky you," I snapped. I couldn't just take a breather. The notecards sent a message, but I felt like a child poking a giant. All it took was one stomp to end everything.

I had already given a set of volumes to Christi. She was coming to return some of them, but also to spend the day reading. It made more sense for Christi to just come here so we could divide and conquer.

"We don't have time to wait, so you better be right about this," I said gruffly. It might have been too harsh. He had no one, and unlike me, I reminded myself, he didn't thrive alone.

That was why he was an alpha.

The bell at the front door rang out. She was here.

I placed one last book on the stack I had on the floor next to me, finally finished organizing the ones I had read today. I twisted my back one way, then the other, and stretched my arms out overhead. Stifling a yawn, I sunk back into the chair.

"I never thought I would say this, but I don't think I can read another word."

Christi smiled up at me from the floor. She had spread everything out around her like a big snow angel of parchment and books. It took everything I had not to tidy it up into neat stacks. She had been humming to herself all day and only now had stopped.

"The bookseller is tired of reading, say it isn't so," she quipped. "I think I'm done for now too. Would you mind if I take this one home, though?" She pointed at a piece of parchment. "I think I have a way to translate it, but I'd have to consult some books to make sure."

"The witch wants to consult the ancient texts? How can I say no to that?"

Derrick had stopped reading a while ago and was laying across one of the chairs, feet hung over the arm. "Finally!" he groaned, jumping to his feet. "I'm calling it a night. You two okay cleaning all this up? Cool, bye!"

I barely caught up to him before he reached the door. "What the fuck?" I asked in disbelief. Sure, I was tired, but I wasn't exactly going to call it a night. I had to do something while I couldn't sleep.

"That," Derrick stated as he sauntered towards the door, "was phase one of *Operation Get Nate Laid*."

I glared at him. "There is no such operation. I'm *paying* her. She *works* for us."

"And that's *never* stopped anyone before," Derrick said, rolling his eyes.

I crossed my arms over my chest. "Derrick, you may have forgotten, but I'm not a people person." Derrick cast me a knowing glance. "I don't *know* her."

"Christi's not people," he said, pointing at me. "This lets you get to know her, and not just as your side witch." He chuckled, and I looked for something in arm's reach to throw at him. "And who says no to a free dinner?"

"What are you talking about?"

He tapped the place on his wrist, where a watch would be if he wore one. "It's that time of night. Have dinner with her before you decide to wimp out. Later!"

Christi lifted her head when she heard me walking back. She had been putting the books in stacks, but none of them related to the topic or source of the volumes. I would have to rearrange them later, after she'd left.

"He left in a hurry," she said, standing up and stretching.

"I tried to organize these a little bit, but I think I made it worse." She motioned to one set of stacks. "These are all the ones we've read through." Another set of stacks. "Those are the ones that need a second look." A third set of stacks. "And these we haven't gotten to yet."

I prayed my eye wasn't twitching at her descriptions. I had them organized by source, topic, and time period, but sure, these three sets of stacks were fine. *Just fine.*

"It doesn't matter," I lied. My wolf opened one eye at that. It had been sleeping, but it had the tendency to do that around Christi. I worked up my courage to ask her to have dinner with me. I leaned against one of the chairs. "Do you want to come upstairs?"

Smooth. I grimaced. The words didn't come out right.

"Why, Nate, I thought you'd never ask," she said, seeming to take it in stride. She motioned to her acid wash jeans and a jewel-toned crop top. "I'm afraid I'm not quite dressed for the occasion."

"I meant for dinner," I corrected, feeling my cheeks growing hot. "But please forget that I said anything."

Christi placed a hand on my arm. "Nate, that was a yes."

My phone buzzed. Joe had texted me with a date, time, and address. Thank god. Christi looked at me expectantly.

"Let me just lock up."

We walked wordlessly through the alley. There was a palpable tension, the electricity of possibility crackling between us. I felt a bit sick, a fluttering in my stomach threatening me. My wolf helped ease my anxiety, excitedly pushing me forward. I swallowed a nervous laugh.

Neither of us laughed as we stepped up to the door. Blood dripped down to the asphalt. A giant red *X* had been painted on the door to my apartment. Christi gasped, but the first thought I had was that I should have invested in security cameras. Reality set in quickly.

Goddammit Alice. Were the calls and texts and fucking notecards not enough? Was Sarah not enough?

I couldn't breathe, and the breaths I could take were quick and fast. Sweat poured from me. The stomachache that had been building made me retch. I knew I would get sick. My whole body pitched forward, and I had to place my hands on my knees to keep from passing out. Panic gripped my chest as my vision went black. My wolf nudged at my mind, reminding me that I wasn't actually dying, I just felt like it.

Christi lightly rubbed my back. "Are you alright?" she asked, her voice shaking. I barely registered that she spoke to me. She repeated the question. I could only nod. She shook her head. "We don't have to have dinner. I'll just clean up here for you—"

I stopped her, my heart finally returning to the right pace. "No. Please. I'm sorry. I got distracted. If I'm alone, all I'll do is think about her. Please, stay."

I investigated the blood further. I ran my fingers through the blood and sniffed. I laughed under my breath. "Animal blood," I reassured her. "Just give me a second and I'll have it cleaned up—"

Christi looked at me for a moment before reading my mind. "You know, your place is a little small. Maybe you could come over to mine. Would half an hour give you enough time clean this—er, to gather supplies? Because I can guarantee salt, pepper, and olive oil, but not much else."

I nodded. I could do half an hour.

"That's not your fault." She paused and shook her head. "None of this is your fault."

My wolf snapped in agreement. I didn't believe either of them.

Chapter Fifteen: Nate

Half an hour later, I stood at her door, holding bags full of
food and a bouquet of flowers. My mother taught me to never
show up empty-handed, and usually that meant wine, but
sobriety meant that flowers were more appropriate.

I let myself in, and I could hear music drifting down the
hall. I loved this record. I dropped the groceries in the
kitchen and looked for Christi. I knew my way around from
the first time I'd visited. Her house was a mix of earth jewel
tones and faded luxury. Every room was a different color,
with various patterns and textures thrown in for good
measure. I hated it. I tended towards minimal, sleek lines and
white walls. So much easier to clean. But my apartment never
felt as alive as her home did.

"Christi?" I called out.

When she didn't answer, I grew concerned. My heart
beat faster. What if something happened to her? What if Alice
had found her too? I smelled only salt and herbs and dog. The
music drowned out any other sounds. Panic propelled me to
search her rooms.

I found myself out in her backyard. My heart fell into my
stomach. I ran to Christi, standing at the edge of her yard.
Her mouth was a grim line. One of her hands held Sadie by
the collar and the other pointed at her ruined gate. Three
shifter men prowled beyond the gate, just out of reach. I

didn't know or recognize them, but I could smell the wolf from here. I bared my teeth, ready to run after them, but Christi stopped me.

"The wards," she explained. "They can't get in, even if they tried."

They snarled menacingly at the edge of her property. Sadie yowled, trying to get away from Christi. I stepped in front of them.

The tallest one, dressed in a severe silver suit, waved in our direction. "The pack says hello," he called out.

With a whistle, they retreated into a car parked down the street. I ran out to follow their trail, but the motor oil and gasoline masked the scent as they sped away. I held my breath until they had driven out of sight.

"I am so sorry," Christi said, her eyes wide.

If anyone needed to apologize, it should have been me.

Her wooden gate was torn off the hinges, the door marred with deep claw marks. My heart sunk. Christi propped it up, but it was useless. It sagged to the sidewalk.

"I found my gate like this. Sadie almost got out, I barely caught her. I couldn't even prop the gate up. They were taunting Sadie, and me, from outside the wards." She took a deep breath, gulping in air. "I couldn't do anything. I just stood there."

"Christi." I reached for her, but she stepped away.

She plastered a smile on her face, even though all the blood had drained out of it. "It's fine," she said through her teeth. Her voice no longer shook. "I caught Sadie. I can get the gate fixed. No harm done. I won't give them the satisfaction of being scared."

"Let me fix it."

"Thanks." Her voice was a small thing. She looked to Sadie. "Come on, girl. Let's go back inside."

I tasted bile. She was wrong; this was *my* fault. This wasn't meant to scare her. It was meant to taunt me. Joe's cure couldn't happen soon enough.

After I inexpertly fixed the gate, I found Christi in the guest bedroom, making up a dog bed for Sadie and arranging a water bowl. She had changed into a brown slip dress that looked just a step up from lingerie. A cream sweater was thrown over it, but it kept falling off her shoulder, leaving bare skin in its wake. She had piled her hair up with a clip, and her cheeks looked flushed. She closed the door, and Sadie grumbled at being left.

"Do you mind if I have a glass of wine?" she asked once we were back inside her kitchen. The situation hung between us, thick with tension but thin like a stretched rubber band. One wrong move and it would snap. I could barely breathe as I moved through it, my body heavy.

I shook my head. "As long as you don't mind if I don't have one."

She nodded, but seemed to forget about it. I watched as she sat at the kitchen counter across from me. I couldn't handle this feeling. My wolf wanted to burst out of my skin if we didn't resolve this soon."

"I'm so sorry, Christi. I should never have involved you."

She shook her head and her jewelry jingled along. I smiled in spite of myself.

"I would have been involved eventually anyway. Ines has friends in the Wilderness who are being harassed by the pack." She explained. "She's been telling me for ages that we should help her friends. I just didn't want to go."

"Why not?" I asked. I needed something to do with my hands, so I started to chop the onions I brought, ignoring the sting.

"All stupid reasons now. The Wilderness is so far away. The Wilderness is dangerous. It wasn't bothering me directly, so why get involved?" She sighed. "Too late for that. The gate was trivial, but they messed up by going after my dog."

Her jaw set and I saw her resolve. I wanted to apologize again, but held my tongue. Nothing I said would make it better. I turned around to set the oven temperature, but Christi practically leapt over the counter.

"Don't!"

I froze. "What did I do?"

"This is a comedy of errors, isn't it?" she said, trying to break the tension as she eased her way around me.

Her kitchen wasn't big enough for the two of us, a fact

that I was now fully aware of as Christi stuck her head in the oven. Her ass practically grinded into me, and I swallowed. Hard. My wolf had woken up and now stared at her lasciviously. Or maybe that was me. What was wrong with me? We were both reeling from the day. My wolf confused danger for desire. Two different kinds of arousal. Bile rose in my throat, and I swallowed my brief panic. I looked back up as Christi pulled herb bundles from her oven.

"You store herbs in your oven?"

She pulled the last bundle out. "Where else would I store them?"

I looked at her for a moment. "You really meant it when you said you don't cook."

"This kitchen is practically ornamental," she quipped, squeezing past me again. "Okay, I will let you work your magic."

She sat at the kitchen island and watched me, providing commentary along the way. The message was clear. There would be no more talk about wolves or Alice or the Wilderness. She picked up the cookbook I had brought over.

"You have got to be kidding me," she exclaimed. She held the book up so I could see the cook on the front, who looked kind of familiar. "This is my sister!" She turned it back so she could look at it. "I can't believe that people actually buy these."

"You're Gianina Reyes' sister? She's like my favorite home cook. I have all of her cookbooks. I wouldn't have even made the connection that you are related."

"Because I am so stunningly gorgeous in comparison? I know," she joked, with an edge.

I understood her misguided self-deprecation. Gianina Reyes looked thinner and more put-together, but Christi looked more real. Especially like this, leaning over the counter, all of that softness on display. Her eyes glinted with mirth, like two more jewels in her collection of baubles and beads.

"No," I said. I swallowed, looking away from her emerald eyes so I could focus. "Because of the last name. Is Reyes a family name?"

"Oh no, that's her married name. She's married to Rachel's brother."

"Really?"

She nodded. "It's a weird sort of circle I've got."

"So then, Owens is your family name?"

Christi sighed heavily. *Oh, shit.* I just stepped in something I shouldn't have. Instead of watching her reaction, I cowardly continued cooking.

"Owens is my married name," she said softly. If my heart could have fallen into the floor, it would have. "My husband, Troy, uh, he died in the early days of the pandemic. Right around the Reveal. He was a doctor. I never got around to changing it back, and I've just gotten used to it now."

I put the lid on the sauté pan so I could turn back to her. "I am so sorry. I didn't know."

She waved me off. "How could you know?" She pushed the heels of her hands into her eyes. "It's just, our anniversary is around this time of year, and it's always a little more raw, you know? It's been a rough week."

Wolves mated for life. I understood loss, even if it wasn't of a mate. But instead of comforting her, I blurted out, "Alice O'Shea is my ex-fiancée. That's why she's stalking me."

Christi took a long breath before saying, "Do you mind if I ask why?"

Did anyone really know the motives of someone as unstable as Alice? I could try.

"My understanding is that her father wasn't going to let her actually marry me, since I wasn't a wolf. This was before the Reveal, so shifters weren't out yet. We were visiting her family upstate in New York and she suggested we go for a walk. We encountered a lone wolf and it lunged for us. I can still see Alice's face through all of it. She seemed so calm. In the aftermath, I figured that she had been frozen in fear. I kept telling her to run." I took a shaky breath, but continued, "I don't remember a lot of what happened. I was mauled pretty badly. But every time I close my eyes, I see her and she's happy I'm being attacked. She wanted it."

Chills ran up my spine and my voice shook when I continued. "I woke up in the hospital. My parents and Alice couldn't understand why I just couldn't go back to my life as usual. I broke it off shortly after that." I grimaced at the memory. "That didn't go over well. The police couldn't, or wouldn't, believe that my ex was stalking *me*. When I joined the pack, I thought I had escaped."

"And now she's the biggest bitch in the country," Christi joked, but neither her tone nor her expression matched the humor of her words.

"In my memories of the attack, she's smiling. She turned me and now she won't let me go. I'm sorry for dragging you into this."

She shook her head and smiled, but the sparkle of mischief didn't return to her eyes.

I focused on cooking again, finally plating dinner. She oohed and ahhed over it like I had spent all day on it. It was just pasta with tomato sauce and arugula on top with semi-homemade garlic bread. The hardest part was boiling the water. She really must not know how to cook. I took the stool next to her at the island. For a moment, I thought the red sauce looked a lot like the *X* on my door. I pushed that thought so deep down that even my wolf wouldn't be able to find it.

"This is really good," she said after a mouthful. "Thank you so much. This was really so sweet."

She touched my leg gently, and I tensed out of reflex. I hadn't realized how much I wasn't used to being touched anymore.

She practically jumped back, almost falling off her bar stool. "I am so sorry. You have been so nice. You cooked me dinner and brought me flowers. You fixed my gate! Shit fuck.

I think I must have gotten my signals crossed, because I kind of thought this was a date."

Oh. *Oh*. Fuck, I was rusty. Of course this was a date. That was how I meant it. It was how Derrick had wanted me to mean it. That was exactly what this was. Here I was, flinching away from her the first time she made a move.

I should fix this.

But Christi had already hidden her face behind her hands. "I am so embarrassed. I am so sorry."

I pulled a hand from her face and took it in mine. I caressed her index finger with my thumb. I could hear the change in heartbeat, smell the subtle change in her sweat. Less anxious, more present.

"I'm sorry. I'm the one who has been misreading signals. I haven't been on a date in a very long time," I confessed. We were both shaken. I couldn't take advantage of her emotions. If my wolf could conflate danger with desire, so could she. But an errant curl fell on her face, and I brushed it back. She beamed at me, and my stomach churned. She leaned in closer.

"Well, I don't bite. Unless you want me to," she winked. "To be honest, it's been a while for me too."

"Then I can't believe just how well we're doing."

The moon shone in through the window like a spotlight onto Christi. She touched my leg again, and if there was a move to be made, this would be the moment.

But I couldn't do it. Not yet.

Chapter Sixteen: Nate

I *liked* her. I was going to fuck this up. This was going to fall into pieces around me because I owed it to her *not* to get involved. Not to get *her* involved.

Shit fuck.

Chapter Seventeen: Derrick

"You don't have to do this," I reminded Nate as I pulled Big Bertha into an empty parking lot.

"I do," he said resolutely. "You didn't see how they tore the gate apart and taunted her. I have to stop it. This has to stop."

I folded my arms across my chest. He couldn't even see that this wasn't about him and Alice, but rather him and *Christi*.

"I've looked into this Joe character," I grumbled. He scoffed. He didn't think the fighting pit at the Dahlia was a good job with *connections*. I'd show him. "He sounds like a washed-up warlock. A dabbler in magic. Not someone with the capital and know how to help you."

"He said he had a patron."

"Where's his business? What's his address? Why are we meeting him in a sketchy warehouse instead of a doctor's office? This stinks and you know it." He pointedly ignored me. "You should have at least told Christi," I lectured. "She understands magic, and *she* could have told you if this was legit."

"I can't," he snapped. "She can't know. I can't involve her any more than I have to."

I backed off. "Fine. It's your funeral."

The scent of the air shifted and I growled. I smelled

shifters—a lot of them. I gave Nate a look that said, *see, I told you*. He shook his head at me and motioned to the door. We both cautiously stepped out of the van. I knew this was a bad idea. How many mistakes had I made because *he* wasn't thinking clearly? We had stooped to a new low.

This Joe person stepped out of the shadows, dressed again like a businessman on vacation. He slicked back his hair and he wore clothes that looked expensive. But what did I know? I wore the same tee shirt three days in a row. Once he stepped near us, the smell of cologne and magic drowned out everything else. He suspected we were stupid and wouldn't be able to identify his shifter bodyguards without smelling them. Joke was on him.

Two shifter bodyguards flanked him. They didn't have any weapons, but that meant that they didn't need to be armed in order to be dangerous. I gave Nate another look. He took a step forward.

Joe opened his arms wide. "Welcome, gentlemen," he exclaimed with a smile, "to our little operation. You don't mind being searched, do you?"

"I do, actually," I snapped, but the grunts didn't wait for our response. They aggressively patted us down. Both Nate and I held our hands up. I could feel him glaring at me.

"Is all this necessary?" Nate asked, in his best keep-the-peace voice. He had used it all the time with Sarah. It was firm enough to be listened to, but polite enough not to ruffle any feathers. "This is just an experiment, right?"

"Just a precaution," Joe said as he strode over. His grunts finished the search, leaving us disheveled but no worse for wear. The amulets that Christi made us hung out of our shirts.

Joe lifted Nate's and appraised it. "Interesting." He dropped it, and Nate finally took a breath. Joe nodded in the direction of the warehouse. "Well, what are we waiting for?"

I glowered at Nate, but followed. This was dangerous. Nate had to see that. It hit me that Alice could be Joe's patron and this could all be an elaborate trap. I kept making eyes at Nate, but he set his jaw and looked straight ahead. He shut me out completely. I wished I could speak telepathically to him. *Hey, dumbass, this is a no good, very bad idea!* And as a person who made no good, very bad ideas, I should know!

We continued to follow Joe as he chatted jovially. "I know it doesn't look like it, but this is all very state-of-the-art. I should know. I made my money in the magitech boom."

I made a show of rolling my eyes, and *that,* Nate decided to see. He motioned for me to cut it out. I instead stuck my tongue out at him. He'd brought me along for a reason. If he didn't want to listen to me, that was on him.

The warehouse was mostly empty except for a small laboratory setup, brightened by boom lights. A solitary medical exam chair sat in the middle of the cavernous room. It was horror movie fuel. I half-expected some mad scientist to run through it, brandishing a chainsaw and hacking us to bits. I hesitated, and one of the shifters pushed me ahead. I glared at him, but moved along.

"How many volunteers did you say you had?" Nate asked, prodding gently.

Joe paused and turned to face him. "We're on the edge of what we can do with magic, Nathan." Nate flinched at that shortening of his name. He began to correct Joe, but predictably, Joe spoke over him. "You are contributing directly to a new discovery." He clapped Nate on the back. "You're a pioneer!"

When Joe began to walk again, I pulled Nate aside, hands clasped on his shoulders. "I can't let you do this. One, this guy is nuts. And two, he's lying. Did you notice how he didn't even answer your question?" I pleaded with him. "Nate, we'll find another way."

He pushed me away and made his way to the exam chair.

"The process should be fairly simple," Joe assured Nate as one of the bodyguards donned blue latex gloves. "We'll take a sample of your blood today and you'll take the first potion. Once we have your blood, we can tailor the second dose to your specific genetic code. Pretty neat, huh?"

I paced behind the wall of shifter bodyguard muscle. Nate rolled his sleeve up like he was under a spell. Could witches still do that? Entrance? Enspell? Enchant? Enchant sounded right. Maybe Joe had *enchanted* Nate! I watched grimly as the shifter took a vial of Nate's blood. Joe had been at one of the benches mixing up the potion. I couldn't smell much except for wolf, cheap cologne, and hot garbage magic.

"Alright," Joe said, producing a glass full of nasty-looking liquid. It was the color and consistency of mixed cement, thick and gray. "Bottoms up!"

Nate took the glass and gulped. He spat it out, all over the floor and Joe's expensive shoes. Joe simply stepped aside.

"Hey!" I exclaimed, pushing the bodyguards aside and expecting them to move. They didn't. I groaned in frustration.

"You'll need to drink all of it if you want the benefits," Joe reminded.

Nate snarled at him. "There's silver in here!"

Silver. I knew this Joe was bad news. He was poisoning Nate.

"How else did you think we'd block your wolf?" Joe snapped, his cool, salesmen demeanor gone as he got in Nate's face. "Did you think this would be easy? Pain produces results!"

I finally got through the mass of muscle. I shoved Joe away from Nate. *Hard.* "That's enough. We're going."

Nate gave me a desperate look. Without any more prompting, he gulped the rest of the potion down, grimacing the whole time. Anger burned in my gut.

"I knew you'd see it my way, Nathan." Joe clapped Nate's shoulder in congratulations.

Nate could barely look up. "When will I know it's working?" he slurred. *Fucking hell.*

"Next full moon, bud," he said with a smirk. "But hopefully, we'll have your second dose made up by then." His face darkened as he looked at me. "I assume you boys can see yourselves out."

I helped Nate out of the chair, glaring at the wolves as I did so. We limped back to Big Bertha.

"You fucking idiot," I complained as I drove Big Bertha back home. Nate was laid out on the banquette behind me, barely conscious. He kept groaning and retching. "If you puke in here, you are cleaning it up."

I was convinced that he was dying. I could barely focus on the road. Every noise he made had me looking back at him in the rearview mirror.

That distraction prevented me from noticing our tail, until the nondescript car, maybe gray, maybe silver, nearly hit my bumper.

"Shit," I exclaimed as the van swerved. The car followed my lane change. "We're being followed."

"The shifters?" Nate slurred.

I looked in the right side-mirror. None of the men in the van looked like the shifters from the warehouse. I couldn't even ask Nate if they were the same shifters as the ones from Christi's house, since he was currently horizontal. He wasn't able to lift his head to look. Either way, someone had warned these shifters that we were going to be at the warehouse.

I counted the men. There were eight of them squeezed

into the small car. They wore varying degrees of nice clothes. "No, different ones. They're dressed like plainclothes cops."

"Cops?"

"No, they just look like cops." We jerked forward as the van got hit from behind. I'd barely gotten the steering wheel back under my control when the car hit us again. I was going to have to steal some healing potions from the Dahlia after this. I heard a *thunk* as Nate fell to the floor. "Fuck me!"

I swerved again, pulling into an off-ramp. The car continued driving on the freeway. I pumped a fist in the air. "Lost 'em!"

I laughed. I could see in the rearview mirror that Nate had pulled himself to his knees. I watched as he vomited, and then passed out.

Nate finally woke up after I had cleaned Big Bertha... twice.

"Have a nice nap, sleeping beauty?" I snarled. I was so mad at him, and I had nowhere for that anger to go. I balled my fists to keep from shaking.

He held a hand to his head. "I feel like I just went on a bender." He blinked hard and sat up slowly. He dry heaved and laid back down, collapsing onto the bed. "I can't make the room stop spinning."

"You idiot," I growled. "You did this to yourself!"

His breath shuddered. "Did it work?"

"How the fuck am I supposed to know?" I paced in his tiny apartment. I felt his walls closing in on me, and I tugged at the top of my shirt. It felt too tight. Everything here suffocated me. "They're making your designer dose now."

I sat on the edge of his bed and exhaled through gritted teeth. Nate was supposed to be the man with a plan. He made good plans and good decisions. What was I supposed to do now that Nate's ideas were shit?

I needed him. I had no one else, no pack, no mate.

Clutching at my chest, I grimaced. "You're not allowed to die on me yet."

Nate laughed, but it came out more like a wheeze. "I don't plan on it."

"We can't just wait around for this to work," I warned him. I tossed his cheap-ass flip phone his way. It hit him square in the forehead. Yet *I'm* the asshat!

"Ow!" he exclaimed. He pulled up his text messages. "Fuck!"

"Yeah. The bitch has been busy."

His phone had lit up the moment we returned from the warehouse. Alice was unhinged and apparently had nothing better to do with her day than to desperately text Nate. Some alpha she was.

The last couple texts were from Christi, but that didn't even cheer Nate up.

> *Call me. I think I'm getting somewhere*
> *You okay???*

Nate threw the phone away from him, hissing. "I don't know how to stop her. Der, when is this going to stop?"

We both knew the answer to that question. It would only stop when one of them was dead.

Chapter Eighteen: Christi

I added another symbol to the whiteboard. I had moved the one that I kept in my office into my living room where I had more space.

Books littered the floor, some opened and some closed, and I returned to my spot so I could move them around. The parchment I'd borrowed from Nate had been written in some kind of ancient runic. I had forgotten I had it, and I felt that I had to hurry. It had looked promising a week ago, but now I wasn't so sure.

I had the alphabet and numbers zero to nine placed in a grid on the whiteboard, and I'd started with a blank square next to each letter and number. At this point, T, H, E, O, and S had symbols from the parchment in their boxes, along with the number zero. Most of the boxes had several possible symbols in them. I didn't want to commit to one and be wrong. I hated puzzles. I liked neat and tidy solutions. Enjoying the journey and trusting the process weren't in my vocabulary. Still, this was the most progress I had made. I finally felt like I was getting somewhere. I had texted Nate a few days ago to let him know I'd made progress, but I got no response. I tried not to let it get under my skin. He probably had with more important things to deal with.

"Movie night! Movie night!" Rachel chanted. She burst into the house, riding Ines piggyback, her hand pointing Ines in my direction.

I groaned as Sadie sang happy songs, twirling around them in circles. "I'm working." I resumed rearranging the symbols I had scrawled on pieces of paper, trying to make them resemble words.

"But it's movie night," Ines complained, hot pink marabou feathers wafting from her pajama sleeves as she crossed her arms. Rachel hopped off, looking equally disappointed. Their sad eyes pleaded with me, but I stood firm. I had a lot of practice doing that lately.

"I know it's movie night," I responded. "That's why I asked you *not* to come."

"You can't reschedule movie night." Ines pouted.

I needed to concentrate, I really did, but they were so distracting. Rachel collapsed onto the couch, pulling Ines close. I wanted to cave and ask what movie we were going to watch, but I owed it to Nate to find a cure.

And Derrick, I corrected myself. I owed it to Derrick to help him find closure. Nate had paid me; this was *a job* for him. No matter how attractive he was or how charming he could be. Regardless of a failed first date. He hadn't called me. I heard that message loud and clear. He was a client. Nothing more, nothing less. The soft caress of the darkness made me shiver.

I groaned again. "Why is this so hard?"

"Yeah, because code-breaking is super easy, everyone knows that," Rachel chimed in.

"Don't you all just have computers to do that?" Ines joined in with a wave of her hand, as though I could just write up an algorithm and have a computer analyze it all. That wasn't a bad idea.

"You know who *could* write something up pretty quickly," Rachel said, serious this time.

I did, and therein lay the problem. Doing this by hand took time. I'd been at it for two days now and had confidently matched only six symbols. I still had to match all the other symbols and rewrite the parchment using the cracked code. It started to feel like too much for just me. What made me think I could do this? And doing it alone would take time. Too much time. I'd fail and disappoint Nate, devastate Derrick. I'd never see them again. They would hate me. *They would run.*

My stomach felt sick and my heart raced. The alternative would be so much easier. All I had to do was hand over the pages to someone else, but I couldn't allow myself to do that.

Dad could do it, but I wasn't going to ask him for help. Not after how our last *chat* ended. He'd probably lecture me on how it was supposed to be hard. *Pain produces results!* No, I needed to do this the long way.

"Where have you gone, mouse?" Ines asked, snapping me out of my darkness.

Still a bit on edge, I snapped. "That is not an endearing nickname."

"Christi."

"It's all lines and circles with no pattern, and honestly,

what I have are just guesses. If it had been based on something, anything remotely magical, I would have figured it out like that!" I snapped my fingers. "But it's all just nonsense. It's worse than nonsense, it's junk!"

"You activated the self-destruct sequence," Rachel intoned low to Ines, foreheads touching.

"I can hear you, and it's not helping!"

Rachel scooched herself off the couch and nudged me. "Christi, you are like the smartest person I know, myself excluded. If anyone can figure it out, it's you. But more importantly," she took my shoulders in her hands very seriously, "what movie are we watching?"

"Just pick something," I said through my teeth, trying to make sense of the symbols in front of me.

Rachel returned to my couch to take control of the television as Ines clapped her hands in excitement. I downed a glass of wine in one go, and then headed into my bedroom. *Goddess, I think I need help.* A little trance couldn't hurt. I wasn't using it to numb myself; I was using it to be more creative, to help my friends.

I found my stash and took two edibles.

"Movie's starting," Rachel yelled, and I rejoined them in the living room.

I continued to work on the parchment, and when the edibles

kicked in, they kicked in harder than I thought. *Goddess, help me*, I intoned. The patterns started to make a bit more sense. When I matched a few more symbols, I had it. The movie droned on in the background. It was like Rachel and Ines weren't here. I grabbed a notebook and started to scribble out the translation. *Oh, fuck*. The parchment didn't outline a cure; it contained something so much worse.

Phone in hand, I stood up, only to stumble backwards and land on my ass. My head swam. *Shit fuck*. I was higher than I'd planned on being, and this was really important. I tried again, walking over to the back door so I didn't block the view of the movie.

"It's Nate," the voice said on the other line. He didn't sound right, but that could have been the drugs. "What's up?"

"Nate," I said hurriedly. "The pelt was a clue! They took the body for a reason!"

"Christi, hold on. What are you talking about?"

"The parchment!" I shouted into the microphone. I held the phone in front of my face, staring in disbelief. What didn't he understand about this? *Come on, Nate! Listen!*

"Christi, slow down. What parchment?"

"It's not a cure, it's a spell!"

The line went silent, and I was sure I had lost him. It didn't matter, though.

"Holy shit fuck!" I exclaimed as skeleton hands erupted from the lawn. *Shit, shit, shit, this was not good*. I had dropped the phone.

I pressed my palms to the glass door, looking out as the hands became arms and arms became full revenants. In a burst of magic, the wards I had around my house lit up. My vision blacked out for a moment, and I felt the drain on my magic. I had etched daisy wheels at each entrance of the house and buried wards in the lawn. That would keep anything from the outside from coming in, but I still had to take care of the revenants on my lawn. First, wolves had destroyed my gate, and now, skeletons destroyed my lawn! I was way too high for this.

"Was that Nate?" Rachel asked, completely oblivious to the incoming disaster. I turned to her and Ines.

"Stay inside, and don't let Sadie out either. I'm going to need chalk. Lots of it."

Chapter Nineteen: Nate

"Christi!" I yelled into the phone. "Are you alright?"

When she didn't answer, I ran as fast as I could to her house, which to be honest, wasn't all that fast. My body ached doubly from the potion. I had spent a couple days sleeping it off. That didn't help me now. My wolf added to the pressure, growling in the back of my mind the whole way. I had Hope and Strength strapped to my back, and I could only hope none of her neighbors called the cops on me. After the incident with Christi's gate, I didn't want to leave anything to chance. Her front door was flung wide open. I could hear the commotion out back, so I let myself in.

"Christi!" I called out in a panic.

Rachel and Ines stopped me at the sliding doors to the backyard. Ines smirked.

"Chill out, bro," Rachel said, clearly intoxicated. I was not going to *chill out*. I needed to help Christi. I might not be back to full strength, but I could still swing a sword. Rachel blocked my path outside. "And you gotta stay inside."

I growled, low and menacing. Rachel laughed at me.

"What is going on?" I snapped.

Rachel smiled, turning me to look outside, "Magic!"

My blood chilled at the scene. Skeletons climbed out of Christi's lawn as though her house was built on top of a graveyard. Half-free skeletons grabbed at Christi from the ground as she ran circles around them, depositing chalk on the ground as she did. A shrieking cry came from the animated skeletons, even though they were mostly decomposed flesh and bone. The sound reverberated in my ears, vibrating into my core. Instinct told me to run, to protect, to fight the threat at any cost. I drew Hope and Strength without even thinking. Rachel touched my arm and shook her head.

I lowered the blades slowly, my eyes locked on Christi. She stopped at the edge of her chalk lines, and the reaching skeletal arms recoiled at the circle, shrieking even louder. Sadie howled from somewhere inside the house. My wolf joined in, drowning any other sounds in my head. I felt my pulse pounding in my ears.

From a satchel at her side, Christi produced a small dagger and a vial filled with gray dust. She poured the vial into her hands, then blew on it. She knelt to the ground, pouring the dust near the edge of the circle, not quite touching it. She took the dagger and slashed her palm. I could smell the coppery blood as it dripped down her fingers onto the mound of dust. She stood, opening her arms wide, blood rushing down her arm and staining her shirt.

"I call upon the Goddess, who reigns over the moon, magic, and beings on earth and below in the underworld. I beseech you, Holy Lady, to bind these creatures and banish them to whence they came!"

The screeching grew louder as the giant arms writhed

within the circle. My head throbbed with the sound. I could feel magic gathering, like static electricity in the air.

"I give you a sacrifice of breath, blood, ash, and bones. My Lady, hear my call and bind them!"

A sound like a thunderclap shook us as Christi drowned in moonlight, a silver spotlight so bright I couldn't see her. That moonlight flooded the circle, and then exploded throughout the yard. Time stopped as we collectively held our breath.

As my eyes readjusted to the dark, I realized the screeching had stopped. Christi collapsed in a heap at the edge of the circle of now-dead grass.

"My turn," Ines said with a smirk. She pulled a baton out of the folds of her robe, and with a slight motion of her wrist, it exploded with hazy pink light, extending to a deadly-looking scythe with pink ribbons streaming from it. She ran into the yard, a hot pink streak in the night.

I ran too, taking Christi into my arms. "Christi, are you alright? Are you hurt?"

She gave me a sleepy smile. "Nate? What are you doing here?"

I wrapped Christi's palm with gauze that we found in her bathroom. Before we came inside, she traced a symbol etched into the wall of the house with a bloody finger. "For protection," she had said.

If that was for protection, I wondered what a bloody *X* on a door meant. Just a warning, I hoped.

Ines returned, reporting that she identified no further threats. She seemed disappointed. Sadie had escaped the guest bedroom and now warbled softly at the back door. I was under strict instructions to keep Sadie inside until the magic died down. Sadie voiced her displeasure.

"Keep pressure on that," I told her, trying hard not to look at the scars on her wrist. I recognized the pattern, and I knew they weren't from magic. My heart clenched. I wanted to hold her tight and not let go. Protect. *I wanted to protect what was mine.* The thought shook me. Why did my wolf doze easily while it had been so insistent and loud before?

"I'll be fine," she smiled, and I had no idea what to do with the woman in front of me. A woman who had deities doing her bidding.

Rachel came out of the bathroom, where she'd been brewing some bathtub healing potion. She handed Christi a glass, and she gulped it down. "Thanks, Rach."

"There's more where that came from. I left the bottles in the bathroom. Drink one every hour until that cut closes," Rachel said seriously, before fawning over Christi. "Bitch, that was fucking epic!"

"Epic?" I questioned.

Rachel jumped up and down. "Super epic. I never get to see real magic like this. Bam! Pow! Explosion! Most magic is boring, all amulets and charms."

"It's not boring," Christi chided, sagging on the couch. "It's practical."

"I take it movie night is over?" Ines asked in a bored voice, picking at her nails. She sat atop the kitchen island, her legs crossed daintily.

Rachel leaned against her legs. "Yeah, Ines, movie night's over."

Ines gave a dramatic sigh, hopping off the counter. "Worst movie night ever. Call me if you need anything. The night is young, and I could still fight fiends if the need arises."

"I'm fine. Nate's with me." *I was?* I was. I wasn't going to argue, not when my wolf chuffed at the words. "I doubt anything else will happen."

"Laters!" Rachel called as the two of them left.

Christi went to clean up, and left me standing awkwardly in the kitchen. I looked at Christi's house to try and find something to do. The urge to clean itched under my skin. I would *not* disrupt this woman's piles. Still weak from the potion, I retreated to the couch. I collapsed, and I realized I couldn't stand up if I tried. I don't think I'd ever been this exhausted. Even my bones felt tired as I sank deeper into the cushions. My wolf dozed happily, which I'd never been conscious enough to enjoy. I yawned. *Keep it together, Nate.* My eyes closed before I knew it.

"You look cozy," she said, emerging from her bedroom. I jerked back to alertness. Her curly hair was wet and thrown up with a clip. She wore practical cotton pajamas and had rewrapped her hand. Even though she wore baggy clothes, I could see the shape of her curves underneath. I wanted to peel them off her and see if her curves looked just as magnificent naked as they did clothed.

What was *wrong* with me?

She'd just banished revenants to hell, yet I thought about sinking my teeth into her sweet round ass and oh my god, why wasn't my brain working? My wolf hummed, a low rumble in the back of my mind.

Christi poured herself a glass of wine. "Can I get you anything? Water? Coffee?"

I remembered her previous offer of instant coffee and declined. "I'm fine," I said, my brain slowly coming back online, despite watching a solitary drop of water bead up at the nape of her neck and slowly travel down the contours of her throat all the way down her cleavage. I reminded myself to make eye contact. "Thanks."

She motioned for me to sit closer on the couch, where Sadie then jumped up and rested her head in Christi's lap. Christi absently stoked Sadie's fur. I tried to sit a respectable distance away from them.

"I'm sorry I scared you like that. I dropped my phone and didn't think, I guess. I'm sorry, I'm a little high." Damn. She'd done all that while intoxicated. It impressed me. I didn't realize how powerful she was. She giggled, wobbling a bit. "And since when do you wield a sword? And a dagger?

Blades?"

I had Hope and Strength in their sheaths on the kitchen island.

"I was the pack beta and couldn't shift at will like much of the pack. Derrick gave them to me."

I would be soaked with blood after those fights for territory, but I always came back alive.

Christi gave me an odd little laugh and a smug smile. "I knew you didn't get those muscles from lifting books."

Was she flirting with me? She had curled her feet away from me, so she leaned in my direction. I didn't remember how to do this, how to play at seduction. I froze up again. An uncomfortable silence passed as Christi sipped her wine, resting her hand on Sadie's head.

"Christi," I said, breaking her out of her staring.

"Hm?"

"Why'd you call me tonight?"

She set her wine glass on the floor. My gut clenched at the thought of the glass tipping over and red wine staining her plush beige carpets. Or worse, onto the bright pink Persian rug. I forced myself to look at her instead and hope that neither of us knocked the damn thing over.

"This was just the beginning," she said solemnly. "You, Derrick, Alice. The parchment I found wasn't a cure. I knew it was about shifters, but I wasn't sure. Nate, it was a spell for controlling a shifter. They skinned Derrick's mate. I'm willing to bet he didn't find a body. Once they had removed her pelt, they could perform this ritual, and she would be under their control."

I felt sick to my stomach. A flayed wolf. There were ways to subdue a shifter. Typically, silver collars or chains would be used to bind them and keep them from shifting. But once bound, the shifter wasn't still under your control. This, though—this seemed unnecessarily cruel.

"Does that mean Sarah's alive?"

Christi shook her head. "She probably didn't survive the flaying. Nate, this is serious. Alice is willing to resort to necromancy to find you. Not only is it illegal, but it's abhorrent. Only a real fucked-up witch would agree to do this."

I thought about what Joe was doing in the warehouse and wondered if it was really that different. He did say he had a *patron*. What was a cure if not another way to control the wolf? As Christi's words sank in, I realized that Alice was not only willing to kill. She was willing to desecrate the dead.

I wiped my face with my hands. "I should have never brought you into this."

She shrugged. "Too late now. They were testing out my wards. They realized they couldn't go through them, so they went under them."

I took her hand, my pulse racing and my breath catching, but my resolve overcame the awkwardness. She gripped my hand harder and sighed heavily. She looked pale, all the color and sparkle drained from her with the moonlight she had summoned.

"Nate, I think you should run," she said. "I don't think there's way out of this. If she's willing to do this to a stranger, I can't imagine what she'd do to you. Even my wards can't keep you safe."

My breath hitched. I had been so singularly focused on the cure. On my wolf. On myself. I failed to see what was right in front of me. Leaving wasn't that easy now. I had a duty to fulfill, and that meant protecting what was mine. My pack. My mate. *Oh god*.

I thought of the scars on her arms and wondered who in her life told her that she didn't deserve to be cared for. They'd probably said that she should just *be* happy. Or that other people had it so much worse than she did. Or told her that she was a disappointment, that she was flawed.

I bared my teeth. I couldn't leave her now. This powerful, beautiful, effervescent woman with silver sparkles in her hair and gentle light in her eyes deserved to be cared for. I swore to God that I would make myself worthy enough to be her supplicant and worship at her altar.

I'd damned us both.

Chapter Twenty: Derrick

I didn't take the news well. Sarah, alive! If not alive, then possibly undead. Anger swirled in my gut. I drank. I had no idea how much.

Sarah sits on top of the closed toilet in the bathroom on our last night together, her long brown hair shrouding her face. I want so badly to touch her, to nuzzle her. To comfort her. She's pushing me away and I feel like I'm breaking.

I cautiously take a step into the dimly lit room, only the night-light shining. She's crying. I hear her sobs.

"Sarah?"

"Leave me alone," she lifts her head to snap at me. I can't do that. The bond between us is too strong. I will never be able to leave her. She's mine and I'm hers. She's my other half, my alpha, my leader, my love. There's no place in the world she can go that I won't come looking.

"Sarah, it's going to be okay. I don't blame you. It's not your fault."

This only makes her cry harder. Fuck, I can't fix this. She wanted them so badly. We've faced disappointment for years. We finally let ourselves believe this time would be different. But our luck ran out and she lost the pups. I held her through it, but now, now she can't stand to be in the same room with me. As though it's my *fault. As though I didn't desperately want pups too.*

"I can't do this anymore." Her voice is raw and wild. I've never seen her like this before, not even in the haze of battle. Her gray eyes fill with more tears. "I can't hope anymore. I'm too old. We just need to stop trying."

Defeat. I smell defeat. I kneel at her knees in desperation, taking her hands in mine. "Don't say that. There are solutions. We can see another doctor. You have a couple more heats left. Please, don't give up."

She pulls her hands away from mine and snarls, "No! You aren't listening, Derrick. I'm done."

I'm shaking as tears well up. Anger balls in my stomach and I lash out, pounding my fists on the floor.

"I can't accept that." My heart racing as fast as my words. "You can't just give up."

Claws find my throat and Sarah bares her teeth at me, ready to snap. "It's an order from your alpha. I don't fucking care if you can't accept it. If you loved me, you would obey."

I'd rather her rip out my throat right now than to feel my heart ache this much. Before I can think about what I'm doing, I stand and punch the wall. We both freeze, stunned and staring at the hole I made.

Sarah shakes her head. "I'm leaving." She stands, and the disappointment in her eyes is worse than her sobs.

"For how long? Where are you going?" I plead as I stalk her through the house.

"Out," she snaps as she opens the door. Before I can respond, she disappears in a flash of fur. Her wolf runs out into

*the night. I don't follow her. I close the door and lean against it,
angry, hot tears running down my face. Slamming the door
behind me, I sink to the floor.*

*"Fuck!" I scream with my fists balled. I pound them against
the floor. "Fuck! Fuck! Fuck!"*

Even dead drunk, I still dreamed. I dreamed about the
cage. I dreamed about two lost souls who wanted nothing
more than to escape. I dreamed about how we made it out
and how I still managed to lose her.

Fuuuuuuuuuck. When I woke up, I felt like a truck ran me
over, and then someone tossed me into a wood chipper. All
that remained were my frayed nerves and somehow my
stomach, which was on a roller coaster from hell and doing
loop-de-loops. Every time I raised my head up, I was
spinning. Not the room—no, the room stayed in place. My
head, though, that was on a sailboat in stormy seas. I
supposed I deserved this after drinking for four days straight.
At this point, death probably wouldn't even feel better than
this; my soul most likely damned to spend eternity in hell
with all the other degenerates and patricides. Someone else—
Nate—would resolve never to drink again. I was not that
someone. Nope, I had the rotten luck to be born an alpha
wolf, and alpha wolves didn't quit.

I sat up in Nate's sad, full-size bed, praying I wouldn't

blow chunks on his sad, white comforter. My stomach quivered like the little bitch it was, but I was chunk-free.

"You look like shit," Nate said from his armchair across the room. He had a book resting on the arm. There he was, the high and mighty Nate I knew. He conveniently forgot that our places were swapped not too long ago, when he was the one passed out and *not* chunk-free. Big Bertha still smelled like his silver sludge vomit.

Ah, Nate, so much better than the rest of us. He wasn't born an animal. That didn't matter, though, did it? He became an animal just the same, like the rest of us.

He crossed his arms. "Now that we have more information, we need to make a plan."

"That sounds like a tomorrow problem. Leave me alone."

Of course, he didn't understand. How could he? My head hurt and I closed my eyes to just make it fucking stop.

"Come on, Derrick. Have some coffee, sober up, and we'll find a way out of this."

"You don't get it. What do I have now? Without a pack, without Sarah, I have nothing! I *am* nothing!"

I knelt on the bed now as if I were begging. I breathed wet and heavy breaths. Like I was catching my breath after a good fuck. My chest burned, and I grabbed at it, wanting the feeling to just go away. I wanted all of this to just. Go. Away.

Nate stared at me, hard and cold. I thought a decade's worth of friendship counted for something. I thought we were pack. Family. Was it so bad to want a family? Why couldn't I have a family? And fuck, why wouldn't that pain in my chest just stop already?

"This was a mistake. I should never have come here," I muttered as I threw myself off the bed. I couldn't meet his watchful, judgy eyes. I stepped towards the door without saying goodbye, just as he had done. But I couldn't stop myself. "I'm going after Joe myself."

He stood up. "Joe?"

"I told you Joe was bad news." I growled. "You didn't listen. You never do. Deal with it. I'm not waiting anymore."

Joe first, then Alice. I would end this once and for all.

"Christi's working on it—"

"Oh, bullshit. You indulge Christi's efforts because you like her."

"Leave Christi out of this. You got a problem with me—"

"Yeah, I got a problem with you, alright," I shouted. We stood nose to nose now, in each other's faces. Who would back down first? It wouldn't be fucking me. "You weren't there. You didn't watch her fade. You didn't stay to help. You didn't even say goodbye!"

Nate stepped back and turned away from me. "Is that what this is about? Because I didn't say goodbye? Of all the stupid shit, Derrick—"

I laughed, annoyed. "Oh yes, let's not forget that you are the smart one. Oh, wise man! Derrick's just fucking stupid. No one wants his opinion on things. Not you! Not Sarah! Definitely not the pack. Even now, you don't trust me. You go off with Christi and it's like I'm not even here, man."

"What do you want from me, Derrick?" he asked, and I could see how much older he had gotten. The bags under his eyes had grown bigger, his hair had gone grayer. Another reminder that time had passed, but I hadn't moved along with it. He clenched his jaw. "Do you need to fight me? Then fight me. I don't know what I can do for you anymore."

"You want to be involved?" I yelled, my arms out. "Get involved. Let's catch Joe in the act." He turned from me, and I forced him to look me in the eyes. "I loved her, Nate, and I've lost her. Nothing we do is going to change that. Either get on board or get out of my way."

Nate sighed. He pulled me gently to the kitchen counter, where five white postcards radiated with malice. I was too hungover for this notecard shit. Each had an image of a playing card in the suit of hearts: ten, Jack, Queen, King, and Ace. A royal flush. I pushed the cards off the counter with an anguished grunt. She skinned my wife and now played literal games with us.

I sunk to the floor and Nate lowered himself next to me.

"Derrick, please. I know you're going through it right now. But please, hold out just a bit longer. Once I'm cured, we'll get revenge. I promise."

I'd stay longer, but if Nate thought I'd take this lying down, he was wrong. I would get revenge. No matter what. With him or without him.

Chapter Twenty-One: Christi

The attack left me shaken. Even worse, Nate was avoiding me. Part of me hoped he had taken my warning seriously—that he and Derrick should run and hide where Alice couldn't find them. The other part of me hoped he hadn't. If he didn't want my help anymore, that was fine by me. But my house had been attacked too, and I was going to get to the bottom of it the only way I knew how.

"I think this is a bad idea, mouse," Ines said as we stepped into the elevator of the Crimson Dahlia and moved the lever to take us down.

"It doesn't matter what you think," I reminded her. She scowled and stepped away from me. I groaned in frustration. "I'm sorry, I'm just so on edge right now."

"We don't have to wait for the wolves," she said as the ancient elevator started moving. "Let's go to the Wilderness, you and me. We can make a difference."

I sighed. If I left now, who would help Nate? I shook my head. "Let's see how this goes first, okay?"

She frowned, but didn't press any further.

I had only been to the caverns of the Dahlia once before, after the Reveal and the formation of the Bureau. Once the coven had set up shop, I figured I would introduce myself. It didn't go well. The coven didn't initiate me as one of their members, and our relationship since had been tenuous at best. The coven looked down on the activities of the various hedge witches, freelance warlocks, and sorcerous spell-sellers. Still, all three frequented the Dahlia, slinging their wares. The coven only dealt with the truly dangerous and harmful. It had taken me a long time to prove to them that I held any real power at all.

The elevator shuddered to a stop and the door creaked open. We stepped out of the elevator and onto the dimly lit floor. Beneath a flickering light was a door with a solitary label: The Proprietor. I shuddered. He gave me a major case of the creeps, but if you wanted to do business with the coven, you needed to go through him first. He handled all requests to and from the coven. I knocked on the door, quickly but loud enough to be heard.

A voice as dark as night and as smooth as shadow answered. "Come in."

The Proprietor sat behind a desk in the almost completely dark office. Dressed in a suit and top hat, the Proprietor's face and hands were obscured by shadow.

If a sigh could sound like the hush of nightfall, his did. "Not you again."

"I'm not here for a job," I explained hurriedly as Ines hissed through her fangs defensively.

I couldn't see the Proprietor's face, but I didn't need to. I heard his annoyance clearly. "Then what can I do for you?"

"I request an audience with the coven," I said, keeping my voice confident and assured. Any hesitation would only result in denial of my request. Only serious supplicants entered the coven's hallowed halls.

"And what do you bring—" The Proprietor shifted, opening out a white gloved hand to me. *Shit fuck*. I forgot about this part. "—for your sacrifice?"

There was an old adage that all magic comes with a price. True names, firstborn children, a voice. Magic required an offering, something precious and something dear enough to make it hurt just enough to be worth it. I sighed as the Proprietor continued to hold out a hand.

Ines held a hand gently on my arm. Her grip and her voice were cold, but firm. "You don't have to do this."

We both knew I wore only one possession worth the coven's price. I shrugged her off and slowly undid the clasp of one of my necklaces. I held it out, and settled the rings in the Proprietor's hand. My wedding rings. Troy would have disapproved. But I already knew how much of a disappointment I could be.

"Wait!" I pulled the rings back to me. "Tell me first, what's so important about *Hysop's Bestiary*?"

His laughter was like the twinkling of stars in a black sky. His hand disappeared into shadow. "You aren't in the position to ask for another boon."

"You and I both know my sacrifice is worth it." My heart raced as I waited for him to call my bluff. Even Ines held her breath behind me. "You tell me what I need to know about the *Bestiary* and I have an audience with the coven. Those are my terms."

Out of the shadow, a gloved hand appeared with a flourish. I let go of the chain. The Proprietor closed his hand around the rings and snatched them back into the shadows. "Excellent," he said, stars in his night sky voice.

"And?" I asked expectantly.

"The secret of the *Bestiary* is not in its contents but in its location. The coven deemed it safer in their possession and paid handsomely for it."

I gaped at the Proprietor like I'd been slapped.

"That's it?" Ines seethed.

I gave her a look even though I agreed. What a letdown. I had hoped for something more, a clue at least.

"It is what we agreed to." The Proprietor purred, sleepy and sultry. "It is what you need to know."

I bit the inside of my cheek to avoid groaning in frustration. *Shit fuck!*

"Shall we proceed?" The Proprietor tapped a cane to the floor.

I nodded. I had assumed that we would be summoned to return later, but the hour had grown late. The coven had already convened for their nightly gathering. The Proprietor opened the trap door in his floor, and I took the first few stone steps down into the crypt.

"Not you," he warned, barring Ines from going any further. She snapped her fangs at him.

"It's fine, Ines. I'll be alright."

She backed away in a huff, and the Proprietor closed the trap door above me. The thud of the wood against the stone echoed through the chamber.

I wasn't sure if it was actually a crypt, but it was easier to think of it that way. It *was* a giant witch-made cave below the warehouse district. The stone steps led the way down to the altar. Magic sang in the air the farther down I went. It sizzled on my skin like electricity. I heard dripping water, though I didn't see the source. The light of the fire beneath the cauldron on the dais ahead guided me on. As I got closer, the coven members placed their brown hoods over their heads and positioned gold masks to cover their faces. They stood in a circle around the altar and the cauldron, facing out to me. One stepped forward—the crone—and waited for me at the bottom of the stairs.

"Who comes before us?" a multi-layered voice echoed through the chamber. It may only have been the crone speaking, but the rest of the coven layered their power over it. It reminded me of an electronic voice distorter or really bad autotune. One voice on top of many others at various tones, pitches, and intonations. My head hurt as I tried to listen to all the voices spoken out of one body.

The crone motioned for me to come forward.

"Christiana Owens," I said, my voice wavering this time.

"The hedge witch," the crone stated in judgment. I took affront to that. I was a hereditary witch and a sorceress, not some lowly hedge witch, and the coven knew it. I frowned, but held my tongue, unwilling to anger the coven any further. The crone pointed at me, one bony finger poking out from the robe's sleeve. "You have made some mistakes, girl."

I fumed, but I knew that whatever I said in this moment would be used against me. I hated that and the person it reminded me of. I stared at the golden mask and waited.

"Yet you have paid the price. What request can we grant, should it be in our power?" the crone asked.

I cleared my throat before answering. "I need to know what Alice O'Shea is planning."

"Is that truly what you desire?"

Shit fuck. The spell for truth swirled around me. I felt the magic bubble inside of me before I spoke again. "I mean, uh, I request. Fuck." I couldn't seem to get the words out and at the same time, I couldn't keep the words in. "Sorry, um, I need a cure for lycanthropy."

I hadn't planned to request that, but truth magic doesn't lie. The crone laughed shrilly. It echoed through the cavern. It reverberated through the stone, causing the floor to vibrate. I lost my balance, flailing until I found my footing again.

"The wolf has what he needs," the crone said dismissively. "He has nothing of value. It was your sacrifice that was offered, not his. What request can we grant you?"

"I'm not important," I answered without thinking, the truth spell still on my lips. This wasn't how I'd planned for this to go. Wind coursed through the cavern, surrounding me in a spiral before the breeze died away. The crone reached out a withered hand and touched my face.

"You may be the most important person in this room." The voices grew louder. "The vessel," the crone intoned.

I held my breath. I knew real divination was possible. My grandmother had called visions to guide her. Divination by touch was rarer. What the Victorians called psychometry could have been magical rather than paranormal. Touching an object could produce a true vision in a talented diviner, but I had never seen it happen without preparation and a lot of help. I closed my eyes in disappointment. This was a parlor trick for humans who didn't know any better. I removed the crone's hand from my face and stepped backwards. I should have known the coven would be useless.

"At least tell me how I can find the necromancer."

"The necromancer is already known to you. All you have to do is look."

That's it? I bit my lip to keep from crying. I sacrificed the one precious thing to me, only to be told platitudes and riddles. *Typical. Useless.* I scoffed bitterly before turning to leave. Each step took me out of the darkness and into dimming light.

"Take heed, witch!" the crone of the coven's voice rang out. "Do not fear the crossroads!"

I did not take heed. I slammed the trap door behind me, drowning out the coven's echo.

Once back in Ines' car, I fought back tears. I had failed. I gave up my wedding rings for nothing. My feet on the edge of the seat, I hugged my knees.

"I'm leaving for a short trip to the Wilderness," Ines explained, "to see the threats to the Aviary for myself." She paused, regarding me carefully. I gave her a look until she continued. "I think you should come with me."

I can't. I wanted to scream it. What difference would I make anyway? Stupid. Useless. *Typical.*

"Next time," I said, my voice small. The caveat sat between us. I knew she would go without me. She knew I wouldn't go without *him.*

"I think it will be good for you. It will take your mind off what troubles you." She nudged me. "We can make a difference, you and I." She sighed, closing her eyes. "It's different there. Greener. Fresher." She opened her eyes, and her red irises shone right at me. I gulped, even though I knew Ines and I knew she wouldn't hurt me. "Christi," she said insistently. "Have you considered this may be the crossroad? That it's time now to make a choice?"

I grimaced. She was right, but what choice did I have? I had come this far. I owed it to Nate—and Derrick—to see this through.

Ines took my head in her cold, gloved hand and patted it

172

with the other hand. This was the equivalent of an Ines embrace, and I almost cried at the intimacy. How long had it been since someone held me? If I loved them, I would lose them. *This way, you're free.*

I shook my head. "Why the face?"

"You don't want to leave because of him. You're thinking he can fix you," she said judgmentally. "But the only one who can fix you is yourself. You are no damsel. There's no knight on a white horse coming. And in my experience, those that do save the damsel tend to lord it over her." She took my face in both hands, forcing me to look her in the eyes. "You want to be able to hold yourself up on your own. It's much more satisfying when you can show them that you don't need them."

"But what if I want him?" I asked, admitting it for the first time.

She smiled, her fangs bared. "That's different. It means you have a choice."

"How'd you get so wise?" I sulked, burying myself further into her passenger seat.

"Experience. Experience is painful. Life is painful. I could offer you release from life, if that was what you truly wanted." She scoffed a bit. We'd met when I was a thrall in the Dahlia. I had just come home, tail between my legs after Troy. Then shortly after, Grandma Ida's health had taken a turn for the worse. In quick succession, I had lost two of the people I cared most about in this world. I wanted to die then.

Ines wouldn't let me. "But that comes with its own challenges."

"No. I don't want to die, Ines," I said with more force than I should have.

Ines was only looking out for me. I just wished she could do it without making me feel so bad about it.

"Good. My life would be very boring otherwise." She sighed. It was the long sigh of an immortal who was very old and very tired. It sounded odd in her youthful voice. "Please come with me."

Ines rarely asked me for anything. She rarely said *please* to begin with. I could see the disappointment on her face. I felt the darkness roiling in thick clouds behind me. I breathed it in, filling myself with it. "Next time."

She shrugged, tossing her hair back, and started the car. We stared ahead in silence the rest of the drive home.

Chapter Twenty-Two: Nate

Neither of my parents could be considered emotional. Even when they fought, it was with facts and figures. They logically debated their side, and whoever argued the best won the fight. They made compromises through bullet points and slide decks. They had planned my future meticulously, both ensuring my well-rounded and rigorous education would set me up for success. Feelings didn't matter when they had the evidence they needed. I followed their lead as best I could, bottling my emotions so they didn't get in the way of the facts.

In the pack, there was order and there were rules to follow. I had to listen to the alpha pair. I had to obey. It kept the wolf at bay if I could be the best beta I could be. But apart from our hierarchy, wolves were driven by instinct and emotions: who you fought with, who you fucked, which pack you waged war on. I had dealt with this the only way I knew how.

My wolf was a wild thing, so I caged it. I'd worked my way up to beta because I could be dispassionate. My worth in the pack was based on how logical I could be. When I fought and when I fucked were based on evidence and orders. Never emotion. Never desire. Never the wanting and yearning I couldn't seem to shake now. I'd kept the wolf at bay. I'd followed the rules. I'd made the plans.

She disrupted all my plans. I ignored all of her calls. I ignored all of her texts. Even avoiding her, I couldn't get Christi out of my mind. I couldn't have her. I couldn't endanger her further. Yet, the wolf kept telling me that she was *mine*. The wolf wanted her, I wanted her. It clawed its way to the surface, scratching constantly at the back of my mind. It drove me fucking feral. Whenever I could, I masturbated to the thought of her, imagining her cunt clenching around my fingers, her head thrown back saying my name. The *only* place I could have her was in my mind.

I could barely control myself. She filled my thoughts, and every damn one of them was filthy. I couldn't concentrate on Alice or running or anything. Everything else lacked meaning. The bond had snapped in. The wolf made me careless. Until I could make her mine, truly mine, the wolf would stop at nothing. Which meant that I had to stay away. I had to protect her.

I dealt with the pressure the only way I knew how. Once the I took care of the physical distraction, I could focus and come up with a plan. I lay on my bed, naked. My dick was so hard. Pre-cum wet the tip as I stroked down. My other hand held the base of my shaft, adding pressure. I thought of Christiana. Of her body. I imagined what she looked like naked. I thought about taking one of her perfect breasts into my mouth, teasing her nipple until it became hard under my teeth. In my mind, I bent her over the bed and allowed myself to lose control. I licked her cunt, lapping her up, fingers plundering her depths. Once she screamed my name, and only then, would I take her. My name sounded so good coming from her lips, even if it was only in my imagination.

The pressure in my dick built, so I started to stroke the tip. In my mind, I took her mercilessly. Hard, fast, thinking only of my pleasure. She wrapped her legs around me and raked her nails down my back. She came again around my dick, and I lost myself. Cum sputtered onto my hand, warm and sticky, as I grunted in pleasure. My dick twitched a few more times with aftershakes, and I was spent. I rolled over, not really caring about the mess in my sheets. I wiped my hand on the pillow and sighed in disgust.

This was why I had to stop this in reality. Mate or no, I couldn't be thinking this way. What would she think if she saw me like this? Disgusting. She didn't deserve that. I didn't know how to be a gentleman anymore, how to actually make love to someone. It was yet another thing Alice had taken from me. Anyone I loved could become a target. I couldn't give Alice more ammunition. I wouldn't be able to give my heart to someone without worrying about the danger.

How would Christi react when the wolf got too close to the surface? I couldn't expect her to handle me when the wolf took control. The wolf was *my* burden to bear. I couldn't burden *her* with the beast. I was terrified of scaring her away.

I groaned into the sheets, then made my way to the shower. For now, I had to keep myself and the wolf contained. If that meant masturbating like a teenager again, instead of actually making love to the woman I desired, well, I had to do what I had to do.

I opened the bookstore and was shocked when Derrick sauntered in, as though the past few days never happened.

"Hey, brother," he said, standing at the register.

I nearly rushed him. "Where the fuck have you been?"

"Following Joe around. Where did you think I was going?" he shrugged. "It doesn't matter. What matters is it's time to get our asses in gear."

"No shit."

"Tailing Joe has been a bust. When he goes anywhere important, his grunts follow him. I can't tell if they are there for his protection or to keep him in line. Do you think Alice would let him work independently?" I shrugged. I didn't know, and my brain hurt from my wolf bouncing around in it all day. Derrick continued, "Until I get rid of his posse, the only thing we really know is that he's working with Alice."

"No," I corrected him, thinking of the facts. "The only thing we really know is that he has a patron and that he has shifter bodyguards."

I still tried to think of Joe as a good man, even if the first dose of his cure made me violently ill. I shuddered to think of what Joe could do to me if he was working for Alice.

"Do you know of any urban shifters? The only way I was

able to find you was because you are an oddity." He pointed at my chest. "Wolves don't like cities, and they sure as hell aren't going to spend their nights on the beach."

It was one reason why I settled here to begin with. The danger for recognition was low. I thought of the wolves who'd taunted Christi and Joe's wolf bodyguards. The bloody X on my door. The pack encroached on my territory, while I dealt with strange wolves. I didn't believe in coincidences.

Derrick looked me up and down distractedly, and then he wrinkled his nose in disgust. "Just what have you been doing up there?"

Of course he would smell it on me.

"Lay off. It's the only thing that's keeping me from her."

We could all be safe if I just stayed away. Maybe Christi had been right. Maybe I should run. My wolf growled at the idea. It wasn't going anywhere without her. That meant I had to stick to the plan, use Joe for the cure, and prove somehow that he'd upgraded from warlockry to necromancy for Alice.

"Why would you want to do that? You were just convincing me to trust her."

I sighed, and Derrick put his hand on his hip, waiting for an answer.

"Derrick, she's my mate."

Derrick scrunched his face up. "That's not possible. I've never heard of a mating bond with a human. How do you know?"

I tried to think about how to put it delicately. "I feel

something."

"I'm pretty sure it's called an erection."

I punched him in the arm. "I mean it. How did you know Sarah was your mate?"

His face fell, and I knew I shouldn't have brought up Sarah. It was too soon, and he was still reeling.

"I always loved her," he says seriously. "She was mine and I was hers. Are you sure you aren't just infatuated with Christi? I mean, you haven't even fucked her."

"And what happens then?"

Derrick exhaled through his teeth. God, that annoyed me. "I guess it would cement the bond. I don't know. *I'm* not the expert on werewolves. Don't you have a book or something to consult?"

I shrugged him off. That confirmed it for me. Even though we'd not made love, once we did, the mating bond would be complete. I would be hers for the rest of my life. Maybe that was the way out. Alice couldn't have me if I was already mated to someone else.

I scoffed. Would that *really* stop her?

"She's my mate," I repeated. Or rather, I was *her* mate.

"Does she know that?"

I shook my head. He waved his hands out. "Then maybe you should tell her that first."

I couldn't. Not yet. Not until I knew we were safe.

Chapter Twenty-Three: Christi

Someone knocked on the door again. I had barely moved in a couple of days, just enough to feed Sadie and take myself to the bathroom. No matter how much they knocked, I wouldn't answer. The darkness had its hold on me and pulled me down. Down. Down. Down.

I buried my head into my pillow and muttered, "Go away."

My grief had spiraled into a full depressive episode, and I wasn't going to leave this bed unless someone plucked me out of it. I had given my rings up for nothing, and that was all I needed to go over the edge. I deserved this for what I'd done.

Maybe I'd imagined the knocking. Who would come to see me anyway? No one bothered to come check on me unless they needed something. Cupcakes. Wine. Amulets. Wards. They didn't really care about me. They cared about what I could do for them. Worthless. Useless. Nate hadn't even bothered making a move when I made it very clear I would be open to it. Stupid. Impulsive. *Typical.*

No one loves you, remember? You are going to die alone, and no one would know until the stink became unbearable for the neighbors. You ruined it, just like you ruin everything you do. Pharmacy. Troy. Failed career. Failed marriage. Troy is dead because of you, and you know it. Everything you do fails, because you *are the failure. You don't deserve love. You'd just fail at that too.*

I sobbed into my pillow as I heard Sadie howling. Shit fuck, did I forget to feed her? *See, you can't even take care of your dog. What a horrible person, you are.* I pushed myself up and made my way to the kitchen, each step a tremendous weight, my body heavy. I got myself to the door and steeled myself to open it. I leaned my head in the middle of the door, too tired to go on.

Then the door started to open and startled, I scrambled backward. Nate stood before me, in a fresh sweater and pressed pants. *Perfect, like you will never be.* I didn't have it in me to be embarrassed at my three-day-old pajamas and unwashed body. *Attractive men like him don't give fat slobs like you a second glance anyway. He doesn't want you either.*

"Hi," he said, strangely gentle in his soft, low voice. "I thought I might find you here."

"What are you doing here?"

"I got a cryptic text message from Ines. I don't even know how she got my number. Plus, I haven't heard from you in a few days, so I'm here to help. We were both really shaken when I left."

The enormity of it clouded my brain. I didn't have the energy to tell him what I needed or how he could help. It sounded fucking exhausting. I wanted to go back into bed and sleep as the darkness cradled me, shutting him out, shutting the world out.

"I didn't ask for help." Not from him, not from anyone.

He nodded, still in the doorway. "I know, but I'm here anyway. I've brought a few things for you, if you're up for it."

"Unless you have some weed and a shit ton of red wine, I doubt it."

"You don't have to do it if you don't want to. Just know that it's there." He shrugged. "I'm going to draw you a bath, okay?"

It *wasn't* okay. *Nothing* was okay, but I guess that didn't matter. My shoulders fell, but I followed him into the bathroom just the same.

"You don't have to wash yourself. You can just sit in the water for a bit," Nate told me as he turned the faucet off. He tested the water with his fingertips, then shook his hand to dry it. "But if you do feel like it, I brought you some soap. There's also a face mask and hair mask. If you don't want to, you don't have to. But it's there."

He set the bar of soap, face mask, and hair mask bottle on the ledge of the built-in bathtub. He had fluffed my robe in the dryer and hung it next to the bathtub.

"Do you need help undressing? I know that can be hard," he said, so matter-of-factly that it caught me off guard. What was he going to do? Undress me like I was a child? Undress me like a lover? *Yeah, right.*

"I can do it."

"Okay, I'll be in the next room, so if anything gets too much for you, just holler."

I peeled off my pajamas slowly. Tears and sweat had dried and crusted on the fabric. I left them in a dirty pile on the floor. I eventually made it into the tub, submerging in the hot water up to my neck.

My muscles started to relax. The hot water felt so good that I dipped my head below the surface. Even if I didn't wash my hair, at least the water got the grime out. Resurfacing, I considered the products Nate had brought. The milky white soap had various flower petals sticking out of it. I took it in my hand and brought it to my nose, giving it a sniff. It smelled nice, subtly floral but mostly fresh and clean. *Fancy.* I was already in the bath. I could at least wash my tits, pits, and bits. I ended up running the bar of soap over most of my body, rubbing the suds into my skin. It felt good to be clean and smelling like flowers rather than body odor.

Let's see what else Mr. Perfect brought. The hair mask, thick and white, smelled like the soap. The container was hot pink, and looked higher end than anything I typically used. Nate seemed as though he'd like luxurious things, even if they were simple. I rubbed the mask into my scalp and ran my fingers through my hair, making sure the mask covered every strand. I piled my hair on the top of my head, letting the mask sit.

The sheet mask had a dog's face printed on it. I laughed

to myself. *He thinks he's funny, doesn't he?* I opened the package and placed the mask on my face. The water had started to cool, so I used my foot to turn the hot water back on. Once the water was hot enough to boil a lobster, I turned it off and luxuriated in the warmth.

You don't deserve this, the darkness hissed. Maybe I didn't deserve this, but that didn't change the fact that he did this for me.

I don't know how long I sat in the bath, but eventually, my fingers and toes grew wrinkled, and I had refilled the hot water countless times. I took off the puppy face mask, setting it on the edge of the tub for another day, and rinsed out the hair mask. Stepping out of the tub, I wrapped myself in a towel and sat on the edge. I felt *better*. Good might have been too strong, but I at least felt less bad. Sufficiently dry, I toweled off my hair and dressed in my robe.

There was a note on my bedroom door, "Walking Sadie and picking up food." In the distance, I heard the washer going. I opened the door and saw that the piles of clothes were gone from my floor. My bed was newly made with fresh sheets and smelling of lavender pillow spray. It looked too nice to go back in to rot, so I put on some soft loungewear and ventured into the living room. I could see that the piles of dishes were gone as well. I bit back tears. Who the fuck did this for someone? No one had ever taken care of me like this. I'd never asked them to.

You didn't ask him, either.

By the time Nate returned, I had curled on the couch with a movie. Sadie ran up to me, licking my hands. Nate held up a white bag takeout bag.

"You want something to eat?" he asked with a timid smile. I nodded. "Great, let me change over the laundry and I'll get you a plate."

               ❦

"What are we watching?" he asked, sitting next to me. *We?* I didn't even have the energy to arch an eyebrow at him. Sadie jumped up next to him, curling into a ball against his leg.

"*Moonstruck,*" I told him, digging in. He'd brought me pad thai, tom kha soup, and green curry with fragrant jasmine rice. He nudged me, and I remembered to take a drink from the bottle of water sitting between us. "It's one of my favorites."

"I've never heard of it."

I faked a gasp. "That is a crime. It's Cher and Nicholas Cage and it's totally bonkers, but I love it."

As we watched, Nate seemed not to know any of the actors, as though he had been living under a rock all his life.

"Not even Fraiser's dad?" I exclaimed incredulously. No, not even Fraiser's dad.

I looked at him sharply. "I didn't ask for this."

"I know," he said, putting an arm around me.

Tentatively, I relaxed into him. This was how you set off

186

the trap. I waited and no tripwire twanged, no cage falling down to box me in. When I looked up at him, he just smiled. No expectations of anything in return. I sank further into him, enjoying the heat radiating from him. He was so warm, it was like snuggling Sadie. When I fell asleep listening to dogs howling at the moon, the darkness didn't close in to consume me.

Chapter Twenty-Four: Derrick

No one left the creepy-ass warehouse where Nate had been drugged. No one entered it either. I thought watching this place would be like the movies, me and Nate being all buddy cop with banter and snackies. Instead, Nate sat in stone silence and nothing exciting happened. *Worst stakeout ever!* Nate had texted Joe with urgency that he needed that cure now. Joe had jumped at the chance.

"Do we call it?" I asked him. We'd been watching for twenty-four hours at least. Nate just pressed his lips together and shook his head. "So, we're just going to wait here until he's ready for you?"

He tossed me a white envelope. *Not a-fucking-nother one.* On the front was Alice's scratchy handwriting: *XO*. I could feel it pulsing in my hands. Hadn't the royal flush been enough of a taunt?

"Open it."

I struggled with the delicate paper, but I managed to pull out the card. In fancy ass gold lettering was an invitation.

"You are cordially invited to a gala celebrating pack alpha, Alice O'Shea," I read. I held it up to him. "Casino themed? Really? You've got to be fucking with me right now."

I threw it to the floor. What a tacky bitch.

Nate shook his head. "I found it on my pillow this morning."

His pillow? That meant the wolves snuck into his apartment while he slept. He collected the envelope from the floor and I shuddered. I understood power plays like this. Hell, I understood alphas like this. My father had been one, and I killed him for it. Not every narcissistic maniac needed a pack of willing fans inflating their ego. My father might have been the white trash version, but he would have thrown himself a gala if he could have.

"This all has to be Alice." I rolled down the window and spat out onto the street. "Joe. The cure. He's working with shifters, experimenting on you. What other pack has that kind of capital?" I asked, knowing full well he didn't have an answer.

Nate walked me through his argument. "I need to know if his cure will work. The full moon is almost here. I have to try."

I sighed. "If you are right—and I'm not saying you're wrong—but if you are right, I still don't see why we can't rough him up a little."

By our logic, this was likely the man who helped kill the only woman I have ever loved. I didn't see why we couldn't torture him just a little after he gave Nate the cure.

Nate gave me a look. "We might be wrong."

"But we might be right."

He sighed deeply. I knew that sigh. That sigh meant the argument was over for now. Which meant I won. *For now.*

He nudged me. "Thank you. For being here and having

my back."

"That's what brothers do." We might fight and I might hate his guts sometimes, but I trusted no one else to be there for me. "I came to you, remember?"

He chuckled. "We might both live long enough to regret that." He shot up and pointed. "Look, there he is."

A shiny black Range Rover pulled into the parking lot. It deposited Joe along with five flunkies before driving away.

"He's traveling awfully heavy for just giving you a cure."

"Not if he's expecting things to go south." Nate shook his head. "Or if he thinks you might go berserk on him."

"All he needs to give me is a reason." I grinned. "Ready to go get neutered?"

***

The warehouse hadn't changed since we were here last. Creepy warehouses tended to stay creepy. Joe continued with his horror movie aesthetic of one medical exam chair and bright lights to illuminate it—except this time, he added straps. I gave Nate a warning glance, but he strode in confidently. He could be so stubborn when he put his mind to it, and he was resolute in this decision. Once again, Joe opened his arms to us with a smile.

"Welcome back, gentlemen," he exclaimed, all teeth. "Well, Nathan, how're we feeling?"

Nate shrugged. "I survived. And it's Nate, just Nate."

"Great, Nathan, just great," Joe said, placing an arm around him. It was such a smooth move, but it got Nate away from me and closer to the bodyguards. Two bodyguards stepped into the space they left behind. I growled at them, but they ignored me. Joe settled Nate into the exam chair. "Now, Nathan, this time is going to be a little different. This dose needs to be administered intravenously."

"What does that mean?" Nate asked as the thugs strapped him to the chair. One of the thugs rolled in an IV pole. *Oh, fuck no.* I thought back to the cage and leapt forward without thinking. The guards created a wall of muscle between me and Nate, but I would shift if I had to. This was turning into straight-up horror movie shit. I flexed, baring my claws.

"Ah-ah-ah," Joe said, waving his finger in my direction like I was a naughty child. The tone of his voice sounded familiar, like he'd chided me before. "Nathan, if your friend doesn't behave, I'm afraid we'll have to call this whole thing off."

Nate's eyes pleaded with me, and I retracted my claws.

"Good boy," Joe said patronizingly. God, I couldn't wait to beat him to a pulp. Maybe I'd skin him alive the same way he did Sarah. The sick fuck. He turned to Nate as one of the thugs hooked him up to the IV. "It means we need to give you the drugs through an IV over about an hour. No risk of spitting it out this time." Joe winked at Nate and motioned to the thug. "Let 'er rip, boys."

Joe strode away from Nate, who closed his eyes as the silver sludge dripped into his veins.

I stood in his way. "The fuck do you think you're going?"

Four of his bodyguards surrounded me.

Joe smirked. "Only one of them needs to administer the cure."

"What if something goes wrong?" I couldn't even smell Nate's panic. *Fuck.* They must have slipped him a sedative with his cure. I remembered that feeling of being hazy, half-awake and half in control. Like a foot that had fallen asleep before the pins and needles started. With Nate out, that left only me with a functioning brain, which was kind of a scary thought. I fought the urge to rip out Joe's throat.

Joe shrugged. "Balto's trained. Aren't you, Balto?"

Balto—*nice fake name, dipshit*—barely looked up from his phone long enough to grunt.

Joe smiled. "See, Nathan's in great hands."

The remaining bodyguards ushered him away as I yelled at him, "It's Nate, you asshole."

I rushed to Nate's side, but Balto grunted again when I got too close. Well, I had a phone too. I quickly snapped a photo and sent it to the only person who cared about Nate's wellbeing as much as I did. My message was simple.

We'll be at your place in about an hour. Need help.

Prowling the warehouse kept me occupied for about half an hour. Anytime I got close enough to touch Nate, I got a growl from Balto. He left me alone otherwise, content to scroll through his sleek magitech phone. Then something started beeping, and I might not be familiar with the medical equipment, but even I knew it didn't sound good.

Balto looked up, scowl on his face. I started to smell Balto sweat in panic. Something was wrong. My hackles raised and I prepared to fight my way out with Nate if I had to. Balto went to fiddle with one of the pumps, and Nate convulsed. My stomach clenched with fear, like being on the top of a rollercoaster before the big drop. I couldn't think, I could only act. Claws out, I dove. Balto pushed me away and into the IV pole. The slash I had meant for him punctured the IV bag instead. Liquid splashed onto Balto as I righted myself. Balto's face went red as he opened his arms to tackle me. I crouched defensively, waiting for him to shift. When he didn't—and not for lack of trying, his face squished with exertion, sweat dripping down his meaty brow—we stared each other down in confusion.

He couldn't shift. Fucking hell, this cure might actually work! Still, I wasn't about to wait for Balto to recover. Dashing through his open legs, I slashed Balto's ankles, and he dropped hard. I pushed him to the side, tugging the IV out of Nate's arm. Blood dripping down my arms, I scooped Nate up and ran as fast as I could to Big Bertha.

Christi stood outside as we pulled into the driveway. She ran to the door before I even got Bertha in park.

"What happened, Derrick?" she asked, throwing the door open and diving for Nate. She checked his pulse and hovered over his mouth. "He's barely breathing."

"Silver, lots of it. I think. I don't know. They didn't exactly tell me what they used."

She stepped aside so I could carry him through the front door and into a spare room.

"Alice?" she asked in a panic as I carefully set him on the bed.

"No, this was all Nate, unfortunately."

She laid her hands on Nate and closed her eyes. "Shit fuck," she swore. We locked eyes across the bed, Nate between us. I could smell her anxiety and fear. *Same, babygirl, same.* She held onto the edge of the bed. "Derrick, I'm not a healer. My mom is, but I'm not."

"Then call your mom!"

Nate's convulsions stopped, but he didn't look good. His skin had taken on an ashy shade of beigey-gray. He lay limp on the bed. I struggled to hear his breathing or even his heartbeat. I wasn't going to stand around and watch the life drain out of him.

"I can't call my mom," she hissed. She mimed a phone

call. "Hey Mom, you know the hot werewolf I've been talking about? Well, he's dying in my house right now."

How was that my problem? I gave her a look and motioned to Nate. "But he is!"

"Just stay here!"

I heard Sadie bark excitedly at her in the other room.

"Come on, man," I whispered, tears in my eyes. I dropped to my knees, resting my head on the bed. I wouldn't take my eyes off him. My chest ached again. Would it ever stop aching?

Christi returned with an armful of potions. She opened her arms and let them roll onto the bed.

"Rachel left these here." She uncorked one of them and started to drip it into Nate's mouth. I thought we'd have to massage his throat or something, but he drank it down. She quickly poured another down his throat. "I don't know how many to give him, but we should be able to give him more in an hour."

She collapsed to the floor. Sadie scratched at the door, but neither of us would move from Nate to let her in.

"Does your friend travel with her own alchemy everywhere?" It was a lot of potions, and I knew this many healing potions cost a pretty penny. "Or is she just rich?"

"She's a *Master Alchemist*. But that's not why I have the potions. Those were from the revenant attack."

"What revenants?" I asked. She had said it so simply, I just knew it involved Nate. My anger at him extinguished quickly as I looked at his prone body. I teared up a bit. *Come on, bro, wake up.*

"The night we found out about Sarah, revenants attacked the house. I'm sorry, I thought you knew."

The puzzle pieces aligned. Nate worried about Alice's pet necromancer hurting Christi. It was never about me at all. I pushed away from the bed. *Goddammit, Nate!*

"Derrick?" Christi looked up at me. "What is Nate not telling me?"

I could ask her the same fucking question. "The short answer, babygirl, is I don't fucking know. He's keeping things from me too."

She laughed hollowly. "Maybe it would be faster if we compared notes."

You're his mate. But that wasn't my secret to tell. Maybe if Nate survived, he'd have to tell her.

"He got tired of waiting. He found some experimental, back-alley cure that some dude was willing to give him in an old warehouse."

Christi gasped, then shook her head. She sighed, brushing his forehead tenderly. "Oh, Nate."

I hated having to deliver bad news like this. "That's not all."

I went to fetch the envelope. Christi took it from me and dropped it like it burned her. We both stared at it on the floor.

"I'm getting really tired of seeing those," Christi sighed.

"You and me both."

"I'm sorry about Sarah," she said sadly.

I shrugged it off. "I'm sorry about Nate."

"What's that supposed to mean?"

I didn't answer her. I stalked out of the spare bedroom, pulling Sadie into my lap. She rumbled as I pet her. I was glad one of us was happy. I hated waiting, but I was stuck with it. Nothing I did would help anyway. Nate didn't need me right now. Christi would take care of him.

I woke from a dreamless sleep to an argument. Honestly, I didn't think Christi had it in her, but she was raising her voice in response to Nate's coolness. Thankful I wasn't on the receiving end, I crept back into her spare bedroom.

"If you don't lie back down, I am going to tie you to the bed!" Christi exclaimed, waving a potion bottle at Nate. Nate sat up, his legs over the side of the bed like he was leaving.

"I'd listen to the pretty lady, brother," I warned him with a smile on my face.

All three of us were relieved he was still alive.

Nate didn't look it, though. He set his jaw and looked stubbornly ahead. "I'm fine," he said with a grimace that definitely did not sell it.

Christi pushed him back down. "Stay there!" she pleaded with him. "You are still unwell."

"If I prove to you that I'm capable of walking myself out

of here, would you be convinced enough to let me go?" Nate bargained.

I leaned against the doorway, fighting the urge to laugh. He was alive. Still a stubborn pain in the ass, but alive. Christi groaned in exasperation, pushing past me to leave the room. I heard a door slam behind her. Both Nate and I flinched. Nate tried to sit up again, grunting with exertion. I helped, propping him up on a pillow. Sadie, oblivious to people arguing, jumped on the bed and curled closely to Nate. She licked his hand.

"I'm fine," he struggled to say through gritted teeth. He wasn't fine, but what I felt was worse. The alpha wolf in me could feel his wolf calling out to me for help. His wolf had been hurting too, and it was coming very close to the surface. I had seen Nate when he was more wolf than human. I had helped him back down after it happened. I knew he wouldn't want us picking up the pieces in the aftermath.

I closed my eyes and focused on my heart. Nate always said he felt his wolf in his mind. Maybe it was different for shifters. It could be an alpha wolf thing. My wolf rested in my heart, the very core of my being. My wolf and I were one soul in two bodies. Or two souls in one body. I am he and he is me. *And we are all together*. I'd laugh at myself for being fucking funny, if this wasn't so serious.

I closed my eyes and focused on my heart, bringing my wolf up. He nudged me, and we climbed into the bed with Nate. Pack. Ours to protect. I called out to Nate from my heart, and I could see him hiding in a corner, black all around him. As a wolf, he barked and snarled. *Go away!*

I called out to him again. I reached a hand out to him, from my heart to his. I knew Nate viewed them as separate, but in my heart, his wolf and his person were the same. *Nate!* I called to him again. The wolf whined at me before settling down. He curled in a ball much like Sadie and fell asleep.

I held my chest, coming back to my body. Sarah had called this *alpha magic.* She'd use the connection to bring our wolves to heel when she needed to. I had associated it too closely with my father and the power he'd wielded over me. I looked at Nate, who dozed off again, less agitated now. My heart ached, and I shook it off. His wolf needed soothing, and I'd soothed it. That was all. No alpha magic bullshit required.

Christi watched us from the doorway, come back in sometime unnoticed. "What did you do?" she asked softly in amazement.

I considered myself plenty amazing at certain things. Fucking. Fighting. Leading... sometimes. I didn't consider this all that special. But the lightbulb came on.

"Doesn't matter," I said, standing up. I looked down at Nate. It was so obvious. How could we not see it before? "I think I know how to beat Alice."

Chapter Twenty-Five: Christi

We stared at the invitation as though it would leap out and bite us. Even Sadie avoided it. It remained where it had been tossed on one of my ottomans. The darkness radiated from it, but I wasn't sure if I was the only one who felt it.

Derrick brought our attention back to him as he tapped the whiteboard with a marker impatiently. On it, he had scribbled a flowchart. He wrote *Nate* in the center with an arrow back and forth to *Alice*. A long line went from *Alice* to the word *Necromancer*. *Necromancer* split into two arrows, one to *Joe* and one to *Sarah*. *Joe*'s arrow had a giant question mark over it. *Sarah* had an additional arrow to *Derrick* with a heart over it. *Derrick*'s arrow led back to *Nate*. *Joe*'s arrow led back to *Nate,* through *Cure,* and to *Alice*. *Alice*'s arrow pointed to the *Aviary*, which led to a poorly drawn stick figure of Ines in a ruffled dress with a scythe. *Aviary* also connected to *Cure*. *Necromancer* shot out to *Revenants*, which then pointed to *Christi*. Derrick had even included my broken gate along the *Revenant* arrow. While it displayed everything we knew so far, it made my head hurt just looking at it.

I tilted my head at one particular doodle. Derrick drew an arrow from my name to Nate's. Above the arrow looked like a stick figure riding a banana with another stick figure. Or was it a dog with two people? Why was one end of the banana so large? I wanted to nudge Ines and ask if she understood the doodle, but she was too busy scowling at the stick figure representing her.

The flowchart ended with an arrow from *Alice* to a doodle that looked like a party. More banana-riding stick figures danced under a mirror ball. I had to give him credit. This was a thorough picture of the problem.

The arrow connecting *Nate* and *Alice* had a broken heart above it. My heart hurt.

Ines lounged on my old leather sofa. Rachel indignantly grabbed Ines's legs and sat underneath them.

I looked to both of them. "Did you see him make this?" Derrick had been here all of ten minutes, and he'd spent most of that time lecturing. I turned to him. "When did you make this?"

"Cards on the table, folks," Derrick ordered, tapping the whiteboard again, completely ignoring me. "We need all the information we can get, and it's come to my attention that not everyone has been sharing." He gave Nate a pointed look. "This is everything I know."

"How come I'm not on the board?" Rachel complained, taking a swig of beer from a bottle she must have found in the recesses of my fridge. I had been trying to cut back with Nate in my life, especially since he was all but living in my house while he slowly recovered from his *cure*.

If Derrick heard her, he didn't act like it. "So pretty much everything is Nate's fault." He tapped *Nate* on the whiteboard. Nate scowled at him. He had recovered from the silver poisoning, but just barely. After he felt better enough, we didn't talk about it anymore. I tried not to let that upset me.

Derrick tapped *Alice* loudly. "Alice is throwing herself a little birthday soirée. Nate's presence is requested."

"I'm not going." Nate folded his arms across his chest. He wouldn't even look at me.

Derrick sneered at him. "You might not get a choice, pal. So far, Alice has skinned my wife alive, terrorized you, destroyed Christi's gate, and sent revenants to propagate her lawn."

"Don't forget the Aviary," Ines insisted. She hadn't been speaking to me either after she'd returned from her quick trip to the Aviary.

Derrick pointed the marker at her. "Yes! Let's not forget the Aviary. Princess, please brief us on that situation."

I couldn't tell if he was being sarcastic or not, but Ines seemed unbothered. "It's surprisingly quiet. Fewer kidnappings. It feels less like a crisis than I expected. The only explanation is Alice's gala. It seems as though all the Wilderness is pausing for her celebration."

"Kidnappings?" Nate asked.

"The O'Shea pack have been regularly taking the children who have sought refuge there."

Everyone went quiet. Ines had never gone into specifics with me. I couldn't breathe as I thought of the littles being taken from me.

"To turn?" Nate asked.

Ines shook her head. "To trap."

Derrick growled, "That fucking bitch."

"Agreed," stated Ines, who wore a deeper scowl than usual.

"That confirms my suspicions," Derrick said, grimly. "We aren't dealing with Alice's full attention right now."

"What do you mean?" Nate scowled, shifting uncomfortably on the couch. He had his body sideways, twisting as far as possible from me. I tried not to read into it.

"I think Alice is too busy planning for her birthday party. I think she's distracted. I think now is the perfect time for an attack."

"The wolf is right," Ines said begrudgingly. "Our next step is clear. Go to the Aviary."

"Pretty, pretty princess has skipped a few steps," Derrick grinned, tapping Joe's name on the board. "First, we need the cure. What stops a shifter from shifting?"

"Easy," Ines said, pointing her fingers so they made a gun. She closed one eye and mimed shooting her finger gun. "Silver bullet."

"Super illegal," Rachel said gleefully. "I love it."

Nate chuckled. "I'd prefer to stay alive, thank you."

Derrick tossed the marker at him. "Not everything is about you! In the warehouse, when the grunt got soaked with the cure, formula, or whatever the hell it was, he couldn't shift. I don't know if it's temporary or permanent, but it worked."

"I won't know if it worked for me until the full moon," Nate said quietly.

I sat on my hands to keep from reaching out to him.

"That hack job?" Rachel scoffed. "It sounds like they just pumped you full of silver. That's not alchemy. It's not even witchcraft!"

Nate winced. He wanted so badly for it to work. I had seen him afterward. Even deliriously ill, he held out hope. I respected that he had his reasons, but Alice didn't seem to be the only one. It was irrational, but part of me was still hurt that he hadn't come to me for help. He was content with letting me pore through his books, but when things really mattered, he shut me out. Regardless of my feelings, I at least thought we were friends.

I looked at Rachel and shook my head in disbelief.

Derrick ignored us, plowing full-speed ahead. "It gave me an idea. We go to the gala. We trap Alice and we dose her up with that cure. Alice loses her power, her pack, her reputation, her control."

"We don't even know if Joe's cure works," I reminded him. "Maybe that shifter had something else blocking him."

"If you get me the formula, I could fine-tune it," Rachel said. "I am the Master Alchemist, after all."

"And if Rachel can't, I know someone at the Aviary who can," Ines chimed in. "It can be a simple exchange. We help protect them, they help us. They have something Alice wants. I think it's the same thing you want."

204

Typical Ines, speaking in riddles. Still, my heart sank. We couldn't ask them to risk it.

"Are you sure?" I asked her. It would be a hefty favor to ask Nate and Derrick. Ines had been badgering me about helping the Aviary, and I was running out of excuses.

Ines bared her fangs. "You do want to control it, don't you?" Ines asked. Nate nodded, entranced. Ines lowered her voice. "They need help and can give us something you want. We need help and can give them something *they* want."

Derrick grinned, flipping the whiteboard around dramatically. A short plan was outlined there. "Excellent! Step one, steal Joe's formula. Step two, refine the formula. Step three, go to the gala. Step four, dose the bitch. Step five, freedom, baby!"

"It's settled then. I'll start making the arrangements. I do have to warn you, it will take some time. Communication is limited."

"Why can't we just leave once we have the formula?" Derrick grumbled.

"It's not like we can just go to the Wilderness whenever we please. These things take time," Ines said pointedly. Train tickets through the Wilderness were expensive, and driving was out of the question.

"You ever wonder about the witches who made the Wilderness?" Rachel asked innocently. "The Reveal happens, and then boom! Hundreds of witches embark on rewilding the West. Huge magical reserves drained overnight, and then they just vanished."

I glared at her. "Rach, they probably died." A feat of that magnitude required sacrifice. "Could we portal through the Wilderness?"

Rachel scoffed. "Do you know how much magical power goes into a portal? It's not just making one hole in space-time, but two! A mouth and a butt!" Derrick snorted, but Rachel continued unfazed. "And we would be crossing a considerable distance. And there's five of us, so then you have to keep the holes open. I am not going to drain my alchemy for a one-way trip! Unless you pay me, and I promise none of you can afford me."

"Fine, but how do we keep Nate safe? This puts him directly in Alice's sights," I pointed out.

Derrick shrugged, "Buddy system? I've got days and the princess has nights."

Ines glared at him, but said nothing.

"What about Joe?" I asked. I tried to put the name out of my mind. There couldn't be a connection to me, no matter what the coven said.

"What *about* Joe?" Rachel repeated. Why was I the only one trying to poke holes into this plan?

"How do we get the formula? And do you really think the guy who promised you a cure is the same one who sent the skeletons after me?"

"Are you suggesting there are two necromancers?" Ines scoffed. "That seems highly unlikely."

"Could the two attacks be unconnected? The coven said the necromancer knew me. My gate was a clear message from the pack, but we don't know about the revenants. Maybe *I* was the target," I pointed out. I had been wondering at that for a while now. Sure, Alice had set me up once, but that couldn't happen twice, right?

Derrick scowled at me. "Babygirl, no offense, but you're not that important."

"Ouch."

"What if it was an experiment?" Rachel said softly. "Or an audition."

Nate perked up at that. "What do you mean?"

"I mean, everything has been small potatoes at this point. One envelope, one call, one text. One attack. Even the *cure*—" She used air quotes. "—was experimental. Sure, the necromancer showed the wolves they can control a shifter in death. But that's one ritual, and a complicated one. The necromancer would need to show their worth to the pack apart from that."

A show of force. Or a demonstration. It started to make sense to me.

"So, she's just a random target?" Nate asked with a growl. I didn't like the sound of it either, but maybe Derrick was right. I wasn't important—or maybe that was the point.

"Not random," I said, jumping up. I grabbed the marker from Derrick. He gaped at me before plopping next to Ines on the sofa.

She snapped her fangs at him. "You smell like a dog."

"And you smell like a rotting corpse."

"Can you stop sniping at each other?" I asked, as Nate told Derrick, "Cut it out."

I finished writing. It was a simple loop: the coven, the Bureau, and the pack. I then drew a big *X* through it.

"I'm not exactly quiet about being a witch," I explained, "but while I work with them, I'm not part of the coven and I'm not part of the Bureau. The necromancer would need to demonstrate significant power. What better way than to target a witch known for warding? First, they tested if they could get past them. Then, they tested if they could get under them. They are practicing for something."

"Something big." Ines mused. "The Aviary is warded."

I nodded at her emphatically.

Rachel sulked, "Again, does no one think alchemy is important?"

"I find it hard to believe that you were just in the right place at the right time," Nate said thoughtfully, but whatever he was going to add to that, he left it in the space between us.

Derrick interrupted, growing impatient. "You leave Joe to me. It'd be a huge *fuck you* to Alice if we take him out."

"Agreed," Ines nodded. "Perhaps we should go hunting?"

Derrick grinned at that. He grabbed Rachel's beer and took a swig.

I sat on the floor with a huff. "What now?"

"We take advantage of Alice's distraction." Derrick said

in annoyance. "We steal the shifter suppressant. Rachel works her magic to fine-tune it. Then we use Nate as bait at the gala. With Alice's attention on him, one of us can pour the suppressant over her."

"And die!" Nate exclaimed. "She'll have security."

"You're being dramatic," Derrick dismissed. "There are four of us. We can make it work."

"So, we just wait?" I asked, uneasy.

"I should know in a few nights if the cure worked," Nate said softly. Nate was being characteristically quiet, but he sat in that on-edge state where it looked like all his muscles were on fire.

I nudged him, and he recoiled. "You okay?" I questioned.

He nodded, his jaw clenched.

Fine then. I frowned, "I'd like to spend a little time on curse tablets and protective spells. Nate is still going to need our protection." I struggled not to say *my* protection.

"And you obviously are going to need my super-awesome healing potions," Rachel chimed in. "I can start work on those until you can get me the formula."

I looked around at the room, Nate included. He wouldn't even meet my eyes, and I wondered if *I* had done something wrong.

"Well, I guess this is it. We're going to take on the most powerful shifter pack in the country. No big deal," I whispered in disbelief.

Derrick pointed at me. "But we're doing it together."

"Thank you," Nate said in a sigh. "You all don't have to do this."

Ines stood up and stared him down. She folded her arms across her chest, one hip popped and her leg sticking out of her frothy gown.

"We'll set up a payment plan."

"She's joking," I said, giving her a look. I turned to Nate and repeated, "She's joking."

The snap of Ines' fangs told us she wasn't, in fact, joking.

"We have a solid plan." Rachel interrupted my spiraling thoughts. She snatched her beer bottle from Derrick. She wiped the mouth on her shirt. "Ew. Anywhoozle, we have a wolf shifter, a sword-wielding werewolf, a scary-ass vampire, the baddest witch I know, and *me*. What could possibly beat us?" Rachel continued, "It's Christi's birthday in a few days." I winced. I didn't like celebrating my birthday, and who celebrated at thirty-eight anyway? "I think this calls for celebration. We should go out!"

⁂

Nate lingered after the war council ended. He collected the invitation, barely touching it with his fingers, and slipped it into his back pocket.

Something troubled him. I could only imagine what he was going through, being haunted and hunted for so long. The end was possibly in sight, either by the cure or by going to the gala to confront Alice.

"So," I said as we both stood in my living room awkwardly. Sadie snored from her spot on the carpet. I couldn't stifle a nervous laugh.

"So," he responded, his voice distant, "happy birthday." I blushed. "I guess this adds to your fee."

As much as Ines insisted on payment, I had no intention of actually billing them. I tried to joke it off. "I guess I'll invoice you."

We nodded at each other. I thought maybe I could clear the air here, but he spoke first.

"I don't think I've properly thanked you," he said sheepishly. "I'm not used to having a friend like you."

A friend. Just what every woman wanted to hear. I had been taking the hint, so now I knew. We were friends. I could deal with that. No more mixed signals or almost-dates. We could focus on him and Derrick and getting safe.

"You took care of me, so I guess we're even." I pushed my hair behind my ear. I bit the inside of my lip to keep from crying. *I saved your life, you asshole. I thought you were going to die!*

"Is that right?"

"It is."

I winced at how hollow that sounded. I would have brushed his arm or given him a hug, but I needed to establish a strict no-touching policy with him. I looked up at his lips and stepped back. We were just friends. There would be no more imagining. I was mature enough to accept that.

"I'll see you later, Christi."

Shit fuck.

Chapter Twenty-Six: Nate

I did not want to go to a nightclub, yet here I was. Derrick was pumped. He wore a suit, actually in his size for once, and shoes with no socks. His long hair looked pomaded or something, slicked back into a bun. He smelled of bad cologne and excitement, making me even more nauseous. This felt like a bad idea before we even started. But I reminded myself that Christi would be here, and she wanted me to be here. This was for her birthday, after all.

What kind of birthday present did you get the woman who was your mate, but didn't know it yet? I settled on dancing with her tonight. It was a poor gift, but the only one I had.

I hadn't properly thanked her for healing me. I didn't know how to. I already feared being a burden to her, and this only added to my debt. I wanted so badly to be with her. I needed to stay away. But then she'd made it clear that we could be friends. The loophole let me have my cake and eat it too. I could keep an eye on her, keep her safe, and protect her, but I could prevent the mating bond from clicking in place. My wolf grumbled at that, and I mentally told it to deal. Soon I wouldn't have to worry about it in the back of my mind anyway.

That got me a snap of my wolf's jaws.

The magic doorway to the club smelled acrid, its

astringency burning my nose. I wondered why Christi didn't smell like that. Even after she performed magic, she smelled salty and herby, like the bundles of herbs she dried in her oven. I grinned at that.

I felt eyes on us, and I surveyed the room, scanning for anyone who might give us problems. I felt uncomfortably hot, sweat gathering at my collar. I could barely take stock of the beings around me, let alone keep us safe. If only I had brought my blades.

Unlike me, fucking Derrick was not on guard. He sauntered in like he owned the place, smiling in everyone's direction. He waltzed up to the bar, which was pretty empty, given that it was still early. A group of men with scales on their faces and arms, dressed in expensive suits with starched white shirts that had the top buttons unbuttoned, paused their conversation to watch us. I gave them a quick once-over to see if Joe was among them. He wasn't, and none of them smelled of the wolves, so I pretended I didn't see them and casually sat at the bar next to Derrick. Derrick leaned against the bar with his most charming smile.

"Stevie, baby," he called over the bartender, and she slithered our way. "The usual for me."

"Of courssssse."

Once the drink was in his hand, Derrick waved me off. "Later, dude!"

"Wait, we haven't found the girls yet!"

So much for the buddy system.

The bartender—Stevie—stared at me. "Sssssomething to drink, sssssir?"

I shook my head. My suit felt too tight and it was too loud, and why was I so sweaty? There were too many beings, and they all had their own heartbeats and smells, mixing together in a cacophonic jumble. The smells gave me a headache; they were too potent and too distinct from each other. My head throbbed with the music. My stomach roiled due to the scents, my nerves, and my head. I made a mistake coming tonight. My wolf was on edge, hackles up, snarling loudly in my mind. My vision blurred. I could barely stand on my own two feet. I wasn't healed enough to be here. I wasn't even sure I wanted to be here. Why was I here?

I hadn't even moved from where I stood, because the idea of wading through all these bodies overwhelmed me.

I started to think that maybe I should just go home, when I saw *her*. It was like the heavens opened up and shone their light in a beam onto her. Christi, swaying to music, a drink in her hand, silver sparkles in her hair. She wore a bright blue dress with silver sequins, making all her amulets and charms stand out around her neck and her wrists. It fit her perfectly, flowing over every curve. The sequins caught the light just right so that she glittered as she moved with the music. When she saw me, she waved me over, a brilliant smile on her face just for me.

And I forgot any idea of going home.

The nightclub of the Dahlia was exactly how I imagined it—dark with neon lights flashing, loud with music vibrating every corner of the room, and crowded with all shapes and sizes of beings writhing to the music or making out on the couches. Giant crystal chandeliers hung from the ceilings, providing sparkling mood lighting along the two floors. I stuck to the small table we grabbed along the wall, watching Christi have fun with her friends as I sipped on seltzer water.

She was beautiful, rhythmically swaying her hips to the beat of the music. She drank Manhattan after Manhattan. Part of me worried for her, but I would protect her. She looked like the promise of a night of reckless happiness, an opportunity for life's greatest adventure. I ached for it.

We were friends. We could still be friends, even if it was just like this. Me, the moth buzzing around her brilliant flame, knowing the moment I touched it, I would die. The flame would consume me. There would be no coming back from it. I would either be with her, or without her, friends nevermore. If I were a good man, I would have walked away. I shouldn't encourage the wolf within me that wanted so badly to possess her. I should have grabbed Derrick and dealt with Alice on our own. I should have kept her from sullying herself for my sake.

I was not a good man.

Christi met my gaze. With curling hands and arms, she motioned for me to join her. Her arms were over her head as she danced without inhibition. I left the table and made my way to her. I kept myself from touching her, as though avoiding her skin would prevent the inevitable. Instead, I swayed a bit next to her, finding my rhythm. I could feel the beat of the music in my blood, as though my pulse set the tempo, my heart racing faster as the song progressed. She rolled her body, her hands pushing up her hair, and she looked so sexy. It was a challenge; there was a wicked gleam in her eyes as she smirked at me. *Game on.*

I stumbled a bit, still weak, but she caught me. I tried to play it off just to see her smile again. I finished two-stepping and pulled her back against me, our bodies crashing together. I rolled my hips against hers in time with the music, her waist in my hands. She looked over her shoulder and winked. She grinded against me in time, shaking her ass as she moved.

"He has moves," she laughed, her head back. I smelled the perfume of her hair, the smell of her body. I hoped that I could hide my erection well enough to dance with her. As the music changed, I grabbed her hands, my arms still around her, and pulled them up to give her a twirl. I stopped her so that she had to face me. Her cheeks were red and she seemed breathless.

I puffed my chest out a bit. "Oh, he has moves."

I twirled her again with one hand, catching her against my body again. She matched my tempo as we swayed to the beat. I dipped her and she laughed gleefully. I wanted to bottle the sound of her laughter. I wanted to drink in her smile and her light so that I could drown in it. It had been so long since another person stirred me like this. Since I felt like I was falling so fast it was almost like I was flying. I couldn't help myself.

A better man would have walked away. But I was not a man. I was a wolf and my wolf howled. *Mine.* I had to have her. She was mine. The mating bond tugged and tugged at me. I could not just be friends with this woman. It had been a mistake to think I could. Ever since she came into my life, I had wanted her.

Fuck it. I pulled her into my arms. With one hand around her waist and one on the nape of her neck, I drew her into me and kissed her.

"Christi," I told her as she looked at me, somewhat surprised, "I am in love with you."

My lips met hers again and again.

I walked home alone. My heart still raced with the thrill of Christi in my arms, her lips on my lips. But I tried to be gentlemanly and do the decent thing. She had been drinking and if she returned my affections, I wanted her to do so enthusiastically and when she was sober. But she hadn't recoiled in horror. I took it as a good sign. My wolf dozed in my mind and I relished the quiet.

When was the last time I felt this content? Not since I was turned. My wolf kept me on edge almost constantly. Not even with the pack did I feel this secure. I felt that maybe we did have a chance against Alice. It looked like my luck was finally turning. Did I detect a hint of optimism? Hell, that too was new. I had Christi to thank for it. She made me feel invincible. I still felt invincible as I rounded the corner to the shop.

Even down the street, I could see the door to the bookstore was ajar. My heart raced as I picked up my pace. By the time I reached the door, I was running. I ran to the door. I paused at the entrance to catch my breath, but the sight confirmed my fears. The bookstore wasn't ransacked; it was just empty. The shelves and chairs remained, but all of the books had been taken. Only ripped and loose pages hung in the air, fluttering down. A fire settled in my gut as I ran up the stairs into my apartment.

That *was* ransacked. My records had been broken; black shards littered the floor. Coffee beans and grounds fell to the floor, their containers tipped over on the kitchen counter. My lamp was shattered, lampshade askew, glass looking like an explosion around it. I bit back the panic as I checked beneath my bed. I laughed bitterly to myself. My go-bag and blades were right where I left them. Whoever did this wasn't looking for my weapons. I turned in circles to survey the damage. Nothing was spared. Anything that could have been torn or broken was in tatters and shards.

I stepped around the broken pieces of my life and slowly made my way to the third floor. The lights flickered as I looked onto Harold's hoard. Or rather, the lack of one. A millennium of collecting priceless artifacts, parchments, tomes, and grimoires, was gone in an instant. The cavernous room echoed as I stepped through it. I wasn't even sure why I walked around to check. There was nothing there. No shelves, no glass display cases, not even loose pages on the floor.

Alice had taken everything from me. My career. My life. My control. Now, she had taken my one escape. The coven told Christi I had what I needed to be cured. All of that was gone now. Any renewed optimism extinguished in my heart.

Dragging my hands down my face, I sunk to the floor and wept.

Chapter Twenty-Seven: Christi

I woke up to Sadie licking my face, her dog breath nauseating me. I lay in the bathtub in last night's dress. *Happy birthday to me*. Somewhere along the way, I had taken off my shoes and dropped my bag. *Shit fuck*. I tried to piece together the night before. We went dancing and I drank. A lot. I remembered Nate just sitting and watching us. I had motioned for him to join us, and he did. Nate danced with me. Nate! Having fun and dancing. But after that, it got hazy. I had flashes of Rachel and Ines dancing with each other, of Ines's car driving us home, and—*oh no!*—of throwing up in the bushes once I got home. My head pounded as I pondered how much today was going to suck with how hungover I was.

I fed Sadie and let her out. I managed to take a shower and change into just a shirt with panties. I sat at the kitchen counter eating cereal straight out of the box when the doorbell rang. My head rang with it. Whose idea was it to install a doorbell? Someone who had never been hungover, that's who. To my surprise, Nate stood at my door with a bouquet of white ranunculus flowers. My jaw literally dropped. When had I told him my favorite flower?

"Come in," I said, cereal still in hand, motioning him inside.

He shook his head. He kissed my cheek and handed me the bouquet. "I can't. I'm sorry."

I quickly put the cereal away and took the flowers to put into a vase. Was he apologizing for something? Did something happen last night that I didn't remember? My brain felt fuzzy. What the fuck was going on?

I returned to the doorway. "Are you sure you don't want to come inside?"

"I'm so sorry," he said quickly. "I fear I may have gotten your hopes up last night, and well—I came to say goodbye."

My heart plummeted and I just gaped at him. I couldn't make a sound if I wanted to. *Goodbye?* But what happened to doing this together? To friends? If the darkness had caressed me gently before, it gripped me now, threatening to pull me—hard—down, down, down. Did I do something so terrible last night that he had to run away from me? *Of course you did*, the darkness hissed, *you always do.*

"I am so sorry," he repeated.

When he turned to leave, I found my voice. "I think I deserve more of an explanation than that!"

I heard him sigh. I saw him shake his head.

"I'm leaving," he said, his back still turned. "That's the explanation."

I stomped in front of him. The whole neighborhood was going to see me in a tee shirt and panties, but I could *not* care less. Thong be damned, I had to get to the bottom of this. With my ass hanging out, I pointed at his chest. "I saved your life!"

He wiped his face and shook his head. "You don't

understand." He sounded resigned, exhausted. "I told you how I feel last night and it was a mistake. Last night was a mistake."

We danced. He seemed happy. *Goddess, what did I do?*

"Please," I begged him. "Can we talk through this inside?"

"If I go inside, I will continue to make mistakes. It's better this way."

"What about the plan?"

"Fuck the plan, Christi," he said, forcefully. Something was in his voice that I had never heard before. "It doesn't matter. None of it matters anymore."

"What did I do?" I felt like dropping to my knees. Why was I reacting like this? Friendships ended, that was fine. I should be able to go back in the house and leave this behind me. No more wolves. No more Alice. No more necromancers. *No more Nate.* I couldn't breathe. "Can you just tell me what I did?"

"You don't remember." He seemed disappointed. Or maybe relieved.

"Remember what?" My voice sounded super casual and convincing. I was definitely *not* about to cry.

He chuckled sardonically. "Some impression I made. You're a terrible liar, by the way. Your voice goes all high and breathy."

"Oh," I said. I made my voice a little lower. "*Oh.* In my defense, I was really drunk last night. I remember bits and pieces."

He shook his head. "You are not making this easier."

"Then tell me what happened! Just rip the bandage off."

Nate strode over to me with a stalking, predatory grace, closing the distance between us. My eyes grew wide as he placed his arms on either side of my waist, hands gripping into me. His gaze darkened, and I couldn't keep my eyes off his lips. This felt familiar somehow. My heart raced and a warmth rose in my gut. I laughed deliriously, but stifled it in the wake of Nate's gaze over me.

"We were dancing—"

"I remember that part," I interrupted softly.

I felt just a bit sick. I could not throw up right now. *Keep it together, Christi!*

"—and then I pulled you close and kissed you."

"You did?" *Shit fuck.* I *really* wished I remembered that.

"I did. Then I confessed that I was falling in love with you."

"And then what happened?"

My eyes were glued on his as he leaned into me. "I realized how drunk you were and how sober I was. Then I panicked, told Ines to take care of you, and went home."

My hands found his waist. I wanted to pull his sweater off and feel what was underneath. I *had* disappointed him. I could barely breathe. "So, that's why you're leaving?"

"I got home and the bookstore had been ransacked. Everything. Gone," he corrected me. "I came to apologize for taking advantage of you, and for ruining our friendship. For involving you in this at all. I'm saying goodbye, Christi. Derrick is on the way now to pick me up. You were right. I should run."

Friends. He thought I wanted to be just friends. I saw his muscles flexing as he touched me, saw his jaw clench as he readied himself to leave. Waiting for me to let him go.

"What if you didn't?" I asked.

He leaned in very close to me. "I'm not joking, Christi."

"I know. But I'm sober now, and I would very much like to know what it felt like." I ran my hands up his chest. "Kissing you."

His eyes closed as he sighed. His arms wrapped around me, and I was crushed against his chest. "I meant what I said last night," he said, one hand tangling itself in my hair.

I leaned into it, lifting my chin up to him. Our noses could almost touch. I could feel his breath against my lips. I felt liquid with warmth, moving from my lips all the way down to settle between my legs. I shifted my hips against him so I rested against his very hard cock. My eyes didn't leave his. He sighed, and his body did that thing where he relaxed all at once.

His voice was barely a whisper as he spoke, "I am falling for you. I'm in love with you."

His lips crushed into mine. The kiss was wet and messy and perfect. The next kiss was even better. His tongue found mine and I sucked on the tip of it. He moaned against my mouth as I smiled. I kissed him breathlessly, not bothering to come up for air. His hands found my ass and squeezed as we found the right tempo with our lips. Blindly, we backed into the door. He wrapped his arms around my ass and lifted me up onto his hips. He lifted me so easily, I didn't have time to be surprised. Pinned between the door and his body, I wrapped my arms and legs around him to meet his lips again. He pressed his weight against me, and I forgot about my hangover. His intensity consumed me, but I rose to match it. His hands slid under my shirt, his hands warm against my skin.

Suddenly he pulled back, his mouth at my neck. "No," he said breathlessly.

"No?" I complained, almost a moan. I needed him and I did not want him to stop.

"No," he responded resolutely. He pushed my shirt back down, but I stayed suspended against the door. "I'm leaving. I can't hurt you like this. There's nothing left for me here." He rested his forehead against mine. "I can't *keep* you."

My heart stopped. Slowly, I placed one foot, then the other on the ground. I caught my breath and took his hand in mine. Then I opened the door and pulled him inside. His eyes pleaded with me to stop, but he followed anyway.

My lips found his again, slower this time, but no less intense. I could feel his heartbeat under my fingers. His warmth enveloped me.

"I should go," he whispered against my lips.

"But you just got here."

He kissed me softly, nipping my lip as he pulled away. I melted.

"Stay," I said, more forcibly. "Stay with me."

He looked at me, and I drowned in those black pool eyes of his. Somehow, he managed to see through to my soul. I didn't have to say another word. He decided. He kissed me and the world exploded.

Chapter Twenty-Eight: Christi

"I am not going to have our first time together be fucking on the kitchen counter," Nate growled in my ear. I didn't remember how I got there, but I sat on the kitchen counter, legs wrapped around Nate. He leaned me back and I could feel every delicious bit of him.

"Why not?" It came out as a whine. I sat up, reaching out to him. "It's better than the front door."

He stepped back, wiping his hand over his face. "Christi, I am trying to make this romantic, and you are not making it easy."

I pulled off my shirt, my legs swinging against the counter. I wanted him so badly. "Who said it had to be romantic?"

"Christi," he growled, but he stepped toward me and put his hands on my waist. I relished the feeling of his rough hands against my bare skin. I pulled him to me, losing myself in him again.

"Wait!" He pulled away again. "I've been tested. I'm good, but you should know that it's been a while. And the last person I had sex with was Derrick, so yeah."

I kissed his neck as he explained. I smiled, pressing a kiss onto his jaw. Was he worried that I would judge him for being bisexual, or just for being with Derrick? I took his face in my hands, kissing him gently. "Who hasn't fucked their friends at least once?" I told him. I even had a secret girlfriend in college. I resumed my trail of kisses down his neck. "It's no big deal." I lifted an amulet around my neck. "Anti-STI. I'm good too, so what are we waiting for?"

He smiled easily now, and I took the opportunity to tighten my legs around his waist. "Oh, what about condoms?"

I laughed. *Take me bed to right now.* If he didn't do something soon, I was going to explode. We needed to stop talking and start kissing again.

I kissed him. "I have an IUD. It's fine."

He pulled away again. *Seriously?* "I'm worried I might disappoint you."

I leaned into him, trying to be both sexy and reassuring. "I'm not disappointed," I whispered. Nate pulled me into him. He lifted his hips against me, and the world stopped rotating. All I could see was him. "Now, stop talking."

"Bed," he whispered in my ear. "Now!"

Fucking finally!

We fumbled our way from the kitchen to my bedroom, shedding his clothing as we went.

"Oh, thank the Goddess," I breathed as he pulled his shirt off. His stomach was solid, but he had a bit of a belly. Despite all the muscles underneath, he actually had a normal body. He kissed me, hard and passionately. He lowered me down before he unbuckled his belt, kicking his shoes off. I quickly undid my bra, discarding it to the floor. Soon there was nothing left between us but our underwear. He practically leaped into bed with me.

I relished in the weight of his body on mine as he explored me with his hands. We continued to kiss, my hands groping his ass, stroking his head. I felt his hard cock against me and I wanted to grind against it. As he grabbed a handful of my ass, he growled in my ear, "I have been waiting so long to touch you like this."

His mouth found mine hungrily as his hands toyed with the waistband of my thong. My whole body pulsed with electricity from his touch. My clit throbbed against him. It made my head spin, dizzying, lightheaded, a little high. It was a head rush. It couldn't just be my hangover. This felt too good. Too right. He kissed my neck, nipping it gently. I sighed with pleasure.

"Oh, Christi, darling. You keep making noises like that and I might come undone."

His voice sounded rough, and I liked it. He rolled onto his side and looked into my eyes with such worshipful adoration before kissing me hard again. I whimpered. He pushed my thong aside so he could use his thumb to caress my clit while one finger played at the entrance of my cunt. I was soaking wet, and I had to hold onto him for dear life.

"Oh Goddess, yes. Like that," I choked out, arching my back. He started to tease me again. He kissed my mouth again, his tongue playing with mine, as he plunged into me, one finger, then the other. I moaned, loudly and gutturally. He smiled against my kiss and slowly started to massage inside of me.

"Louder, darling. I want the neighbors to hear you."

His thumb toyed with clit as he pushed his palm up. I felt a burst of pleasure. I was close, I knew it. Too fast, it was happening too fast. I wanted to enjoy the feeling a bit longer, but I couldn't help grinding my hips into his hand. I reached for him, stroking him through his boxer briefs. When I started to pull them down, Nate shook his head and grabbed my wrists with his free hand. He held them above my head, gentle but commanding. My insides twisted and fluttered in response.

"I'm not done with you," he growled. I opened my mouth to protest, but his mouth was on my nipple, sucking and nibbling. My vision darkened. The friction of his thumb against my clit became unbearable, so I bucked my hips faster.

"Yes," he whispered in my ear. "Come for me, my darling."

I no longer felt in control of my body. While I bucked against him, I made short, breathy moans that grew louder and louder. No inhibitions could stop me now. I was loud and needy. Had it just been a long time for me, or was sex always supposed to be this good? I hadn't even taken his cock yet.

"Yes, Christi," Nate said, kissing my shoulder. "Tell me

who makes you come so hard. Say my name."

I came without warning, Nate's name on my lips. My legs shook and I threw my head back. He smirked and kissed me gently as I came down from my orgasm. He slowly extricated his fingers, then wickedly popped them in his mouth to lick me off.

"Fuck," he exclaimed, relaxing next to me on the bed. "You even taste good."

I was shocked, but a giggle erupted from my lips. I was still on high.

He held me in his arms, stroking my hair. "Do you think you're ready for more?"

"Please," I murmured.

He shook his head, kissing me hard. His lips were on mine, hot and passionate. He didn't hold anything back, tongue forcing its way into my mouth. I was overcome with wanting again. That was it, wasn't it? I had wanted him for so long.

He grabbed hold of both my thighs. "Have I told you how luscious you are? All your curves, so many places to grip and bite." He ran his hands up and down my upper thighs and hips. "I've dreamed of being trapped between your soft thighs, licking you until you come again and again."

"Nate," I breathed.

He plunged both fingers inside me, and I cried out. He smiled, hungrily. "That's my new favorite sound, my darling," he said, lowering his face between my legs. "Let's see if I can make you scream louder."

He lowered himself down and started to lick at my folds as his fingers mercilessly drove in and out of me at a steady clip. I moaned and grabbed at his head. His tongue circled my clit, and I arched my back in pleasure.

"Yes, Christi, that's it."

"Are you always so vocal?" I asked, my eyes closed while he sucked and nipped at my labia. I held back a moan. "Mmmm, like that."

He stopped for a moment, and I caught my breath. He grinned, my juices coating his face, a naughty gleam in his eye. "Only when I fuck," he said with a wink.

Who was this man? Gone was the silent and sensitive Nate I was used to. He had been replaced with some kind of sex god. And I liked it.

"So, you better get used to it." He ran his teeth along my thigh, placing a sweet kiss there. "That didn't come out right. I mean I like to talk dirty." More thigh kisses. "But it's you, darling. You bring it out in me."

With that, he sucked at my clit and I came again, hard. Stars filled my vision, and I panted like a wild animal. His fingers hadn't stopped, playing with me through the sensitivity.

"I don't think I can wait any longer," he said, wiping his face and using the same hand to stroke his erection through his briefs. "Give me one more, and then I'll take you."

I felt so sensitive and his fingers felt so good inside me, it was like I could come on cue. This time, I sat up and grasped his shoulders.

"Nate!"

"Christi," he said my name deliciously. His eyes were hazy with lust. "My darling, I'm going to try to make this good for both of us, but I'm not sure I can control myself anymore."

"This is you controlled?" I laughed. His eyes narrowed, and I realized that he meant it.

"Christiana, this is me trying very hard to control myself."

Chills ran down my spine. Goosebumps erupted on my skin. I shook my head. "I don't want you to control yourself, not with me."

He grinned, showing all his teeth. "Careful what you wish for. You might find yourself with the wolf instead," he said, kissing me deeply as he finally pulled his boxer briefs off. "God, love, you are so beautiful." He ran a finger along a stretchmark on my hip. "Your body is amazing. Next time, I'll take care to appreciate it fully."

I had come three times in about five minutes. I could only imagine what his idea of *appreciating me fully* meant. He looked glorious, his cock standing straight up against a trail of hair starting from his belly button. Like an arrow, *sit here*. I bit my lip. *Next time.*

"Lube?" he asked.

I pointed to my nightstand. "Top drawer."

He rummaged through the door, and I heard something start vibrating.

"Next time, I'll have to use some of these toys on you," he chuckled, clicking the vibrator off. He poured some lubricant in his hand and stroked his cock a few times. I didn't think wolves could purr with pleasure, but he did. His cock glistened, and he climbed back on the bed. "I might not be able to last long, love."

I was pretty sure I would manage. There was always a next time. *If there was a next time.* I caressed his face. "I don't care, just don't hold back. No holding back, please."

"Never," he said. "Come here."

He pulled me beneath him, and I felt him at my entrance immediately. One of his hands found my breast and the other pulled my leg up. He lifted my hips a bit and slid a pillow underneath, relieving some of the pressure of holding myself up.

"Hold on," I said, repositioning so that my hip didn't lock up uncomfortably. I tried to look sexy while doing it, but there was only so much you could do in a middle-aged body. "Okay, I'm good."

"You're so wet and ready for me. Let's see how well you'll take me."

He sheathed himself in me with one long stroke. I felt every inch of him stretching me exquisitely. He had warmed me up thoroughly and I still felt tight against him. I moaned as he exclaimed, "Fuck, love, you feel even better than I imagined."

He started thrusting, grunting as his hips ground into mine. At first, he was steady and I matched his rhythm, lifting my ass up so he could hit deeper.

"I'm yours," he said as he sped up. He pounded into me relentlessly, and I could only dig my hands into the sheets as I moaned deeper.

I felt him spasm inside me as I cried out again. Tears streamed down my face as the orgasm tore through me. He groaned gutturally as he came, and we both collapsed in an exhausted heap. I loved the feeling of his weight on top of me.

He kissed my shoulder as he pulled out. I dug the heels of my hands against my eyes, trying to get rid of the tears. What was that? I didn't cry after sex. Ever. But it was good with him, oh, it was so good. I felt empty but sated. Fuck, why hadn't we done this sooner? I kissed him as he lay on his side next to me.

His hands brushed away my tears, caressing my face. "You have all the pieces of my heart now, Christi."

As much as my heart swelled at the words, I could only hope that he hadn't noticed that I didn't say them back.

Chapter Twenty-Nine: Derrick

I laid on the horn of Big Bertha. Once. Twice. Thrice for good measure. *Come on, Nate.* This was all his idea, so where was he? He had called me in a panic last night. I had helped him pack the rest of his belongings into Big Bertha. He'd told me to be here. Sure, I was half an hour late, but come on, how long does it take to say goodbye? No one ever said goodbye to me before leaving, so I didn't know.

When honking didn't draw any attention, I let myself in. The slam of the door behind me was much louder than I anticipated, though I wasn't exactly trying to keep quiet. Sadie padded over, and I gave her my hand to sniff. Sometimes I thought the dog was the only one who was happy to see me. I'd miss her when we were in back in hiding. I dropped my backpack to the floor.

"Hey, sweetie," I told her, sitting on my heels to give her ears a rub. "Where is everybody, huh?"

I stumbled into the kitchen and took off my dark sunglasses. That might not have been the best decision, as my head throbbed with the light. I put the glasses back on. What a shitty hangover. Now was not the time for one either. Going out on the lam required street smarts and cunning. Since Nate had neither of those, I needed to be in tip-top shape.

"Hello?" I called out. "Anyone home?"

I could hear voices, and I took a big sniff. Christi was

definitely home. Nate had joined her. And—you have got to be kidding me. I smelled the change and could throw up. *The idiot.* We were supposed to be leaving!

I knocked on Christi's door. Nate answered in only his pants, barefoot and shirtless, with Christi behind him, barely covered in a large tee.

"What's up, party people!" I exclaimed. Neither looked happy to see me.

"What are you doing here?" they asked together, almost on cue. *Ugh.* This was not going to be fun. Well, I could *make* it fun, at least.

I dramatically took a big whiff. "Wait a second. Something smells different." Nate started growling. I grinned widely and pointed both fingers at them. "You guys did it." I added a body roll for emphasis. "Fucking finally."

Christi gave me a horrified look. Oh, poor little witch. For wolves, this was just a part of life. Everyone knew everyone's business.

"Relax, babygirl. I smell the mating bond between you. Buuuuut—" I waggled my eyebrows like a cartoon character for emphasis. I was mostly fucking with Nate. I did feel a little bad for embarrassing Christi, but she needed tougher skin if she was going to hang with the big wolves. "There's only one way for the bond to solidify."

"Seriously, Der," Nate asked, letting go of the door. His gaze darkened, and I could sense his wolf. He had been so eager to be rid of it. *Look who's in control now!* He would fight

238

me if he felt I threatened them. "What are you doing here?"

"You told me to be here," I said, as much authority in my voice as possible. *Play wolfy games, get wolfy prizes.* I'm *the alpha, bitch.* "Bertha's loaded up. It's time to go." I motioned a finger in a spiral. "So, let's roll."

Christi's face fell as Nate took a step closer to me. I could hear the low rumbling from his chest. I threw my head back in annoyance. *Ugh.* I hated dealing with mated pairs. But fine, I'd do it, since he made me.

I inhaled deeply and puffed out my chest. I straightened my back so I stood full height. From the depths of my body, I summoned my wolf.

"Nate, outside," I commanded. "Christi, put some clothes on." I turned to Sadie, who looked at me with her adorable black eyes. "Sadie, keep being a good girl."

Christi stifled a nervous giggle behind Nate. I smelled her discomfort, but also her fear. She was full of anxious energy, like a rabbit ready to run. *Interesting.* It was a familiar smell that caused pressure in my chest and a lump in my throat. I forced the emotion down; I couldn't go *there* right now.

Nate followed the command begrudgingly. "What?" he snapped once we were in Christi's backyard.

"What happened to *we have to get the hell out of here*? Or even *I have to keep her safe, Der*? Hm?" I argued, perfectly fine getting in his face. "We were supposed to be on our way to Wyoming!"

He wiped his face with his hand and shook his head. "Fuck."

"Yeah, I know you did. So, what now?"

"She's my mate. I can't leave her."

How inconvenient. I grew impatient, and more importantly, I grew tired of this backwards, forwards, upside-down, right-side-up logic of Nate's. First, we had to stay put. Then, we were going to the Wilderness. Cure? No cure. Cure. No cure? We had to leave. Now, we couldn't leave. *Stop this ride, I want to get off!*

He was supposed to be loyal to *me*, but I was feeling very much dragged around by him. Was it too much to ask for some consistency? I set my jaw. Since he was no longer thinking clearly, I had to make the hard decisions.

"We're leaving."

"Put yourself in my shoes, Der. What if it were Sarah?" he pleaded with me.

What a low fucking blow! Right to the chest. *Bullseye.*

"Fine! I didn't want to go to stupid Wyoming anyway," I said with a sigh. God, I was tired of this shit. He owed me big time.

Nate closed his eyes and exhaled. "Thank you."

"Don't thank me yet." I poked him in the abdomen. "You're out of shape, brother."

Nate arched one eyebrow. "Have you seen yourself lately?"

Funny. Well, I wasn't laughing.

"I mean combat shape. We need to train before we head into the unknown. We know that there are wolves and necromancers. When's the last time you fought a wolf shifter?"

His silence told me everything I needed to know. I ushered him back inside to his mate. She wore some clothes now and sat patiently with Sadie.

"Christi, I assume you can handle yourself when there's magic involved. But can you fight if it's hand-to-hand?"

"If you need me to outrun someone, I could do that," she said. "I can focus my efforts on warding and protection, but I'd rather not fight if I don't have to."

Nate caressed her arm. I kept myself from groaning. *Oh, brother.*

"And you likely won't," he said reassuringly. "But we should show you some self-defense moves, just in case."

I exhaled through my teeth. I wanted to argue, but that was hard when I agreed. "Maybe we can get you a gun. What about Pinky and the Brain?" They stared at me blankly. "Pretty, pretty princess and the chaotic chemist? The blood bitch and the pocket rocket?"

"Ines and Rachel?" Christi offered.

"Yeah, can they fight?"

Christi shook her head. "Ines, yes. Rachel, I wouldn't put it past her. She generally sows chaos wherever she goes."

"I need them here," I ordered. "I need to see what we all can do. We'll start drills today. Then, pretty, pretty princess and I can work on getting that cure from Joe."

"Why can't I do it?" Nate asked, offended he wasn't invited on *my* stealth mission.

"Joe knows you. And keeping you away from him means keeping you away from Alice." I clapped my hands at them. "Okay? So, let's get a move on!"

Nate and Christi looked at each other. Some kind of telepathic communication happened between them. This time, I did groan.

"What?" I snapped, my wolf snarling. I could use an excuse for a good fight, but I thought of better fun the *three* of us could have. Fun mental picture, but Nate would kill me before that happened. Too bad.

"Can we shower first?" Christi asked, sweetly. Oh, little witch, welcome to the pack. Clothing was optional. Touching was mandatory. There were no secrets between wolves. She'd have to learn that soon.

"Fine," I dismissed them. "Do what you have to. Where can I put our stuff?"

Nate growled low, more of a vibration than a sound. He didn't even bare his teeth. Subtly, he made sure that he placed his body between me and Christi. This was going to be *so* annoying.

"What stuff?"

"Need I remind you that you no longer have a place to live. Big Bertha's out front, full of our shit. I can sleep there, but I'd rather take a bed if you have one."

Christi directed me to her guest bedroom. I gave them a half-hearted salute, happy to finally begin preparations.

By the time Nate and Christi were finished, I had installed my coffee maker in Christi's kitchen and had started making food. The body had to be nourished properly to be efficient. Christi's cabinets and fridge were devoid of real food, mostly just witch ingredients. No one could subsist on herbs and spices.

I fed Sadie a piece of bacon from the pan. "I bet you like that, huh, sweetie?"

She nudged my leg and sat like a show dog. Who was I to say no to that? She was simply the cutest. I dropped her another piece, warning her in a whisper, "I know it's good, but I don't want you to develop bad habits. I'll get in trouble with your mom."

Finally, Nate and Christi emerged from her bedroom. They looked more disheveled after their shower.

I looked them up and down disapprovingly. "Look, I get it. You're mates! Get all the cardio you want. It's good for training. It's good for morale. But do you have to be so fucking loud?"

Even music in my headphones hadn't drowned it out. Christi blushed a bright crimson, but Nate was unbothered. Nate reached over and grabbed a piece of bacon from my

243

plate. I narrowed my eyes at him.

"Wear earplugs," he responding with an unapologetic grin. He chomped down on the piece of bacon and grimaced. He spit it out into the sink. "What is that?"

"Tempeh. Full of protein," I responded. "I also made eggs, spinach, and some rice and beans. You gotta eat right to make gains."

Nate poured himself a cup of coffee, making up a plate without the tempeh. His loss, more for me. He set the plate down, and then made up a plate for Christi. *Ew*. I was happy for Nate, really, I was. I considered myself lucky for having been able to bypass courtship altogether.

"Thanks," Christi said softly. "And thank you, Derrick. This looks amazing. I'll never say no to someone else's cooking."

Nate grumbled. "Maybe I take over the cooking from now on."

They laughed together, a casual intimacy that had seemingly developed overnight. If I examined the ache I felt at that, I would lose the focus I had recently gained. I'd start with Joe and work my way to the top. Alice was the real threat, and she needed to be taken out. My anger needed to burn hotter than anything else. Revenge first, feelings later.

Chapter Thirty: Christi

I heard the crash of the gate, and then Rachel's voice rang out, singing at the top of her lungs. *Great.* Well, it saved me from having to send them a text. I ran out to the backyard to find that Ines and Rachel letting themselves in through a side gate. Ines held two bags and supported a drunk Rachel. I would have sworn it was a full moon tonight.

"Christi!" Rachel called out, trying to run my way, but Ines held onto her shirt. "It's your birthday week! We decided to have a slumber party!"

"Rachel decided it, *and* pre-gamed it. I am merely the delivery service," Ines stated in her deadpan manner.

Sadie joined us, barking belatedly at the intrusion. When she saw Rachel and Ines, she circled around them happily.

Rachel frowned at Ines. "Don't be a bitch."

"It's too late for that," I mused. "The couch is available or the office, but Derrick beat you to the guest room."

"Ah, man," Rachel complained, but Ines shrugged.

"Can we all just come back inside and maybe drink some water or coffee?" I ushered them into the house.

"Ew, gross," Rachel groaned, pointing at us. "Wait, why is Nate here? Did you seal the deal after your makeout sesh?"

I huffed. "Everyone seems way too involved in my sex life today." I muttered under my breath. Looking back at Nate and Derrick in the kitchen, I felt conflicted and confused. I didn't want to invite more doubt from other opinions. "Can we just drop it for now? He needs a place to stay, so he's here too."

Ines gave me a look, and I tried to match it with a look that said *later*. She shrugged. "Confirmed."

I corralled them back inside and made a pallet for Rachel. After some coaxing, Rachel curled into a ball and fell asleep.

Ines complained very loudly. "Ugh," she groaned, her nose turned up in disgust. "It figures the moment the wolves move in, there would be orgies."

I couldn't blush any more if I tried. Could everyone smell it? Was I just giving off pheromones? I wasn't even a wolf, for the sake of the Goddess. Derrick sat up a little straighter and gave her his predatory grin.

"What, princess? Upset you didn't warrant an invite?" he challenged. Behind the sunglasses resting on her nose, Ines rolled her eyes.

"Behave, both of you," I admonished. I turned to Ines. "Any updates?"

"I bought tickets through the Wilderness for the thirteenth."

Friday the thirteenth, an auspicious omen.

"Plenty of time to whip you all into shape."

"And after the full moon," Nate chimed in, leaning against the counter, "we'll see if Joe's cure works on werewolves."

It distracted me, knowing that there was an Adonis underneath the neat sweater and slacks. I'd suspected it, but now *knowing* it was true stirred something in me.

Derrick jumped up. "There's no time like the present. Let's get those asses moving!"

Later that night, with Nate sleeping soundly, I snuck out of my bedroom. My heart ached. All this talk of mates and love just felt like too much. It felt like all my breath was being sucked out of me. *You can always start over. Be free.*

To my surprise, when I walked into the kitchen, Derrick already leaned against the counter with a cup of coffee in his hand. In the dim light, he looked less like a hardened wolf and more like an abused mutt. Sadie slept on his feet. I laughed with my mouth closed. I guessed if Sadie liked him, I could get on board too.

"You're up late," I said, as I started to make tea.

Derrick laughed, but it was a sad, ironic sound. "I wasn't joking when I said you two were fucking loud," Derrick countered. "You know, I can always bring someone back myself. I can scream with the best of them." He paused. "Nate never sleeps, so at least one of you is in a dazed stupor."

That was news to me. What else was I going to discover about him? I sat at the kitchen counter with my tea. Derrick stayed standing, staring at me. I didn't quite understand how it all worked, so I asked. "What kind of life can a wolf have after their mate dies?"

"None of your business," he said, teeth bared. Then he sighed, setting his coffee cup down. His features hardened and he set his jaw. "That's not fair. Nothing matters after Sarah. That's it." He shrugged. "Wolves pine over their mate once they are gone, but they can find love again, just like a human would. Wolves mate for life, but just because you can't have another mate doesn't mean you can't be in love. Mates are like spouses, I guess. I don't know. I'm not an expert. You should ask the egghead in your bed. He'd probably give you a better answer." He yawned and stretched. "I'm not only here out of loyalty. The only thing keeping me from jumping off the nearest cliff to join Sarah is my anger. I'll have my revenge or die trying."

"But what if there is someone else out there? You don't think there could be a chance for happiness?"

He laughed, baring all his teeth. "No one would ever be like her. She freed me," he said. "We were caged together and she freed us." He gave me a lazy grin. "Now, there might be a good fuck out there for me. What dog doesn't want to be petted?" He gave me a discerning look. "What's with the questions? You worried Nate is going to die on you?"

My stomach clenched at that. I hadn't thought of that possibility. No, my concern ran deeper.

"I was married. Before the Reveal," I confessed. "My husband, Troy, he was a doctor. We met in graduate school, got married because everyone else was and it seemed like the next step. We were going to separate, had talked about divorce. He wanted kids and I kept pushing it off." I couldn't bear telling Troy the truth, that I didn't want them. "And then he got sick. And what kind of person leaves a dying spouse? I'm not sure I deserve a second chance."

He leaned over and held my forehead to his. It was strangely intimate, his hand on my neck. Then he kissed the top of my head, petting my hair. I had forgotten that shifters were just as touchy-feely as I could be.

"It's too late for that now," he told me, "because you've got one. You know, I couldn't give Sarah what she wanted either. I never thought of leaving, but sometimes giving up is the right thing."

Before I could ask him about what he meant, he licked my face and retreated to his bedroom. Sadie trotted behind him. *Traitor.*

I rubbed my cheek, wiping off his saliva. Still, I stayed up thinking. A second chance. Did it even count if I didn't have a choice?

Nate stirred when I came back to bed. He wrapped his arms around me, enveloping me with his warmth. I could already feel the sticky sweat between us from our skin contact. I pulled off my sweatshirt and tossed it to the floor. I already ran warm, but sleeping with Nate felt like sleeping in a furnace. He resumed his position, nuzzling my neck and kissing my jaw, working his way up my neck to nibble my earlobe. I leaned my head back, inviting him to continue. It was easy to give in to the pleasure. Like Derrick said, who didn't want to be petted? I craved this, even if I didn't understand it. Even if I couldn't explain why, or if, I wanted it.

"Talk to me," I murmured. "Tell me about the pack."

I didn't want to talk about wolves right now. I wanted to keep the curtains drawn and forget that anything outside this room existed. But I needed to know. I needed to understand what I was in for.

"Well, I showed up shortly after Sarah and Derrick killed the former alpha." Nate started. "The pack was a mess."

I tried to school my face. I didn't want Nate to see my disgust at the casual violence of it all. Knowing the shifters had different social rules didn't make it any easier to swallow. I had a hard time imagining Nate like that. But then again, he stashed two blades underneath my bed.

"And when I showed up, I showed up angry." His brow furrowed. "I had just been turned. I had left my fiancée and my family. Alice stalked me relentlessly. I found out about a pack in Colorado. This was before the Reveal, so I didn't even know if I was going to find real shifters there. I wanted someone, anyone to feel the pain I felt. Derrick and Sarah were barely adults, barely literate. They looked to me to be the adult, so I stuffed all that anger down and I got shit done."

"Sarah and Derrick needed strong wolves to reinforce them as the alpha pair. But they also needed to reinforce the bonds of the pack to repair the wound left by the alpha's death. There was a lot of fighting, in the pack and against the other packs in the area, who thought this was a great opportunity to try and take over our territory. I was new to the pack, but also new to being a wolf. I didn't know what was normal and what wasn't for shifters."

I stayed very quiet as I listened, my hand on Nate's chest, my eyes locked on his in the dark.

He shrugged. "It was different for me. Growing up, I was always *different*. Being Black was hard enough. Being bisexual and Black was out of the question. You remember what it was like growing up; anyone who was different was made fun of. It had gotten better in college, but I hid a lot of myself."

I nodded, though I knew I would never understand what he had gone through and what more he could face.

"The pack made me feel accepted, including all of the secret parts of me." He told me, rubbing my arm. "I felt free to be me, including the wolf that I hated. I could be bisexual and still manly. I could be aggressive, but respected. I was *the* beta. And as a beta, I was respected, adored, and feared. It's seductive. When Derrick started bringing me into their bed, it felt like a reward for a job well done. I respected them, fought for them, and I would have done anything for them. I loved them. I loved him. But most of all, I loved being pack."

Chills ran up my arms, goosebumps causing the hair on my arms to stand up on end. Nate didn't speak after that, just held me while waiting for my reaction. I swallowed the silence. I hated the tension but I couldn't leave the words unsaid. "Why leave then? If you felt that way."

"Sarah was in heat. She and Derrick had been trying. They wanted me to help them. I wouldn't. Then, I started to get messages from Alice again. It was enough to tip me over the edge. I wanted to protect them, so I left."

Derrick's grief made sense now. He had lost the love of his life, but he also was free from the secret. I tried to remember if he'd ever said the word *mate* in reference to Sarah. Nate called Sarah Derrick's mate, but not Derrick. I didn't know wolf shifter dynamics, but I did know Derrick.

"It's so sad." I murmured without thinking. "It must have been so difficult for Sarah and Derrick, to know that they weren't mates, but the pack needed an alpha pair. To keep the pack from falling apart, they had to keep up appearances."

Nate sat up. "What do you mean?"

"I'm your mate, right? You'd never let me be with someone else."

He grinned at that, and I knew I was right. He kissed my bare shoulder. "You're mine."

I tried not to grimace. I hadn't decided if he was *mine* yet. "Maybe I'm wrong. Maybe wolves can have more than one mate. But Derrick loved you. He loved her too. Would his mate really let him share? Sarah sounds like a shrewd woman. She took down the previous alpha. She knew she needed to look strong, and what could be stronger than an alpha pair?"

Nate sighed. "I don't know how I never saw it. I just assumed—I thought we were brothers," he snarled. "I'm going to kill Derrick for lying to me."

I rubbed his arm, coaxing him to lie down with me. He pulled me into his arms and I relished in our closeness. "He's still mourning." I reminded him. "Mate or not, she was still his wife."

"His *wife*. *Hm*. Let's get married," he whispered in my ear, his hands in my hair, his breath hot on my neck. I couldn't breathe. I lay there frozen. I shut my eyes and hoped he would think I fell asleep. He lifted himself up on one arm. "I'm serious, Christi."

I turned to kiss him, resting a free hand on his abdomen, dangerously close to his crotch. Maybe that would distract him. When he waited for a response, I tried a new tactic.

"It's been one day," I laughed. "I know the sex is good, but it's still new. You've had a rough few days." I left a lot unsaid. *Please don't pin all your emotions on me.* I felt the darkness looming over my shoulder, its tendrils reaching out to caress Nate's skin. I swallowed hard.

He rested his head against mine, our noses almost touching. My heart fluttered, coming back to life for a moment before stopping again.

"If I'm honest, you stole my heart the day you tried to rob me."

You can always leave. Run away.

I tapped his head softly. "I think you are thinking with your wolf and not your head."

I reminded myself to breathe after holding it in. I thought of the grounding techniques therapists had taught me over the years. *Name one thing you can see, smell, taste, hear, and touch.* But it didn't work, because all I could see was Nate's dark eyes, all I could smell was his stupid, fancy soap, I could hear the hitch in his breathing, I could still taste his lips on mine, and all I could feel was his heart beating under my hand. Just Nate.

"We aren't a couple of young kids, darling. I know what I want out of my life, and it's you. Tomorrow. Today. I don't care, as long the world knows you're mine." His voice was husky and low, full of love and hope.

I couldn't handle it any longer. Sitting up, I sighed. It was over the moment I said *yes.* He pulled away reluctantly so I could fully untangle myself from his embrace.

"Nate," I warned him, "marrying me won't stop Alice. You've seen what she's willing to do. And she's a wolf. Wouldn't it be easier to go back to the way things were before—"

He snarled as he pulled me back in his arms. He rolled over on top of me, and my heart jumped with the thrill of it. I had never seen this side of him. There was a lot that we still didn't know about each other, facets that had yet to be discovered. He bared his teeth at me. "Before? You mean before she ruined my life?" he growled. "Why the hell would I want that? It's her fault, darling. She made me what I am, and then she hunted me when I didn't thank her for it. She set me on the course that led to you. You can't rid yourself of me that easily."

"I'm not a wolf," I told him with a whisper. He kissed me, hard and possessive. I would be lying if I said it didn't cause me to melt inside.

"That doesn't seem to be a problem. The wolf wants who the wolf wants. Mine has picked you."

I could feel him growing hard. He nipped at my ear, but if he thought that was the end of discussion, he was wrong.

"So how does that work? The wolf? Are you just a human consciousness inside a wolf?"

He rolled off me with a sigh. Shaking his head, he chuckled.

"What?" I exclaimed. "My education on werewolves has been through shifter romances. You can't blame me for having a flawed perception. Shifters aren't exactly known for being forthcoming."

Most shifter packs were insular and secretive. It was one thing that set the O'Shea pack apart. It had become too large and too powerful to ignore, its leader too charismatic and striking not to stay behind the curtain.

"Think about it as two minds. When I'm human, the

human mind is in control, but the wolf mind is still there. When I'm a wolf, the wolf mind is in control, but the human mind is still there. Sometimes control slips, usually close to the full moon, but not always."

So, the wolf wanted me, but so did the man. How odd it must be to have two minds in one body. But I could only think, *Poor Nate*. "Why do you want to get rid of it?" It was an honest question, and I couldn't quell my curiosity.

"It's...complicated," he responded, tracing circles on my hip with his fingers. I propped myself up on one arm to get a better look at his face as we talked. "Imagine getting sick." I winced. Between Troy and Grandma Ida, I could imagine illness quite well. "It's not like a cold or something where if you rest, you can recover. You never know what the day is going to bring, because you are no longer in control, the illness is. Maybe it's a good day, and the illness is barely a thought in your head. Maybe it's a bad day where the illness consumes you. You could eat right, exercise, do everything you can to keep the illness manageable, but nothing helps. You lose days just being sick. Weeks. The illness takes over. It becomes part of who you are."

He paused to kiss my bare shoulder, collecting his thoughts. "There's a sharp line now in your life. Before the illness and after the illness. You become a different person. You mourn the person you were and who you could become. You would do anything to get back to that person, to the *before* you. Even if you know that you will never be that person again, you still have to try."

Tears welled in his eyes, and my heart dropped into my stomach. I had no idea. All this time, Nate struggled and I didn't see it. I stared at him, unable to say anything, do anything to make it better. I squeezed his arm. He kissed my hand. "It's worse, because this was forced on me. I never wanted this. I didn't have a choice. When the wolf is in control, I have my life taken away from me." He sighed. "That's why I want a cure. I want to be able to have a choice. It's why I want to be with you too, marry you. Not because of Alice. And not just because of the wolf. I want to make the choice, and I'm making the choice for me."

He kissed me tenderly. "Think it over, my darling. I'll still be here when you decide."

When. Not if.

Chapter Thirty-One: Derrick

Be stealthy. Be *stealthy*.

"Do, do, doooo," I sang under my breath, making my way through the warehouse. "Do, do, doooo. Do, do, dooo. Do, do."

Either Joe was stupider than we thought, or he did not care about this cure at all. What idiot kept their abandoned warehouse-laboratory unguarded at night?

I rummaged through the drawers and cabinets, trying to find something, anything that we could use. Using my phone as a flashlight, I waved it behind the doors I had opened. As I searched, I realized that *I* was the idiot. Joe didn't lock up the warehouse because there was nothing here. Nothing of use to us anyway. The drawers mostly held loose papers and pens, some notebooks. One held a dusty old book. Nate would love that, but time ticked down. I shut the drawer quickly; I'd wasted enough time already searching for a whole lot of nothing. Empty glassware filled the cabinets. Where had Joe produced the medical equipment from?

He must have a second location. I swore under my breath. This was a bad plan, and I was stupid to have suggested it. A potion with this much potential wouldn't be stored here. Dejected, I restored the central hub back to its all abandoned hospital glory. I was making my way out, quickly and quietly, when another door caught my eye. This didn't look like an exit. Dark gray and heavy-duty, the door looked like a walk-in freezer, with a metal latch to open it.

Just my luck, it didn't have a lock.

A blast of cold air hit me as I stepped inside. The door slammed behind me, making the same padded *thud* as a refrigerator door. White fiberglass walls insulated the room, keeping it frigid. Wolves ran hot, and cold never bothered me much. It had to be freezing for me to feel it. Along the white walls were metal shelving units—and on those metal shelves were row after row after row of clear, plastic bags full of silver-colored poison. *Bingo!*

Joe wasn't making anything in the warehouse, but he definitely stored it here.

I grabbed as many bags as I could, wanting enough samples for Rachel to analyze and a few more to bring with us to the Aviary. Arms full, I looked at the shelves. I grabbed one more bag to be safe. What if Joe showed up while I stole his shit? I'd need to disable his shifter bodyguards somehow.

Careful not to open the bags and spill shitty shifter suppressant on myself, I tried to use my foot to lift the handle. The floor was slick with condensation, and my other foot slid farther and farther away from the door. About to do the splits and covered in silver sludge, I nearly fell over.

The door opened, and I didn't have time to worry about who was behind it. I was just grateful to have been saved. My foot fell to the floor and I righted myself. Ines held the latch, a hand on her hip. Pink ruffles surrounded her. So much for stealth. She stuck out like a beacon. Everything about her screamed that she did not belong here.

"Are you finished playing?" she snapped.

I heaved a large breath, gathering up the bags in my arms. "You were supposed to stay in the car," I snapped, making my way out of the fridge room.

She latched the door carefully behind me, avoiding the slamming sound I had made earlier.

"It was boring in the car."

Ines yawned delicately next to me, sitting on blood, red leather seats. She drove a sexy, black Citroën DS convertible that had been heavily updated. I'd been jealous the moment I saw it. Now that her trunk was full of the miracle solution, we waited to see if Joe would return to the warehouse.

I scowled at her. We were supposed to be alert. She volunteered for this! "What's the matter, princess?" I teased. "Too early for you?"

She smiled at me with all her teeth. Her fangs subtly overlapped her lower lip, drawing attention to her pink lip gloss. "No, simply bored."

Everything bored her. She leaned back, pushing my knees over so she could cross her legs and place her boots on my side of the dash. I got lost in all her pink fluff. I shoved it over on her side so I didn't look like a kid who puked up cotton candy. She pulled her legs in, sitting cross-legged in the driver's seat. She pulled her round pink sunglasses down at me and narrowed her red eyes. I supposed she meant it to be threatening, but she wore a bow in her hair. How threatening could that be?

"Don't touch me, wolf."

I poked her arm and she hissed.

"I mean it," she said through her fangs. "It's bad enough I have to smell you without your dirty paws on me."

I laughed. I could show *her* dirty. She looked too clean, too innocent, but her eyes resembled mine. *Animal. Inhuman.* She snapped at me for emphasis.

"Stay on *your* side then."

"It's *my* car."

We were nose to nose when a black Range Rover pulled into the parking lot. We had parked Ines' car in a corner of the lot shadowed by a freeway overpass. It was as inconspicuous a spot could be in a large, empty lot in front of a large, empty warehouse. Bright solar-powered lights illuminated the rest of the parking lot. In spaces like these, it was easy to see why the witches rewilded much of the coast. This was a useless wasteland of concrete.

We both sat up, hands on the dash to watch as Joe stepped out of the vehicle flanked by his usual shifter cronies. Ines reached into her pocket and pulled out a pair of opera glasses. As she held them up to her eyes, I gaped at her.

"Do you do anything normal?" I seethed. All my attention was now on her and her dumb opera glasses and not on our likely pet necromancer. "Why can't you just use binoculars like the rest of us?"

She scoffed. "These *are* binoculars. They're antique!"

I gave her an exasperated grunt before turning back to Joe and his cronies. At least we knew that he still used the warehouse. I couldn't understand his game, though. Nate never paid him for the cure; Joe gave it freely as part of his *research*. Nate's silver overdose convinced me that Joe's experiment was likely a bunch of bullshit. Which meant our good old friend Joe had to be doing something else. So, what was it? Was Joe researching a cure or something more insidious? Did Joe know that this stuff could suppress a shift? If so, had he figured out if it was permanent?

Why would *Alice* want a shifter suppressant, anyway?

Maybe Joe actually performed necromancy on dead puppies in there, using the cure as a front.

The Range Rover drove away once Joe and company entered the creepy warehouse safely. I wanted to burst in there action-movie style and kidnap Joe, but I'd promised Nate no torture. This was purely a smash and grab. We had what we came here for—watching Joe's movements was just the cherry on top. We had set up Joe to come to the warehouse, after all. Nate had sent him a text saying he knew more werewolves who were interested. Joe bought it hook, line, and sinker, the dumbass. Balto must not have told his boss about his snafu with Nate's second dose.

I wondered if he could shift again and how well his tendons were healing. Tendons were notoriously hard to heal with magic and potions. In my defense, Balto deserved it.

Ines and I watched in silence as no one entered or exited the warehouse. I fidgeted in my seat. It was good and all that we'd gotten samples of his cure, but that didn't stop me from wanting to go in there again. I wanted to know what he was doing. I wanted to know if he was the man who'd killed my Sarah. Unless I interrogated him, I would never know.

"Fuck it," I said, standing up and ready to hop over the door. "I'm going in."

Ines pulled me down by the bottom of my tee shirt. Instead of moving me, she ripped the fabric. "Sit down," she hissed, the fabric still gripped in her gloved fingers.

We both looked down. She recoiled a moment, dropping the part of my shirt she'd torn off, as if she'd forgotten her own strength. Dazed, I sat down. She shuddered and pointed to the warehouse. The bodyguards had left the building, but waited in a line at the door. *Interesting*. The bodyguards might not be Joe's. *Very interesting*. I *knew* they had to be O'Shea pack.

"What are they waiting for?" I asked aloud.

A sleek, black town car pulled in front, answering my question. Did all villains have a fleet of black vehicles at their disposal? I looked at Ines with her pretty little black cabriolet. I raised an eyebrow. She glared at me and pointed, urging me to look on. I scrunched my nose up at her mockingly, but followed her direction.

A few more shifter bodyguards stepped out of the car. I couldn't smell them from this far away, but not many males could achieve those muscles that without shifter DNA or steroids. One of them held the door closest to the warehouse open, making it impossible to see the passenger clearly as they stepped out of the car. From this distance, all I could only make out the color of the person's suit (gray), the color of the person's hair (black), and their general shape (rectangle).

I would bet money that these wolves were the same ones who'd tailed us after Nate's first dose. If only we could identify them.

Ines had the binoculars, and she leaned over as far as she could to see better with them. She practically stood up, her ass out and the rest of her hovering over the dash of the car. One of her hands used the steering wheel as leverage as she bent over for a better look. I definitely paid attention to the wolves, and not to her butt.

The whole thing happened in slow motion. I watched as she dug the heel of her hand into the wheel. I saw the wobble of her skirts as her foot shook on the seat. She started to lose her balance. One delicately booted foot slid off the leather driver's seat. The opera glasses tumbled out of her hand as she pitched forward. Her hand slipped, landing right on the horn. The horn, honked in a cavern under the freeway, sounded loudly and echoed across the parking lot. If the person in the town car hadn't noticed us yet, they sure did now.

Ines started shouting rapid-fire in another language as she plopped inelegantly into the driver's seat. I swore under my breath as the bodyguards ran in our direction, yelling commands and making hand signals. Once Ines found the gas pedal, the car peeled out of the parking lot. My heart racing, I held on for dear life as she shot onto the freeway like a bat out of hell. Ines weaved in and out of traffic. I hated this feeling, the out-of-control, whooshing of adrenaline as we sped to certain death. It was why I rode motorcycles back in Colorado. I would rather face down death in a situation that I chose or created, where I could at least go down fighting.

Ines still yelled things that I didn't understand. Served me right for not going to high school and learning a language like someone normal. I held my breath until she stopped in a parking lot along the coast. I had no idea where we were, but I knew it was nowhere near Christi's house.

Once the car screeched to a halt, she swung the door open, got out, and slammed it shut, nearly taking it off the hinges. She gathered up all of her pink ruffly bits into her arms and turned in a huff. She stormed out onto the sand before throwing her arms out and screaming at the top of her lungs.

She wiped her hands on her dress, walked back to the car, and calmly sat down in the driver's seat. I had never been more confused, frightened, and turned on in my life.

As we drove wordlessly along Pacific Coast Highway, I knew two things for certain. One, Joe was not working alone. And two, Ines absolutely terrified me.

Chapter Thirty-Two: Christi

"Have I mentioned that I think this is a bad idea?" Nate said, his arms crossed and his mouth a thin line. "Because it's a bad idea."

I held a wine glass in my hand and quickly poured the fuck-me-up potion into it.

Rachel grinned at me, wiggling her fingers together like a mad scientist. "Don't listen to him. I think this is a great idea!"

Nate gave me a look from across the kitchen counter. He persisted. "No offense, but if Rachel thinks this is a good idea, then maybe it's not a great one."

Rachel scoffed. "I'll have you know that this potion is specifically designed for Christi. I've designed it based on her weight, height, tolerance levels, and added a little extra oomph for maximal trance inducement. It's a proprietary blend of mushrooms, THC, ketamine, herbs, and spices. If it wasn't illegal," she grinned widely, "I'd patent the shit out of it."

After the Reveal, many anthropologists reexamined Paleolithic cave paintings. Viewing the paintings from a magical lens, they suggested that the journey into the cave represented the journey to the Underworld. The cave was a sacred space for communication with the spirits and the gods. Sensory deprivation within the cave produced the vision. The results of this holy vision were painted on the cave walls.

When I told my grandmother about this, she'd said, "shit fuck, of course they are!" I inherited many things from my grandmother, including her penchant for swearing. There was a reason the coven met in a cave. My grandmother, living in suburbia, didn't have access to caves, but she was a flower child. She'd trained me using good old psychedelics.

"That doesn't reassure me." Nate came over to my side of the counter and gently took the glass away from me. "You don't have to do this."

What choice did I have? We needed to know what we were getting into by entering the Wilderness. I had to at least try to divine what Alice had planned. We needed to know what Alice had found at the bookstore. She searched for something, especially given the *Bestiary* Jessica had sent me to steal. The coven wanted to keep it out of her hands for a reason.

I could question why I hadn't thought of this sooner, but when I looked at Nate, I knew why. My feelings propelled me to act now.

I took the glass, held my nose closed, and chugged the potion. Now all I had to do was wait.

Nate led me to the bedroom. "I'm by your side."

I laughed. "Not much help you can do while I'm in the trance." I lay down on my bed and rolled onto my side to look at him. His brow furrowed deeply, and I wanted to reach out to smooth it. "I know what I'm doing."

"I know." He said through gritted teeth, squeezing my hand tightly.

Rachel's potion worked quickly. I felt like I was floating, then flying. Once my vision blacked out, the trance began.

At first, I could only make out shapes and patterns. If they had any significance, I wouldn't know. Divination was an art as much as it was a form of magic. It required more practice than I gave it, and I was not naturally a clairvoyant like Sophia. I would never put the weight of something like this on her frail shoulders.

My vision became clear and I stood at a crossroads. Was this what the coven meant? Or was my mind just playing tricks on me?

A dusty highway beneath my feet, I looked out at desert, complete with Joshua trees, small brown shrubs, and tumbleweeds. The mind was a funny thing sometimes. I'd likely watched a film with a similar scene or seen an advertisement with the same imagery. My brain clung onto the coven's warning and tried to make something of it. Still, if magic guided me here, it meant something. I walked in the heat to the Y in the road. In the middle stood a wooden signpost. I couldn't make out what the signpost said, so I reached up to wipe the dust off.

"Christi," a familiar voice rang out, pulling me away from the sign. I turned in shock and panic. In the middle of one of the roads stood Troy, whole and healthy.

"Troy!" I exclaimed as nausea rose up in my gut. *Why would the Goddess be showing me this?* I didn't need to see him. I looked back to the other side of the road. I could choose to follow Troy or forge ahead on the empty road. He reached for me. *It's just a vision*, I reminded myself, even though I felt like I was going to be sick. *It's not real.* I looked again from Troy to the empty road.

I began to walk toward Troy, but no matter how far I walked, he was always just out of reach. No matter how far I ran, I was still stuck in front of that damned signpost. It looked like Troy stood even farther out on the road than when I started walking. The road stretched out past the horizon. I wiped the sweat off my brow and leaned forward, hands on my knees to catch my breath. When my hands met tulle, I realized that I wore the black dress from my dream. When I looked behind me, I saw a trail of blood. Troy still beckoned me to come closer, and as much as I wanted to, I got nowhere.

He held out my necklace to me, my wedding rings dangling from his hand. A reminder that I had betrayed our vows. My breath hitched as I stifled a sob. I couldn't save him.

I hitched up the heavy black dress and turned to the empty road.

At the other side of the fork, another figure beckoned me

forward, but it wasn't who I expected. Sophia as a young child waved in my direction, darting off with a laugh. My heart hurt at how happy she sounded. I don't think I had ever heard her that carefree. I left Troy behind to follow Sophia. She giggled as I chased after her, occasionally looking back at me.

"Hurry, Zia!" she called out. "Catch me!"

But soon too, the distance between us became greater and greater, until her cries of *catch me* became cries of *don't leave*. Tendrils of dark shadow clawed at her arms and legs, pulling her farther from me. As she disappeared into the black on the horizon, I heard her screaming. I heard screams echo hers before I realized that they were mine. The darkness on the horizon billowed forward like a thundercloud on land. It engulfed everything it touched, spreading its inky blackness across the desert. I turned and ran, closing my eyes in hopes that would keep the darkness from catching me.

When I opened my eyes, I stood in front of the signpost again. The darkness had gone and bright sunlight was left in its wake. I got nowhere. I huffed and sat at the base of the sign, black dress billowing around me. *Wake up! Wake up, wake up, wake up!* Nate had been right: this was a bad idea. I'd learned nothing, and now I was stuck in a trance where I'd seen my dead husband and watched as the darkness engulfed my niece. Blood drenched the sand where I sat.

The longer I sat, the more the blood spread from me, until I waded in it. It didn't matter if I stood or sat or swam. I dog-paddled in the blood, trying to keep it from going over my head. This wasn't a trance or a vision or anything useful; it was a *nightmare*. My muscles grew tired from the exertion, and I knew I couldn't keep paddling. The blood kept rising and rising until I finally sank. The weight of the dress pulled me down. Down. Down. I couldn't breathe, and I tried to swim up to the surface. But there was nothing gain purchase on, no detritus to push off from. Just blood.

If I couldn't go up, I would have to go down. I opened my eyes instead of scrambling blindly. I thought the blood would be thick and sticky, but it acted like red-colored water. Even though I could see clearly, it confirmed my suspicions. Nothing floated in the water but me, and the road appeared to be very far below me.

My grandmother could control her visions. She made her trances and dreams knit together in ways that made sense. As I dove down, quickly running out of air, I wished that she were here. I wished someone else were here to guide me and help me make sense of it all. But even my grandmother had told me that sometimes visions didn't tell you what you wanted, but showed you what you needed. I failed to see how I needed this.

Just when I felt like I would pass out from lack of oxygen, my fingers touched the uppermost tip of the sign.

When I opened my eyes again, I stood at the crossroads just like before. The sun shone brightly, heat rising from the asphalt. Not a drop of blood to be seen. No trace of darkness looming on the horizon. I screamed in frustration. Was there a choice I needed to be making? I tried both roads at the fork and neither got me any farther. I looked behind me. It looked like the road went on forever, continuing until it blinked out on the horizon.

"Is that what you want?" I yelled to the blue sky. "You want me to go *backwards*? Fine!" I gathered up the dress and left the fork in the road behind to walk the singular highway. The world changed with each step I took. Eventually, I heard birdsong and the buzzing of insects. The blinding heat cooled as a light breeze caressed my skin and wicked away my sweat. Grass sprouted and flowers bloomed. Day turned into dusk, a violet twilight hazy with the setting sun. The bright full moon had risen overhead.

I walked until orange and purple sunset faded into silver and indigo skies. I walked until the stars glimmered into existence. I walked until I was awash with the moon's glow. I kept walking until the trance faded into that same darkness I had tried so hard to escape.

Chapter Thirty-Three: Nate

Derrick and Ines returned from the warehouse with several bags full of Joe's "cure." They filled Christi's fridge, Derrick grumbling that we needed space for food. Ines collapsed onto Christi's couch dramatically, pulling a layer of her dress over her head to block the light.

Derrick took me by the arm. "Joe's our guy."

I nodded gravely. My heart sunk. If Joe was Alice's necromancer, then I doubted his cure was going to work at all. My body ached with exhaustion. I wiped a hand over my face. I tried to remind myself that the Aviary could help me as well. All wasn't lost if this didn't work. My wolf whined in the back of my mind, circling around and around, unable to calm itself.

I had allowed myself to hope, and it looked like I would only end up disappointed again.

Rachel slapped one of the bags of the cure. "Nice work, guys, but I need the protocol if I'm going to be any help."

Derrick glared at her, a low rumbling coming from his chest. "What do you mean *protocol*?"

"Recipe, ingredient list, steps, something!" she exclaimed exasperatedly. "I might be able to take it to the alchemy to analyze it, but it would have been quicker if you'd brought me a lab notebook."

I looked to Derrick, who gritted his teeth, a muscle in his

jaw twitching.

"Lab notebook?" I asked. My major had been in the humanities and was over two decades old. I gleaned most of my impression of laboratory work from television and novels.

"It's a notebook where you write down your protocol and your observations for your experiment," Christi chimed in from her seat at the kitchen counter. Her voice was still heavy with sleep from her trance, but she had insisted she was fine and wanted to work. She buried her nose in a large map, and she spoke without looking up. "It's pretty much a record of what you did, how you did it, and what happened when you did it."

Rachel looked at Derrick expectantly. "You didn't happen to find one of those lying around, did you?"

Derrick groaned loudly, in frustration. Ines shot up from the couch. Her eyes narrowed at Derrick.

"I am trying to sleep!"

Rachel and Derrick argued loudly in the living room.

"Without the protocol, the best I can do is guess."

"Fine," Derrick capitulated, which was unlike him. "What about my portal idea?"

"It just doesn't work that way," Rachel snapped.

Derrick continued to poke her. "I don't see why not.

Portal in a bottle. You can carry it with you and it will take you anywhere you want to go. You just drop it on the ground and bam! Portal!"

Rachel flung her arms out dramatically, knocking over some of Christi's knickknacks. Nothing broke, but I winced just the same. I followed her around, trying to pick things up and prevent further damage as she paced.

"Portals don't work that way. You have to know both openings and closings. You can't make a portal without knowing your position on the exterior of the portal. That's problem numero uno, pal! You have to know your starting position. Do you want to lose yourself in space-time? Because that's how you lose yourself in space-time."

"Okay fine, you know your starting point. Then why can't you make a portal to anywhere?"

Rachel groaned. She looked over to Christi as I picked up the last knickknack. "Christi, can you please help me out here? If Derrick won't listen to the Master Alchemist, maybe he'll listen to you."

Christi didn't look up from her map. "I'm not getting involved. It's all you, Rach."

They continued to bicker. We all were getting frustrated. Trains to the Wilderness ran infrequently. Waiting felt wrong. We wanted to be doing something. Derrick grumbled about his failed stakeout and Christi, shaken by her vision, wouldn't even talk to me about it. Ines had retreated into Christi's office, needing to make some calls. It was clear she too was upset, or at least pricklier than usual. I was getting anxious as we moved closer to the full moon, unsure if Joe's cure would even work. To say the house felt tense was an understatement.

I came up behind Christi and rubbed her shoulders, moving her curls out of the way to kiss her neck. I felt the goosebumps erupt over her skin. Smiling to myself, I mentally logged the response. I enjoyed finding each of Christi's erogenous zones.

She sighed, rolling her shoulders back. "Can I help you?" she asked, playfully.

In response, I ran my teeth along the nape of her neck. She melted against me.

"I'm sorry, but you being here is just so distracting," I said, in between kisses.

"I'm just sitting here. You're the one distracting *me,*" she quipped. "I was doing fine until you came over."

"Get a room," Rachel groaned at us. A paper ball hit me, but I was undeterred.

"It's my house!" Christi said, shutting down all complaints.

I paused my kissing and returned to rubbing her shoulders. I looked at the map she had been studying as I kissed her cheek. "What are you working on?"

She took her pen and traced a section of the map. The map looked familiar—what used to be California, Oregon, and Washington state before the Reveal. The three were now called the Pacific Coast. Not quite a state, not quite autonomously run, all because of the Wilderness. The green on the map denoting the Wilderness started in Southern California, near what used to be Joshua Tree National Park. It engulfed the Sierras and forested areas from there to the coast. Only the LA metro area was spared. A strip of brown ran along the length of California's Central Valley—even the shifters respected the farms that fed the area. Green covered the rest of the coast, sparing only San Francisco and Seattle.

Much of the Wilderness was just that, wilderness. The witches had returned the areas to nature, which allowed the flora and fauna to move back in. It also allowed for shifter packs to flourish. Not every pack was like the O'Sheas. Most were small family groups that lived together.

Christi had been tracing each of those areas with a red pen. Several red circles dotted the Wilderness on the map. She had traced almost all of Western Washington—the O'Shea pack's territory. I'd spent so long trying to avoid that area as much as possible. Now it was our destination. Christi tapped a small blue circle close to their borders.

"That's the Aviary."

Christi placed the end of the pen against her lips. "I'm struggling to see how we are going to help them." She frowned. "It's such a small territory compared to the O'Sheas."

"If Alice has control of it, they need our help."

She nodded. "I know that. It's just that Ines keeps talking

about kidnapping at the Aviary. It doesn't add up. From what we've seen, it's not exactly Alice's mode of operation. Same with the bookstore. There has to be more to it that I'm missing. A connection."

I kissed her cheek. "It's not all on you to figure it out."

She bit her lip and hummed softly in disagreement. I rubbed her shoulders again, resting my cheek against hers. She turned. "I wanted to ask you something."

"Go ahead."

"I want to see my family before we go."

"That wasn't a question," I pointed out.

She playfully slapped my arm. "It was coming. You were just impatient," she chided, but her face has gotten brighter, and her eyes glinted with the spark of something. "Do you want to meet them?"

The bond had been working on her. She continued to avoid my question, and my wolf could still feel her hesitancy towards our bond. Of course, I had noticed that she hadn't returned my declarations of love. Despite what she said, I could be patient. I was willing to wait until she was ready. I smiled to myself. This was a big step.

"I'd like that."

Ines made a frustrated grunt behind us, throwing the door to the backyard open as she entered dramatically.

"Those idiots with the train have sold out all the cargo space," she scoffed. She grimaced in annoyance. "As if that was possible! We now have to use one of our two bags for the cure."

"What does that mean?" I asked.

I knew we were allotted two bags each for the trip, but that was where my knowledge ended.

"It means that we each must bring a cooler full of the cure instead of actual luggage." She huffed. A piece of her hair fell out of her bun. She made a muffled scream as she crossed her arms and blew the hair out of her face.

Derrick sauntered over with a smile on his face. "Oh no, how will you survive without all your dresses?"

"How will we keep the cure cold for almost three days?" Christi asked, trying to defuse the situation. I shrugged.

"I'll have to get some dry ice from the alchemy," Rachel said, resigned. "You all owe me big time."

I was about to bet either she or Ines were going to complain about the expense, but Derrick interrupted. "We wouldn't have to worry about this if we had a portal," he insisted. This time, we all groaned in response.

"I'm not joking," Rachel added indignantly. "I quit my job for this!" She didn't wait for a response, storming out of the back door and into Christi's yard.

Christi looked over at Ines, and gave her a look. This was apparently new information to all of us.

Ines sighed. "I'll go speak with her." She narrowed her eyes at Derrick. "And if you bring up portals one more time, I will not hesitate to gut you. I have been looking for an excuse."

Derrick made a motion to zip his lips.

Later in bed, Christi leaned on her folded arms, and I ran my fingers along her back lazily. She had three blue butterflies tattooed on her left shoulder that I traced over and over. There were so many things about her that I hadn't even discovered yet.

"You know, we haven't talked about your family. I don't even know if you have siblings."

My stomach hurt at that. I barely spoke with them after I left, even after the Reveal. I was so ashamed of what I had become and later, of how I had behaved. I had spent so much of my adult life apologizing to my parents for my existence, all the while knowing that the wildness inside me wasn't just from the wolf.

"It's just me and my folks. Mom is a Superior Court judge and my father is Professor Emeritus of Philosophy at the University of Chicago."

"So distinguished," she teased. "Do you miss it? Chicago?"

No. Yes. Maybe. I missed more than just the place. I missed who I used to be. I missed the future I could have had there. I missed the man I was and the potential he had. But that man didn't exist anymore.

"I always got the feeling that my parents would have

been happier without me," I confessed.

"There's the rub," Christi said softly, leaning into my touch. "When you're a kid, you don't know any better. Then as an adult, you see that your parents are just human, with all the flaws that entails. Eventually, you realize that your parents can be a mirror, reflecting every bad quality and small hurt you have. By then, you are reflecting back all their disappointments and failures. I still have trouble wrapping my head around that one."

My wolf smiled at that, proud of how astute and reflective our mate was. She wasn't wrong. Both my parents had clawed their way to the top of their fields amidst racism and sexism. They were smart and fiercely independent people who failed to understand how I too would become fiercely independent.

"They weren't easy parents to have. I spent a lot of time with my grandparents growing up."

My wolf listened for Christi's easy breathing. I knew she wasn't asleep, though her eyes closed.

She made a noise of agreement. "I miss my grandmother all the time."

"I'm lucky, Pops is still kicking at 95. Your house is a lot like his, full of music and food and people. He always tried to get me out of my hiding spots to talk, but I'd rather be reading. Still would."

I hadn't thought about his house in years. I remembered Pops putting his records on and telling me to listen, *really listen*, to the music. I remembered my grandparents dancing in the living room and stealing a kiss when they thought I wasn't looking. I remembered what happiness once felt like. Sunlight streaming through the window, curtains billowing from an open window, lying on my belly with my latest book from the library. I remembered hope and joy and the lightness of being a child. I remembered looking at my grandparents, old, gray, and wrinkled, and thinking that was what love looked like.

That was what I missed about Chicago, what I missed about my life before the wolf. That promise of happiness.

What was it about Christi that made me want to divulge my secrets to her?

"I'm not surprised," she said, her voice thick with sleep.

We both should be getting rest, but I wouldn't change these whispered words in the darkness together for anything. Even though we had the curtains drawn, moonlight shone through the crack and made a line of silver light on Christi's skin. I kissed it.

I heard her stifle a sob. My wolf immediately was on guard. "Hey, what's wrong?"

She shook her head, gulping down tears.

I rubbed her back as she cried. I waited until I could hear her breathing evenly, and the wolf in my brain calmed before speaking. "It's okay, whatever it is. It's okay."

She sniffled before she said in a small voice, "I don't know if I deserve this. You know, when Troy died, I felt relieved, because I was finally free. What kind of shitty person thinks that?"

She started crying again, and I pulled her into me.

I understood, of course. In the pack, I had felt freer than I ever did, but I was more trapped than I would ever be. I had hated that the pack hierarchy had kept the wolf at bay. I'd gained more control, but I'd hated that I embraced the wolf that I so despised. I had learned to love and loathe myself. When I'd finally left, there had been a lot of emotions, relief being one of them.

When Christi pulled away, she wiped her face and laughed. "I'm sorry. You know, I've never told anyone about that."

I kissed her forehead. "Your secret's safe with me."

I love you, I wanted to tell her. *I'll protect you*, I longed to tell her. *It doesn't matter*, I pleaded with her in my mind. *It doesn't matter because you're* mine.

Chapter Thirty-Four: Christi

Derrick led us down into the fighting pit of the Dahlia early in the evening. The fight had already begun and the noise was unbearable. I wished I had brought earplugs as we followed him to a spot in front.

The full moon meant that Nate missed this peculiar field trip. I tried to remind him of the buddy system, but he reassured me that he was a bigger threat as a wolf than a target. I didn't believe him, but I didn't push. He insisted that he needed a night to himself regardless of the full moon. He hoped so badly that the cure would work, but he didn't want us there if it didn't.

"Now will you tell us why you dragged us here?" Ines tried to yell over the din. She crossed her arms and popped a hip, annoyed. She looked like she didn't belong here, cotton candy softness compared to the grotesque scene in front of us. I tried not to look as some kind of creature had its arm ripped off by a vampire in the ring.

Derrick pointed at the fight. "Some of you didn't grow up in a cage, and it shows!"

Rachel stood on tiptoe to yell in my ear.

Unable to hear her, I put a finger in my other ear to drown out the noise. "What?"

"I said, is he serious?"

I threw my hands out and shrugged, shaking my head.

Maybe I could ask Nate later what Derrick's past was like.

Derrick continued. "We are going to get up close and personal with the wolf shifters soon. You need to know just what we're up against. I fight the next round, and then you'll really see what a wolf shifter is capable of."

Ines scoffed. "You brought us here to watch you die?"

Derrick childishly stuck his tongue out at her, and then puffed his chest out. "I'll have you know that I'm the reigning champion!"

The fight distracted me when blood splattered on my face. I wiped it away with a grimace and shook my hand to get it off. I looked down at my dress. Blood had splattered onto it as well. The dress ruined, I ran my hands down it to wipe them off too. I protected people with wards, talismans, and amulets. At all cost, I tried to avoid harming anyone with magic. I tried not to cry as the creature, whatever it was, was dragged out of the ring. Dead. My stomach lurched, and I closed my eyes to let the wave of nausea pass. I wished Nate were here. Then I could at least feel his warm, strong body against mine instead of being jostled around in a sea of people.

Ines looked impassive as she watched the cleanup. She shook her head as Derrick jumped into the ring. "Idiot," she said, but I only could read her lips.

Rachel climbed up the ropes of the ring with a whoop. "Go Derrick!" she cried. She fell to the floor with a jump, raising her arms high with her hands balled into a fist. "This is awesome!"

I didn't share her enthusiasm. The vampire had remained in the ring, and she now wiped her mouth, blood still dripping down her face. I grimaced as she spat out guts and gristle. I agreed with Ines. Derrick was an idiot, and we were going to watch him die.

Derrick shed his clothes, his underwear landing on Ines' head. She pushed them off with disgust. Rachel pointed at her, laughing. I didn't understand why they seemed fine. As Derrick waited for the fight to start, he began to transform.

I had never seen a shift. It was just as disgusting as the fighting. Gray wolf enveloped him as bones cracked through skin and reknit in a different configuration. Muscles tore and stretched. Before anything could bleed, his skin molded to the new form. He screamed as his nose elongated into a snout, his ears lifting to the top of his head. I covered my ears to drown it out.

A bell rang. Derrick pulled his shoulders back and howled. I didn't know a howl could sound more like a roar. The vampire had been crouching, ready to start, and she was on him in a flash. My heart stopped as Derrick's claws caught the vampire in midair. He used her momentum to spin around and toss her away. She landed on a wall and fell onto the spectators. Derrick hyped up the crowd by turning his back from the vampire and howling in our direction. *Fucking Derrick*. I cried out as the vampire jumped up on the ropes and tackled him from behind. She managed to bite him this time, pulling away a giant chunk of his bicep as easily as if it were a chicken leg. He swatted her back, which seemed to only make her angrier.

She moved in a blur, biting and slashing whenever she made contact. Even though Derrick made a show of trying to catch her, he barely missed her each time. He played with her. He waited until the vampire had her fangs at his giant neck, and then he struck. With one slash of his claws, he mauled her face, skin and blood falling right off it. Bone crunched—and I flinched—when he grabbed her head in one hand. He pulled her off his back using her head and broke her neck as he flung her to the floor of the ring. Using his muzzle, he separated her head from her body with a crunch. I couldn't watch.

"Awesome!" Rachel screamed, one arm in the air. "Yeah! Go, Derrick!"

I pushed through the crowds and ran up to the main floor. I threw the bathroom doors open and vomited in the first trash can I could see, unable to make it to the toilet.

Later, after he bought us celebratory drinks, Derrick threw one arm around my neck. "Welcome to the pack, babygirl."

When we returned home, Nate was already gone. *Not a good sign.* I fed Sadie and changed into some pajamas. Nate had left a shirt on the floor. It wasn't going to fit me, but I held it to my chest. It smelled like him. I couldn't imagine him as the monster Derrick became in the ring. I knew Nate was a werewolf, but I hadn't really thought of what that meant. I wasn't sure if I wanted to run or hide. Instead, I just climbed into bed, Sadie following close behind, and I tried to fall asleep.

I tossed and turned until I heard howling from outside. Trying to sit up, I saw stars. Something hit my wards. I threw off my covers and tiptoed as fast as I could out into the living room. Rachel still slept on the couch, unaware of the commotion. Derrick was nowhere to be found, likely asleep as well. I felt the wolf's cry deep in my soul. How could they sleep through this? The howling turned into whining as I stepped closer to the sliding glass door that led outside. A giant white wolf scratched at it. Its muzzle dripped with blood and viscera. Fear froze me in place and my heart raced as I decided what to do. The wolf obviously wanted in. But was it friend or foe? I looked back to the bedrooms. I could call Derrick, but then I imagined him as the terrible wolf-man and shuddered. No, I would have to make this decision on my own. The wolf howled again and I held a hand to the glass.

Sadie sang behind me, her feet excitedly tapping on the floor. If this were a rogue werewolf, she sure was a terrible guard dog. The wolf lowered its tail behind its legs and continued to whine. I knelt down, and moonlight streamed through the glass. I finally saw the wolf for more than its size and bloody maw. Eyes like two black pools pleaded with me to let it in. Let *him* in. I knew those eyes.

I couldn't breathe as I opened the door.

I didn't risk moving. The wolf circled me, sniffing at my face, my arms, my legs, leaving a trail of blood in his wake. Satisfied, he darted off into my bedroom. If I needed more proof, that was it. Surely, Alice's wolves wouldn't know the way to my bed. My heart raced as I caught my breath. I placed a hand to my heart, just existing for a moment.

I gave Sadie a look as I closed the door. "Stay out of the bedroom or he might eat you."

Sadie grumbled before circling into a ball at the edge of the glass.

"Good girl." I patted her on the head.

I tiptoed back into the bedroom, holding my breath. Closing the door behind me, I took stock of the room. I had seen the wolf run in, but I couldn't see the wolf now. He was giant, so I couldn't have lost track of him. I searched through the room, listening for the whining and looking for the blood trail. I lowered to the floor, lifting the sheets so I could see underneath the bed.

There, among discarded shoes and storage boxes of unused jewelry, were two black eyes looking at me in the dark.

"Hello there," I said gently. I tried to remember what Nate told me about the wolf. I knew he recognized me as his mate. I knew that Nate was somewhere in there. But I also knew that the wolf had a mind of his own. I didn't want to scare him, especially since Nate had been so anxious about the change this full moon. The wolf must have picked up on that. I wasn't sure that he wouldn't bite at me if I held out my hand. I didn't know if the blood was the wolf's or something—someone? —else's.

I settled on coaxing him out with words. I used the voice I had reserved for the littles when they were small, higher and more of a sing-song cadence than my true voice. "Come on, you handsome fellow. I haven't met you yet. You want me to see you, don't you?"

The wolf whimpered, but crawled a little closer. *Nate,* see me. *If you are in there,* please *see me.*

"Come on, caro mio," I whispered, my voice in its natural register. "Come to me."

The wolf crawled until his black nose touched mine. Nate hadn't warned me about how awesomely intimidating the wolf was. I had grown up with big dogs, but the wolf Nate, he could eat Sadie for lunch and be hungry for more. Without meaning to, I scrambled back in surprise and fear.

As I splayed out on the floor, the wolf finally moved from under the bed. I sat up. My room remained dark, but I could see the wolf's brilliant white fur. He sat patiently for me with a little huff.

"You stay there," I said, standing. I turned the light on and smiled. "There you are."

I had never seen a wolf so beautiful or so large. He had

ghost-white fur with the barest tint of silver along his spine. Two silver lines began from the tips of his ears, down his snout, and under his eyes. Red stained his muzzle and down onto his chest and paws. The wolf was pure muscle, lean and trim. His eyes and nose were a deep black. I didn't have to kneel to look into his eyes.

I knew I should be afraid, but something told me I knew the man inside the wolf. Somewhere behind the wolf mind was Nate. I reached out and gently stroked the fur along his neck. The wolf huffed once and circled around me again, whining. A deep rust spot formed where he had been sitting. The blood wasn't just from his face.

I gasped. "You're hurt."

He nudged my back, then darted for the bed. I knew it could get me bitten, but I grasped his tail without thinking. The wolf paused and gave me a growl. I released him.

"Let me help," I cautioned. I could see the wound clearly now, a long gash along his haunch. "I'd remind you that I'm a shit healer, but you were out of it then too." Still, I knew how to help if he'd let me. I pointed at him to stay. "Don't you dare go under that bed!"

If he did, I couldn't pull him out again. I ran to the bathroom and collected a large jar and an old towel. When I returned, the wolf squeezed into a corner of the room, back to the wall. I almost laughed. I'd seen Nate do that so many times. Now I understood why.

"Come here, gorgeous," I coaxed, holding up the jar. "I'm

not going to hurt you."

He huffed, unconvinced. I sat on the floor and opened the jar. I hoped curiosity would bring him to me. I smelled the salve inside the jar and even rubbed some on my own skin. *See, this is some good shit!* The wolf sniffed once, twice, and plodded over to me carefully.

"You have to promise not to bite me if it stings, caro," I warned him. I had no idea how much the wolf understood me, but I spoke to him as if he could anyway. "You'll be unhappy with yourself in the morning if you do."

I stroked the wolf's neck as I worked the salve into his haunch. He didn't even flinch.

"Good boy," I said softly.

My mother, who *was* the healer, had made the salve for small cuts and bruises. I doubted it would help a gash like this, but it couldn't hurt. I found a ratty tee shirt and wrapped his leg. The wolf nuzzled my face. I began wiping the rest of him down with the towel, trying to remove the worst of the blood. The viscera wiped away—I tried not to think too hard about that—but the blood stained the wolf's white fur bright red. The wolf's chest rumbled as I toweled him off. I had almost finished by the time I realized he purred like a cat.

"I bet that feels better." I stood and patted the bed. "Come on up. You don't sleep well as a human, but maybe you'll sleep better like this."

If a wolf could raise an eyebrow, Nate's wolf would. He eyed me skeptically.

I shrugged. "Suit yourself."

I turned off the light and climbed into bed. My heart finally stopped pounding and my breathing felt steadier. I laughed. I had a giant wolf in my bedroom. Even weirder, that wolf was my—well, what exactly was Nate? My boyfriend? That sounded so juvenile. We were a long way from high school. My partner? That sounded better. He *had* asked me to marry him. That felt too heavy. I settled on caro mio, which managed to escape my lips tonight. *Dear one*.

I loved him. I did. But those feelings were mixed with a stronger cocktail of fear, anxiety, and distrust. It made me want to run. I wasn't successful at my first marriage. How could I possibly be a good mate?

Nate's wolf jumped on the bed and settled in beside me. We barely fit in a king-size bed, and I scooched over to make room. He nuzzled my face again before closing his eyes. I fell asleep with my head on his fur.

Chapter Thirty-Five: Nate

I saw Christi's horror before I felt the change. The moment the shift began, she recoiled. She didn't scream, but she did leap out of the bed in disgust. I couldn't blame her. My bones broke, elongated, shortened, and reknit in the right skeletal formation. My skin sagged and stretched. Fur gave way to body hair. My jaw opened and closed and opened again. The wolf's snout separated to form the rest of my face. All while I grunted, shouted, and yelped in pain. As quickly as it started, it finished. Wolf was now man.

I collapsed in a heap, naked and panting. Christi reached for me, but I scrambled away.

"Don't touch me."

"Nate," she whispered. She looked me up and down. I turned my face away so I didn't have to watch her revulsion. I felt her touch my leg. "Oh, Nate."

"Leave me alone," I pleaded, voice husky and raw from the change. My wolf growled at me loudly in my mind. It wanted Christi's comfort. My stomach and jaw tightened. I never wanted her to see me like this. I thought if I had a cure, she'd never have to see the animal. I had a chance to be normal again, and it hadn't worked. Bitter tears streamed down my face. I hated that she had to watch and pity me.

"Oh, Nate, caro mio," She sighed, caressing my face.

Please stop. I turned from her, but she held me firmly.

She held me against her chest as I wept. I didn't deserve her even touching me.

I had allowed myself to dream of what I could have, what I should have, and maybe even what I would have. I had imagined marrying Christi. Dancing in the living room and stealing a kiss just like my grandparents. I imagined tidying her piles and having her beautiful chaos disrupt my order. For the first time, I let myself want something. Really *want* something.

The cure didn't work, and I was still a wolf.

"I hate myself, I hate the wolf, and I hate her for doing this to me," I whispered shakily. Sometimes good people did bad things that you couldn't forgive. Sometimes bad people did good things, so you forgave them. But there were some people who didn't deserve forgiveness, regardless of how good they were or what good they did. Alice had hardened my heart. I learned how to hate. I learned how to kill. She may have created the wolf, but I fed it. I carried that guilt with me.

I would never again be that boy reading books on a sunlit carpet under a summer breeze.

"Why couldn't she have just let me die? She killed me that day. The least she could have done was let me die," I cried. My chest ached, and I clutched it to soothe the hurt.

Christi took both of my hands. She kissed the top of one, then the other. She wiped my face before kissing my cheeks. She kissed my lips so softly and tenderly that I cried again.

Now that I started, I didn't think I could stop. Once released, it felt like I would never be able to carry it all again.

"I see you, Nate. I know it doesn't mean anything if I say it. But I've seen the man and I've seen the wolf. They are both you. And I love you."

"I'm a monster." I whispered, burying my head in her shoulder. I felt her shake her head.

"You are the most beautiful creature I have ever seen."

She didn't understand the wildness inside me. She didn't understand that I could never be whole, as long as I had the wolf in me. But I could forget that for a little while in her arms. She loved what I showed her. For now, that was enough.

We made love slowly and I fell into a fitful sleep. When I awoke, the blood had been cleaned from the bed and the carpet. My body ached, joints burning and muscles stiff. My eyes were puffy from tears. I lifted my head. When both it and my heart felt heavy, I buried my head back in the pillow and dozed a little longer.

When I walked out of the bedroom sometime the next day, having slept over twenty-four hours, Christi sat on the sofa, petting Sadie. It seemed suspiciously quiet.

"Where is everyone?" I asked, my voice still hoarse. I could barely move; exhaustion had settled in my body and mind. I was wrung out, and if I never felt anything again, I thought I would be okay with that. Still, I had slept off the worst of the change, even if I still limped about.

"Out," she said simply. Her tone of voice suggested that she had asked them to give us some privacy. "There's dinner in the fridge if you want it," she told me from the sofa. "Derrick made a tofu stir-fry."

The change made me starving. I was ravenous enough to eat Derrick's rabbit food, but I still wrinkled my nose. "Is that all you have?"

She laughed softly. "I also ordered delivery from the local steakhouse." She had been teasing, thank god. "You're welcome."

I ate the steaks over her kitchen sink and followed them with a pot of Derrick's thick, muddy coffee. When I felt human enough, I sat with Christi.

I took her hands in mine and squeezed. "I'm sorry you had to see me like that."

She sighed, but gave me a small smile. "I meant what I said." She let it hang heavy between us. *I love you.* Man and wolf. I rested my head against hers. She caressed my face. "You don't have to apologize for who you are. Thank you for trusting me." She gave my face a pat, and the teasing light returned to her emerald eyes. God, I loved her. "I do have questions."

"Questions?" I asked, kissing her palm. She nodded. I motioned her on. "By all means, then."

"Your leg," she noted. "I'm a terrible healer, so what healed it?"

"The change," I responded.

She nodded, biting her lip. "That's good to know. How about what happened?"

I didn't want to worry her, but there was no point in secrets now.

I had been ambushed. I knew my territory and my usual route. The only animals out at night were racoons, coyotes, and the occasional dog in the yard. We lived in a beach city. As Derrick had said, it wasn't exactly a wolf haven. Shifters tended to stay away from cities and humans. I had been so distracted by the fact that the cure didn't work that I didn't smell them coming. They smelled familiar—Joe's bodyguards. They cornered me and I fought my way out. My wolf had to kill two of them. Another wolf followed me. I didn't realize it when I ran, but I led them straight to Christi's doorstep. I had been prepared to defend Christi's home with my life. The shifter hit her wards and ran off.

After I explained this, I kissed her. She had protected me.

"Your amulet? That should have protected you!" she chided. She touched my chest. "Where is it?"

"Darling, it's on the nightstand. I couldn't have put it on as a wolf."

"I'd feel better if you wore it all the time. I've had to heal you too many times already, and it is *not* my specialty. Warding is," she said emphatically. "This is why I wanted someone with you!"

"I know, love. I'm sorry." I held her close. "I think they were trying to scare me. I don't think they were supposed to hurt me."

"I don't want to stay here any longer than we have to," she said, her eyes full of tears that didn't fall. My chest hurt as I heard her voice break. I caused this. "The sooner we can stop Alice, the better." She took a shaky breath. "I'm so scared."

"So am I, love. So am I."

Chapter Thirty-Six: Nate

I needed to stop fucking it up with Christi. My wolf snapped at that. It wanted so much for her to just accept us and be done with it. I didn't want to talk about it. I knew that I needed to convince her that we were worth it. Especially if I didn't find a cure soon. Especially if we couldn't stop Alice soon. My wolf paced in the back of my mind. Christi may have said the words, but we both held back. My wolf didn't like the bond being solely on our end. It needed completion, one way or the other.

Before she had left for her family's house, Christi tried to prepare me for dinner. She was nervous, and I had reassured her as best as I could. I was already hers; her family wasn't going to scare me off.

"It's just Mom, Giana, Dusty and the kids," she'd said. "It's going to be a little hectic, and there will be tears—likely from me, since we have to leave Sadie. But I promise you, we can be home and in bed by nine."

I didn't tell her that the morning of the dinner, I had a *new* message on my *new* burner phone.

`rsvp, XO`

Another reminder that Alice knew where I was and how to find me. As though her wolves roughing me up during the full moon wasn't enough.

It didn't matter. We were bringing the fight to her.

I stood with Derrick at Christi's sister's door, bouquet in hand.

"Flowers, huh?" Derrick smirked.

I shrugged. "It's rude to show up empty-handed."

Derrick didn't take the dig, but he chuckled to himself.

"Did Christi warn you?" Ines asked from behind us, and I jumped. Neither of us heard or smelled her. Rachel peeked out behind her, a foil-covered pan in her arms.

"How the fuck did you do that?" Derrick exclaimed, but Ines only smiled at him with her fangs showing.

"Are you both ready for the chaos?" Rachel asked, laughter in her voice.

"Chaos?" I questioned, my heart racing. I could be in comfy pants right now, five slices into a delivery pizza. I could barely keep my eyes open, body still ragged from the shift. But I gritted my teeth and plastered on an easy smile to disguise my discomfort. I needed to show up for Christi. She wanted me here.

Ines laughed sardonically. "Gird your loins, gentlemen," she said, winking before opening the door and crossing the threshold.

I agreed with Ines; this was chaos. All my senses were assaulted at once. My head hurt immediately. Music played over speakers, mixed with people chatting and small children laughing. The room was warm, due to people's bodies and cooking in the kitchen. The smells made my mouth water, savory garlic and onion mixed with sizzling butter. Baked goods smelled of chocolate and vanilla. Women's perfume, floral and soft. I wanted to flee and vomit at the same time.

My wolf kept me standing in place with a growl.

"Come in, come in," Christi's nephew Liam said at the door, like he paid the bills on the place. He was short for his age and had a bright blue cast on his arm. He motioned with it. "This is my house!"

"Is that how you greet us, munchkin?" Ines admonished him, scooping him up into her arms.

He pushed her off. "Aunt Nes, I'm trying to be cool!"

"Very well," Ines said. "Can you inform someone of our presence?"

"I'll race you!" Rachel suggested.

He ran as fast as he could through the house with Rachel on his heels. Derrick and I exchanged a look.

Sadie padded over to us, and Derrick went to his knees. "Hello, beautiful girl. I've missed you." Ines glared at him, and as though he could see her, he quipped, "I'm talking to the dog."

"Ines," a voice very similar to Christi's called from the kitchen. "Is that you?"

"Who else would it be?" Ines answered as we followed her into the kitchen. The woman looked like Christi but was taller and slenderer, a woman whose image graced cookbooks everywhere.

She handed Ines a wine glass filled with a dark red liquid. "Fresh from the butcher. There's more where this came from in the garage fridge, but it'll be cold, so you better enjoy this one while it's warm."

The woman then looked at us, and Ines disappeared into the house with the glass.

"You must be Nate and Derrick. I'm Giana, Christi's sister. Everyone's outside with the kiddos. There's a cooler with beer and water, and we have wine on the counter. Nate, it's all non-alcoholic, so please help yourself. You'd be surprised how good they make alcohol-free beverages these days." I nodded, feeling warmth rise to my face. I hadn't expected this. Christi had warned me of her family's potential missteps, but she hadn't prepared me for their kindness.

Giana waved for Rachel as she took the flowers from me. "Hey, Rach, can you put these in a vase?" Arms empty, Giana was free to embrace me. I tensed with surprise. "You are so sweet. You didn't need to do that."

I froze, unsure of what to do, so I did what came naturally and asked how I could help. Giana waved me off before becoming distracted by the music. "I love this song!"

Christi danced into the kitchen, her cheeks flushed, holding a glass of red wine. She and Giana burst into laughter, singing a verse of the song. I realized in that moment just how beautiful Christi was like this, with sunlight in her hair and a smile on her face. How could I have missed that? We had been spending too much time in the dark recently.

"Hey, guys," Christi said. She gave me a quick peck before wrapping her hand in mine. "Follow me."

Liam ran through the backyard with a tan man with straight black hair. He threw Liam a ball, and Liam caught it with glee. A graceful older woman in a bright blue caftan waved Christi over from a retaining wall.

"Mom, this is the man I told you about," she said, her nerves palpable. "Nate, this is my mom, Donna. She's an artist."

She waved Christi off. "I dabble."

"It's nice to meet you," I held out my hand, and she ignored it, moving in.

"Oh, Nate, we hug here. I'm delighted to meet you," she said, hugging me. "I'm quite upset that Christi hasn't brought you around sooner. It's been ages since she's brought a man home."

"Mom!" Christi said through her teeth. "Please behave."

Donna looked confused, but I knew it as the fake confusion of mothers everywhere who embarrassed their children. "I'm behaving."

"Christi!" Giana called from the house.

Sorry, Christi mouthed, leaving me with her mother. I shifted my weight uncomfortably. What did I say to this woman?

Donna saved me from having to make conversation.

"You know, after Troy, I didn't think Christi would ever find someone. It's just been so long."

What was that supposed to mean? Christi was a beautiful woman who was vibrant and smart. How could she not find someone? I was the one who didn't deserve her, that was certain.

"I love your daughter, Donna. She's the most amazing woman I've ever met."

Donna patted my shoulder half-heartedly. "That's kind of you to say."

I clenched my jaw and excused myself before I said anything I regretted.

"Tough crowd, am I right?" Rachel joked, popping up behind me. "Donna's a bitch, but we love her. You met Giana. That's my brother Dusty over there."

Derrick had just caught up with us, a beer in hand, but at the sound of that name, he looked over in disbelief.

"That's Dustin Reyes," he said his jaw dropped. "*The* Dustin Reyes! Later, brother!" He slapped me on the back, jogging over to the other man.

Rachel groaned, "Oh goodie, another golf fanatic."

We stood in silence for a moment, watching Christi run around with her nephew, catching him when they reached the other end of the yard. Liam wrestled Sadie and tried to ride her, which the dog accepted reluctantly. Christi waved at me with a little smile when she saw me staring. I gave her a small wave. They seemed happy. The whole family seemed happy and loved and taken care of. A pit started to form in my stomach. I was taking her away from this to fight my battle. How selfish could I be?

"*Happy families are all alike; every unhappy family is unhappy in its own way,*" Rachel said softly.

"Tolstoy?"

"What? Just because I'm a potion jockey doesn't mean I don't read." She scoffed at me. Looking at her, you wouldn't think reader. You wouldn't even think Master Alchemist. Her hair was done up in two buns like mouse ears. She wore a men's vest and baggy black jeans that overtook her small frame. Alchemical symbols littered her tan skin; her eyebrows and nostril pierced with rings. I had to hand it to her. She had a sense of style, even if it wasn't my taste.

She winked at me, toasting me with her beer bottle. "Welcome to the Bianchi refuge for the magical and the weird," she said nonchalantly. "Now that you've been adopted in, you might not be able to leave."

Bianchi. My blood ran cold. "What did you say?"

"You might not be able to leave."

I shrugged it off. It had to be a coincidence. Christi couldn't be connected to Joe. Could she?

"This is a lot," I finally breathed. Rachel continued speaking, but I only half-listened. *Bianchi. Joseph Bianchi.* The necromancer would be someone Christi knew. My mind raced as I started to panic.

"It was a bigger deal in high school. On Sundays, all our

friends would hang out at the Bianchis." I winced at the name. "It got quieter and smaller when Christi went away to college, but when she came back home, she started bringing in strays, like Ines, and you. She's like that."

"Like what?" I asked, because it was the right response. I barely paid attention as my mind repeated the name in my head. *Bianchi. Bianchi. Bianchi.* Over. And over. And over again.

"The summer before senior year, my parents found out that my sleepovers with the neighbor girl weren't so innocent and well, you remember what it was like. They threw me out. Dusty was just getting started in the pros, so he wasn't around. Christi literally took me to her house and told her parents I was staying. She shared her bedroom with me for over a year. That's just who she is."

I looked at Christi, laughing and playing with the kids. There was no way *she* could be connected to that slimy con man. She seemed free and wild and bright, soft curves and soft curls and soft smiles. I wondered what it would feel like to be accepted into her sphere like that, to feel her warmth. She still held back from me, just slightly.

It had to be a coincidence. Christi would have told me if she knew Joe. Wouldn't she?

Rachel caught me staring and continued, "They're good people. I mean, their dad's an asshole, but Donna, Gigi, and Cece, you couldn't ask for better friends. Or family." She narrowed her eyes at me. "You hurt her, and I will *kill* you

308

and dissolve your body in the alchemy. They will *never* find you."

"Noted," I laughed. This was the longest Rachel and I had spoken. She was always tinkering with something at the house or arguing with Derrick about portals. I tried to push Joe from my mind. "Thanks, Rach. I needed this."

"You'll do great." She punched my arm lightly. "You have to!"

Chapter Thirty-Seven: Derrick

I was hanging out with Dustin *Fucking* Reyes. I used to relax by watching his PGA Tours. The Golf Channel was one of the few that came through in the compound. He'd been the best until his injury. I had wanted to be him. I had wanted him. Now I was in his backyard!

"I'm a huge fan," I confessed.

He smirked. "I can sign something before you go, if you want."

My jaw dropped. "Yeah, thanks, man!"

He raised his beer bottle to me. "Don't worry about it. So, you're, uh, a werewolf like Christi's man?"

Christi's man. She must have been telling her family about him. I would have save that to tell Nate later, when he moaned about her and their mating bond.

"I'm a wolf shifter," I corrected. It was an important distinction, and he needed to know. "I used to be *his* alpha."

Dustin nodded with a smirk. My heart swelled. I'd impressed him. *Fuck yeah!* Inside, I pumped my arm and jumped up and down. Outside, I just gave him a chin nod. Sadie had escaped the children and now sat at my feet, looking up at me lovingly. I would miss having a dog to spend time with. I gave her a few pats, and she chuffed.

"Cool. I know you're going up there, but have you ever thought about moving up north? Go *full* wild?"

Much of the Wilderness was land purchased by coalitions of shifter packs. We had considered it in Colorado, but we never had the funds. Besides, some brave humans—too closed-minded to accept that magic existed in the world—also lived up there in off-the-grid bunkers, preaching about the apocalypse. I should have been offended by his assumption that I was a wild animal, but fuck it, Dusty Reyes could call me whatever he likes. I tried to play it off smooth.

"Nah, man. I like it here. I'm the reigning champion of the Crimson Dahlia's fight pit."

He nodded his head again, taking a sip of his beer. "Cool."

I looked from him to Rachel, who was now wrestling her nephew. I looked back to him. "Are you sure you're related to the pocket rocket?"

"That's a good one." He laughed, but it was a single syllable. *Ha.* "You take care of my baby sister, okay?"

I nodded a solemn vow for my hero.

"Thanks."

We continued to drink our beers together, and I would *never* forget this.

I wandered into the kitchen to find another beer, before I realized the cooler was outside. I had been so starstruck, I forgot. Nate stood next to Giana—and *fuck*, I would let that woman stomp on my balls—telling his glasses story. I had heard it so many times, and honestly, it wasn't as charming as he thought it was. There was a nervous edge to his voice, so I wasn't going to add to it. He deserved for Christi's family to like him. But still, he name-dropped both of his parents like that mattered. No one cared who your parents were unless you murdered them. I would know.

"So, what happened?" I asked with an easy smile, butting in.

He looked at me in confusion for a moment before continuing, "I needed reading glasses. That's why I couldn't read. Once that was fixed, I was reading through all my classes."

"Yet there's a conspicuous lack of glasses on your face right now," Giana said, pointing a wooden spoon covered in tomato sauce at him. God, it smelled good. Maybe Dusty would be willing to share. We *were* pals now.

He laughed. "There are some advantages to being a werewolf."

"Super awesome wolf vision!" I chimed in.

Giana slapped me playfully. *We* were pals now. "Hush," she exclaimed. "I think it's sweet that your mom went to bat for you. Our dad always tried to help with our problems, but he usually made them worse." She looked sad for a moment before pointed the spoon at me. *Yes, mommy?* "Oh Derrick, the sauce is vegetarian, and we have salad and roasted veggies. Christi told me you don't eat meat."

"Thanks, G. I appreciate that."

"It's nothing," she said with a smile, shrugging one shoulder.

"I don't know, I think you and Dusty should adopt me."

I wasn't completely joking, but she laughed anyway. Nate, however, seemed determined to *ruin* the best day of my life. He crowded me back until we ended up in a living room corner. Ines slept on one of the pristine white couches next to Christi's niece, who scribbled in her journal. *Weird.*

"What are you doing?" he snapped at me.

I motioned to him. "I'm helping you. Making you look good."

He waved his arms wildly at me. "*This* is *not* helping!"

"I haven't even asked Giana and Dusty for a three-way. See, helping," I said, only half serious.

Nate groaned exasperatedly, but leaned in to me. "We need to talk."

I leaned in closer. "We are talking."

Nate shook his head. "I mean, about important things. Christi's family name is Bianchi. Joe's full name was Joseph *Bianchi.*"

"That had to be a fake name, Nate. No evil villain is stupid enough to use their own name," I tried to reassure him, but his brow furrowed deeper.

"No, but an arrogant man might," he suggested. "And the coven said—"

"The coven also called Christi a *vessel*, so I think it's safe

313

to say they were speaking in riddles."

I wanted to catch Joe as much as he did, but I wasn't going to grasp for leads where there weren't any. I was about to tell him to calm down when Christi came over to us.

"Hey, darling," he said, giving her a kiss. *Ew*.

"Hi," she smiled brightly, all googly-eyed at him. She was so whipped already. Just as much as he was, even if she didn't know it yet. "Why are we hiding?"

"We were just chatting," I told her, winking at Nate. This Joe stuff was all in his head. "He's all yours."

"Don't go too far. Dinner's almost ready," Christi told me. I nodded, heading back outside for the beer I had meant to grab in the first place.

Chapter Thirty-Eight: Christi

"Hey," I smiled at Nate as Derrick sauntered away. "Sorry I've been so occupied. Can I get you anything? I can get you a seltzer or some tea. I know where they stash the fancy coffee."

He smiled warmly at me, hiding his teeth. "I'll be fine with water. Your family is," he paused, searching for the right word, "lively."

"I warned you." I had seen him chatting with Rachel earlier. "I trust Rachel filled you in. She can't keep a secret to save her life."

We stood in the hallway, awkwardly staring at each other. I wanted so badly for him to like my family. I squeezed his hand. I usually knew what to say to people. I was a people person, for the sake of the Goddess. Yet, his nerves made *me* nervous.

"Speaking of secrets—" he started.

"Okay, people," Giana called. "Dinner is on the table. We will not be waiting for any stragglers."

"I guess we should—" he started, motioning his thumb to the table.

I nodded my head. "Yeah," I said, snapping out of my worry. "Let's."

Nate stopped me, holding my wrist as I turned around. "Wait."

"What's wrong?" Now he *did* worry me. I couldn't read the look on his face.

"It's nothing," he said, shaking his head and releasing me. "We'll talk later."

I sat next to Nate, creating a buffer between him and Mom. I obviously wanted to torture myself further. But then he smiled at me again and the butterflies fluttered. *Shit fuck*.

Mom tapped me to look at her, and when I did, she pulled my hair back. "Is that a love bite on your neck?"

Where was that giant hole to swallow me? Because this was it. This time, I really would die of embarrassment.

I pulled my hair back down and flicked her away. "It's nothing, Mom," I said through my teeth.

"What's a love bite?" Liam asked innocently.

Sophia sighed as only a teenager could. "She means a hickey."

"What's a hickey?"

"It's a—" Ines started. Rachel cackled and Derrick joined in. Nate blushed deeply purple at this point, staring at the table. I couldn't blame him.

"Don't answer that," Giana snapped at Ines. Then she pointed at each disruptive person, Mom first. "Can we quit it? Christi's an adult." Then Rachel and Derrick. "Grow up, you two." Sophia. "We'll talk later." Liam. "You'll understand when you are older. We'll leave it at that."

Dusty cleared his throat. "Sophia, why don't you say grace?"

"Do I have to?" she complained with just a touch of boredom.

Dusty closed his eyes and took a deep breath. "Liam, champ, why don't you do it?"

"Jesus, please bless our food. And thank you to the Holy Mother, the great Goddess, for the bounty of the harvest," he said solemnly, before grinning and shouting, "Let's eat!"

Giana pointed out the various dishes on the table. "Okay, so we have a pork tenderloin with cherry chutney, goat cheese whipped potatoes, smashed broccoli, and a fennel salad. Then baked rigatoni, smoked salmon, chili-marinated olives. Oh, and Rachel brought lumpia!" She passed the dishes around the table.

Derrick gave a big sigh. "I would ask to marry you, but I like your husband too much. I am serious about the adoption, though."

Giana made a face. "Two children are enough for me."

"Fair."

"And don't forget to save room for cupcakes!"

"If you sing *happy birthday* to me, I am leaving!" I warned her.

Giana laughed me off with a knowing look.

"What kind of cupcakes?" Liam asked, already halfway through his plate.

"The best kind," Sophia told him. "Chocolate with vanilla frosting."

"Yum!"

I turned to Nate as he passed me the baked rigatoni. "This is why I don't cook."

Both Nate and Derrick piled their plates high, with Ines's plate empty and Rachel's with a nibble or two of potatoes. Those two were talking in low voices, and Rachel wore what I called her flirty face. She had been trying to get with Ines for years. And well, Ines enjoyed the chase more than anything.

"So, Nate—" Mom said over the noise of our side conversations, "Cece tells me that you took over the bookstore. I've been meaning to stop in for years. It had such a large collection of herb craft tomes."

"Herbal remedies aren't in demand as much now with the newer, better healing potions coming out."

Rachel puffed up at that. "You're damn right, they are," she chimed in, but Ines shushed her.

"The store still has the collection," Nate winced, and I squeezed his leg under the table. He corrected himself. "Sorry, it *had* a collection. We had a break-in recently. I'd appreciate any suggestions you have for replacements."

"There's nothing quite like healing with your hands," Mom said wistfully. "I'll have to stop by, if you all come home."

It was like a bomb had detonated in the room, but instead of exploding out, it pulled us all in. Everyone went quiet and still at the same time.

"Mom!" I chided in a loud whisper. "Please!"

Nate, the only one unfazed, continued chatting with her

like nothing happened. "You should bring some of your art when you do. For purchase, of course. I'd like to have something on the walls when I reopen."

"That's so thoughtful of you, Nate." Mom gave me a look, and I chose to ignore it. I didn't need her meddling in my business.

"There's a couple of places on Main Street for rent, Donna," Nate continued in the charming way that drew me to him in the first place. "You should really think about opening a gallery. It's just what the town needs."

"See?" Giana hissed at Dustin. She had been trying to get Mom to open her own gallery for years. Dusty just drank his wine and shook his head.

"Thank you, Nate. I appreciate that." Mom turned to me. "Christi, I don't know why you can't marry a nice man like him."

He was working on it. I only had a chance to mouth *sorry* at him before the doorbell rang.

Chapter Thirty-Nine: Christi

I jumped up to answer the door, since I was closest. My heart dropped into my stomach when I saw who it was.

"You again! What are you doing here?" I hissed at my father. I stepped onto the porch and closed the door behind me.

He held his arms out to me. "Is that any way to greet your dear old dad?" he asked. He pulled a small box out from behind him, a stupid magic trick he had used to surprise us when we were children.

I was not amused.

"Happy birthday, honey," he said, holding the box out to me.

I folded my arms and stepped back. "Did *she* pick it out or did you?" When he didn't answer, I seethed, keeping distance between us. Of course, he wouldn't pick out something himself. No, he sent his new wife to do it. She understood what a woman my age wanted, considering we were the same age. I repeated through gritted teeth, "What are you doing here?"

He made a big show of putting his hands up in surrender, box conveniently disappearing. He placed his hands quickly into his pockets. Always putting on a show. That was Dad. It didn't matter how you felt or what you did, as long as you looked good doing it. And if you felt horrible inside, even better. I felt like I was ten years old again, crying at the kitchen table over homework. *Pain produces results, Christi!* he'd remind me.

I wanted him gone before anyone else figured out he was here. Especially Nate.

"Your mother told me you were going to do something stupid, so I came here to talk you out of it."

I scoffed. "Who thought it was stupid, Dad? You or Mom? Did she use that word, or did you decide it for yourself?"

"There's no need to be hostile, honey. Let's go inside and talk."

Inside, there would be witnesses. Inside, he would have backup, so he could berate me even better. Bystanders would see that *I* was being overemotional and overreacting. I didn't need an audience for that.

I laughed bitterly. "Go home, Dad. Whatever you are here to say doesn't matter, because my decision is already made regardless of what you think about it. I don't need to hear your opinion, because I could not care less."

"Christiana, be reasonable!"

I opened my mouth to respond, but the door behind me burst open.

"Christi!" Nate rushed to my side, pausing at my shoulder.

Derrick followed and shrugged with an uncharacteristic grimace. "He heard yelling."

And he'd come out to protect me. My heart swelled at that for a moment before my father's face lit up.

"Nathan!" Dad exclaimed, walking over to Nate.

"It's Nate," the three of us yelled in unison, correcting him.

Dad shooed me and Derrick away. Maybe I learned a thing or two from the wolves because I growled at him as he moved closer to Nate.

"It's you," Nate grumbled in barely concealed anger. "You nearly killed me."

"You know each other?" I questioned, putting myself between them. I faced Nate. "How do you know my father?"

"Your father?" Nate repeated, looking over my shoulder. "I knew it!" He pointed emphatically at Dad. "He's our necromancer!"

"What? No." I spoke before I fully understood what he said. My father, the necromancer? He was a piece of shit, but he wouldn't go out of his way to hurt me. Would he? I turned on my father. "How do you know Nate?"

"Let's just say we have mutual interests." I looked to Nate, who was being held back by Derrick. My father smirked. "How'd the full moon go for you? I'm eager to know the results."

Nate spat at him.

Realization fully dawned on me. My father *was* Joe. Joseph was a common enough name, so I didn't have to think too hard that to convince myself it could be a coincidence. I had been so very wrong. My anger built as I thought of Nate lying in my spare bed with silver poisoning. I thought of Nate's wolf being stalked by Joe's—no, my father's—bodyguards.

"You have got to be kidding me," I exclaimed incredulously. "You came here to tell me *my* choices are stupid when *you* are working with the wolves! You're warning me that they're dangerous because you know just how dangerous they can be! How dare you?" I stepped closer to him, my finger pointed at his chest. He stepped backward. "You gave Nate false hope! You attacked my house! What is wrong with you?"

He held his hands up in supplication again. "Christiana, I don't know what *lies* these men are telling you. I *did not* attack your house. You're my daughter! And I explained to Nathan that the cure was experimental. Who are these men to you anyway, honey?"

He tried to push the blame onto me, like I made this a bigger deal by overreacting. Just like he always did.

I pointed at Nate, who Derrick had released. "That's my mate!" I couldn't see Nate's grin, but I felt it beaming behind me just the same. "You almost killed him! I should report you to the Bureau! Or better yet, let the coven deal with you. You know how they love to take down errant witches!"

"Honey—" he entreated, but I held firm.

"I could say a lot of things about you, Dad," I said bitterly. "But I never would have thought you were evil. You are working for *killers*! For what? Money? Like you don't have enough of it already. Does that sit well on your conscience?" He didn't stop me from continuing. "You really don't care as long as you end up on top at the end."

"Let me explain—"

I held a hand up to stop him. "No, you need to leave. Now!"

The door behind us opened.

"I'd wrap this up if you want dessert," Giana said with a hand on her hips. She sighed and looked at my dad. "Hi, Daddy. I'll see you on Wednesday after school pick-up."

"Sounds good, sweetheart." The door slammed behind Giana, and my father's smile disappeared. He sneered at me. "You've been spending too much time with the wolves, honey. They know how to manipulate easy *prey* like you." Nate snarled, but my father waved to him over my shoulder. "Just wait, Nathan, my Christiana is a bit of a wilted flower. Delicate, temperamental. She makes it difficult for anyone to truly love her. You'll see."

Hot tears welled in my eyes. *How dare he!* I didn't say anything as he walked away. Nate came up from behind me, wrapping his arms around me, nuzzling into my shoulder. Both he and Derrick growled, a low rumble I felt more than heard.

"He can't be the necromancer," I whispered as my tears finally fell. "He just can't be."

Derrick gave a hollow laugh. "I thought he just hated

Nate. How can he hate his own daughter?" He petted my head. "I don't understand fathers who hate their own children." He shook his head and walked back inside.

I couldn't breathe. I felt like the wind had been knocked out of me. I turned to Nate. "This is all my fault."

My father, working with Alice? It seemed inconceivable. I should have told Nate about my father ages ago. I had wanted to believe in his innocence, in his goodness. How could I have been so stupid? Stupid. Useless. *Typical.*

Nate kissed my forehead. "You are not responsible for your father's actions."

Even as we walked quietly inside, I couldn't let that feeling go. The darkness didn't need to pull me down this time, I was already neck-deep in it.

Chapter Forty: Christi

"What's with all the commotion?" my mother asked when we came inside.

The darkness beckoned me to follow it, and I wanted nothing more than to surrender to it. But I focused on the heart of the matter. I wanted to lash out at Mom for even speaking to Dad. I felt the fury deep in my bones. She bore some responsibility for how I felt right now.

But I didn't want to upset the littles, so I plastered a smile on my face and shook my head. "It was nothing." I sighed, my mind changing as soon as I got the words out. "Actually, no, I think we need to leave."

"Leave?" Mom asked incredulously.

I pushed past her to find Sadie so I could say goodbye, but Mom followed me.

Unable to stand it, I turned to her and unleashed. "I can't believe you. You called Dad!"

Mom's lip quivered and I rolled my eyes. *Unbelievable!* I just about had enough of my parents today.

"I had to. I thought maybe he could talk you out of it," she explained. "Cece, you might not come back."

"Mom!" I chided in a loud whisper. I tried to remain calm in front of all my family and friends. "Please!"

"Christi!"

"No, we're leaving!"

Sophia stood up and screamed at the top of her lungs. Sadie joined in, howling. It sounded like an eerie keening, a banshee's death knell. What else was going to happen today? I didn't think I could take anymore.

"They can't leave," Sophia shouted, quick and desperate. She grabbed onto my arm. "Zia, you can't leave. You can't. You can't leave. If you leave, you won't come back."

My heart sunk as Giana looked at me, her eyes wide. I took Sophia into my arms and caressed her hair. Dustin swept up Liam, and Mom ushered guests into the other room.

"I'm not going anywhere, bug," I told her, petting her hair. "It's just for a quick trip. I'll be back, you'll see."

Her hot tears wet my shirt, but I could feel her breathing calm. I forgot all about my father.

"Why don't we have a cupcake in your room? Just the two of us. You can tell me all about it. I'll be right back," I told Nate, who nodded.

"We're in no hurry. Do what you have to do."

After a few cupcakes, I had sung Sophia to sleep, and placed a protective amulet around her neck for sweet dreams. Giana cornered me in the hallway. Her face paled, and she shook with terror.

"My daughter hasn't slept in days. She's saying that you all are going to die," Giana whispered manically. "She seemed better today, but—I don't know how to fix this, Cece." She leaned against Sophia's door.

"The amulet should help prevent any prophetic dreams," I tried to reassure her. "This is intense, but it's clear she's gifted. Grandma would know what to do."

My grandmother had trained us both in the old ways, Giana in illusions and me in protective magic. If anyone could understand what Sophia experienced, it would have been her. My heart hurt at the thought.

"Seance?" Gigi suggested.

I bit my nails. If anyone had crossed into an afterlife, it would have been our grandmother. I shook my head. "Grandma didn't have unfinished business."

"It was worth a try." She sighed heavily. "Dusty and I will need to have a talk."

I pulled her into a hug. "You'll figure it out," I told her. "You're a great mom. The best mom she could hope for."

She was certainly better than ours, who called up my traitorous father to tell on me.

Giana pulled away and wiped her face with her hands. "Is he worth it?" she asked pointedly. Not *do you love him? Is he worth it?*

It punched the air out of me, and I took a moment before nodding.

"That's all I needed to know."

"I can't believe she called him," I said, still angry.

"She's worried about you, Cece. We all are." She shook

her hair out and put on a fake smile. "I'll be out in a minute, okay?"

I nodded, but I watched as she tiptoed back into Sophia's bedroom and sat next to her bed, caressing her hair as Sophia slept. I crept out of the hallway, careful not to disturb them.

Mom and Dusty were in the kitchen, putting dinner into storage containers and washing up the dishes. Dusty always was Mom's favorite. She handed me a cup of tea and another cupcake, smirking.

"I like him," she said in a stage whisper.

"No one asked you," I snapped, still on edge.

Dusty laughed, chiming in, "For what it's worth, I like him too."

"Some judge of character. You like *Derrick*."

Dusty nodded. "He's a fan."

I rolled my eyes.

Mom motioned to the living room. "He's in there, waiting for you."

"He can wait a minute longer," I told her. I gave her my gravest of looks. "You shouldn't have called Dad."

"I didn't know what else to do."

I felt a pang of guilt. I shouldn't treat her so harshly, given the nature of my trip. Still, I couldn't bring myself to forgive her—not when my father had treated me so poorly. "He's dangerous, Mom," I warned her. I looked to Dusty as well. "I think you all should stay away from him for a while."

Mom looked at me helplessly, like I just asked her to stay

away from her grandchildren. They didn't understand. I don't know why I expected them to. I sighed and left the kitchen.

Nate stood up when I entered the room, nervously plucking at the bottom of his sweater. "Everyone left, but I wanted to make sure you got home alright," he said. "I should warn you, though, Derrick was quite emotional about leaving Sadie here."

I smiled. So was I. There were days when I only got out of bed because Sadie needed a walk. In the worst of my depression, I still made sure that Sadie was taken care of, even when I couldn't take care of myself. I couldn't imagine going to sleep and not being able to cuddle her.

I knelt down so I could wrap my arms around her. She licked my face and pawed at me. I took her ears in my hands, massaging them, but also making sure she looked at me. I looked into those dark eyes and I knew that she knew.

"You be good, okay? Be patient with the littles, they don't know how annoying they can be for you. I don't know how long I'll be gone, but I'll come back to you, okay? I'll come back. I love you."

I wrapped my arms around Sadie one last time before we left. For the first time, I had to admit to myself that I was terrified. Even during the attack on my house, I had so much adrenaline running, and I'd been so high that I couldn't feel afraid. But now, I was so scared that I wouldn't make it back home.

He had to be worth it, I told myself. I loved him.

Chapter Forty-One: Nate

The moment we left the house, Christi apologized.

"I am so sorry. It's not usually that hectic. I mean, it is, just in a different way. My father was horrible and my mother didn't act much better, and I feel like I ignored you and *I* was the one who invited you. But I really did have to help with Sophia and shit fuck, I'm rambling. I'm going to stop talking now." She ran a hand through her hair, which had started to frizz with the sweat of her anxiety.

A curl fell into her face, and I brushed it behind her ear. When she looked down, embarrassed, I lifted her chin with my finger. I caressed her blushing cheek. She grimaced, so I gave her a smile and motioned for her to walk with me.

"Your family seems really nice."

"Thank you. I happen to like them. I know you come from something different."

"*Different* is the right word. My parents aren't warm people, but they care in their own way, even if it's from afar." I tried to keep my voice even. I had done a lot of thinking while I had waited for Christi. I wanted to keep her mind off things for a little while longer. "I don't think I've told you this, but I told my parents, after the Reveal. About why I left, why I couldn't come home. But the damage was already done, you know?"

Christi laughed hollowly. "It's like putting a bandage on a

bullet hole. Dad never understood why I left my career after the Reveal. He thought I should have continued to pretend." She sighed angrily. "Then he turned around and joined a magitech firm. The hypocrite." She scowled, balling her fists up. "It wasn't just the magic, you know. It was never about the magic. It was always about me. No matter what I do, it's never good enough for him."

That resonated all the way into my bones. I wanted to draw her into me and hold her until this all went away. I didn't want to provoke her further, but I needed to know. Now was as good a time as any. I spoke the words as gently as I could. "Your father was the one who offered me the cure. Did you know?"

"If I did, do you think I'd invite you to my sister's house and expose you to that shitshow? I'm sure I could think up better ways to mess with your head." She huffed. "I'm sorry. I should have said something the moment you said you were working with someone named Joe. We could have gotten to the bottom of this so much sooner. This is all my fault."

I took her hand and squeezed. I should have known better than to prod. I had never seen her that upset, had never heard her yell even when she had been furious with me. I didn't know she had it in her. While my wolf smiled at the ferocity of his mate, I worried about her. So much had happened in the space of a few hours.

"Your dad's not in the picture at all, is he?"

She shook her head. Her eyes grew distant, and all I

wanted was to bring her back to me, to make her smile light up in my direction again. "Giana keeps a relationship with him for the littles' sake. Goddess, they aren't little anymore, are they? But I tend to steer clear. You can probably see why."

I understood that. Sometimes it was easier to stay away than to force the relationship. I loved my parents and I knew they loved me, but the man I became was in spite of them instead of because of them. I bumped her shoulder as we walked.

She sighed. "Every choice I make adds to his growing lists of disappointments. He really is such an asshole. But I didn't believe he could be cruel. Nate, I still don't know if I can believe he's the necromancer working with the O'Shea pack."

"Do you think he'd attack your house?" I asked carefully. Because that was the heart of the matter. Christi was never hurt. Scared, maybe. Shaken, very, but not a scratch on her. Either her wards were very good, or she was never the target. My hand went to the little wolf around my neck.

"I don't know what to think anymore," she said softly. "I barely got through that interaction with my father, and now you're asking me to make sense of it. Nothing makes sense. My father is at the very least on Alice's payroll. My niece thinks we're all going to die. And my mother called my father to tell on me. At this point, I should only trust Gigi and Dusty, but who knows, maybe they're sleeper agents for the fae!"

She said it with a laugh, but I could see the overwhelm in her eyes. I wished I knew how to make this better. This was a very specific kind of hurt that only a parent could inflict. It wasn't just the act of letting their child down. It was perhaps confirming what Christi already knew: that her father was not a good person. Or worse, it was helping her understand that not even *she* was safe from his actions. Instead of being the disappointment, Christi should have been disappointed in her father. Beneath his car salesman veneer, he really didn't give two shits about her.

It hadn't been personal when he pumped me full of silver.

But for Christi, it wasn't Joe the necromancer harming her. It was Joe her father.

"You lied," I said, trying to joke.

Her eyes lit up, ready to meet the challenge. "Oh, did I?"

I consulted my watch and made a big show of it. "You said I would be back home in bed by 9:00, and it is 9:15."

"I do remember making that promise. I'll have to make it up to you somehow." She paused and turned to me. "Thank you, I mean it. This was important to me, and you were there, with no complaints except the one." She kissed me in the middle of the street. "It's why I love you."

If she didn't look like a rabbit ready to run, I would have celebrated. My wolf howled in the back of my mind, ecstatic, but I knew if I held her too tightly, she might bolt.

I was starting to understand her hesitance, apart from

334

the events of the evening. Pictures covered the walls of Giana's house. There was a photograph of teenaged Christi and Rachel, holding diplomas and making peace signs. Another was of Giana, staring into space as though the world was her oyster, and every cookbook cover she had posed for. Of course, there was a picture of the kids as babies and a wedding portrait of Giana and Dustin. But next to that portrait had been another wedding portrait, with Christi in a white gown laughing at a bald man with light brown skin in a tan linen suit. Both of them had love in their eyes and a future together. That had ended.

I wished I could explain it to her. The mating bond, how it felt to me and the wolf. She would have to settle for my actions. I would spend my whole life convincing her that I wasn't going anywhere, if I had to. She had declared that we were mates. She had all but completed our mating bond. My wolf howled in celebration. I wouldn't scare her off. For now, I settled for putting her at ease.

"It's the sweaters, isn't it?" I joked.

She laughed. "Oh, it's definitely the sweaters." She stopped again for a kiss. "I've never felt this way for someone. I'm scared. I don't want to lose you."

I caressed her face, and she leaned into my hand. My wolf was ready to howl at the moon, to tell everyone that would listen that she was in love with me. "I love you. I want to spend the rest of our lives together."

I watched as Christi's smile turned to horror. Green

flames reflected in the green of Christi's eyes, and I turned. The whole neighborhood milled around Christi's house. Eerie green flames engulfed it, and before I could say another word, Christi made a run for it.

<hr />

Derrick held Hope and Strength, guarding the threshold as Rachel belted a bandoleer of potion vials. Ines held a screaming Christi from the flames.

"Someone call the Bureau," a neighbor yelled, but Derrick shut them up.

"Don't be a stupid fuck," he shouted, before pointing at a bystander. "You! Go to the Dahlia. Ask for the Proprietor and tell them Derrick sent you. He'll know what to do."

The neighbor nodded and ran off. I helped Ines hold Christi back. I had failed. I'd failed to protect her. This was all my fault. All I could do now was ensure she stayed safe.

"Christi, there's nothing you can do," Ines cried over her screams. "You can't save it."

"Let go of me!" Christi kicked and elbowed in vain.

I stood in front of her and took her face in my hands. "Darling, there's nothing we can do."

"It's all I have," she cried, her forehead against mine. My heart broke at the helplessness of it all. She sagged in my arms, falling to her knees. I knew the feeling and for a second, I was back to the floor of the bookstore full of empty shelves. Anger burned in me. It was one thing to destroy me, but how dare someone hurt my mate.

"Nathaniel!" a voice bellowed over the noise. Alice had finally come to collect. "Nathaniel!"

It might have been Alice's voice, but the body that came out of the flames was Sarah's.

I turned to Ines, panicked. "Get them out of here," I pointed to the onlookers.

"On it!" She disappeared in a streak of pink.

Derrick tossed me my blades. *Idiot!* Luckily, I caught them by the hilt. He growled low and I held him back with an arm.

"Let me go," he ordered darkly. His eyes had gone cold and his jaw set.

"It's not her," I reminded him. "Derrick, I know it looks like her, but that's not Sarah."

"I know."

Backed by green flames stood Sarah, naked and gaunt, surrounded by animated skeletons. Our worst fears proved correct. Necromancy.

My heart dropped as Christi dashed into the yard. I knew I had to trust her—I had seen her powers in action, but still I worried for her safety.

I couldn't think about that right now. I set all my feelings in a box and locked it tight. Instinct guided me now as I gripped Hope and Strength tighter.

Ines and Rachel attacked the skeletons as they kept

coming, climbing over the fence and popping up from the ground. Ines gleefully brandished her scythe, slicing through the skeletons like a hot pink grim reaper. I could hear Rachel's laugh as explosions of colored potions splattered onto the skeletons. Each drop caused fractures that cascaded through the skeletons like dominoes, ending in a blast of bones. Christi ran from corner to corner of the yard, trying to contain the attack. I could only do so much with my blades. I focused on the joints and heads, slashing between the bones. Time seemed to stop as I surveyed the fight. I could hear my heart beat pulse in my ears. Skeletons kept coming. Erupting from the ground. Crawling over fences. It was like we kicked a nest of spiders.

I looked for Derrick and found his wolf. We nodded. This was not the first time we had fought together. We started towards Sarah.

In life, Sarah had been a formidable opponent. Not only did her wolf have speed and strength, but even as a human, she was ferocious in a fight. She fought dirty, going for the eyes, the hair, the groin. She'd use her nails to scratch and mar while she kicked you where it hurt. Whatever spells reanimated her had amplified her skills. She anticipated every hit I tried, disappearing in a burst of speed, only for her to reappear and hit me in my blind spot.

Derrick waited and watched, unable to hurt his wife.

"A little help here," I pleaded, trying to get him to snap out of it. Sarah kicked me in the side, flattening me to the dirt.

I tasted grass and minerals and spat blood.

Derrick finally growled, baring his teeth in a snarl as he lunged for her. She managed to fling him off her with a thrust of one arm. Derrick landed in a thump, his wolf giving a whimper. I inhaled sharply. I needed to find a weak spot, some opening that would allow me to strike.

Christi took a nasty blow from a group of skeletons. I couldn't split my attention trying to look out for her. I needed to trust that she'd be fine. A flash of light in her direction told me I was right. I had to focus.

I turned back to Sarah. There was something off about this fight. For one, the skeletons swarmed Christi, Rachel, Ines, and now Derrick, but ignored me completely. While Sarah landed hits on me, she held her punches. I knew they could have more power behind them. She threw Derrick across the lawn with one hand. I only fell to the ground. She should be making easy work of me. Even though I expended effort trying to fight her, I was not nearly as taxed as my friends. I managed to dodge Sarah, ducking under her arm as it swung towards me. I kicked her back as I turned around, and Sarah stumbled in a jerking motion.

"Sarah," I cried out. "Focus on Sarah!"

I couldn't tell if they could hear me. Rachel laughed manically in the center of the yard. Skeleton pieces flew through the air as she dropped her bombs. Christi, who had righted herself after that blow, a nasty bruise purpling on her face, nodded at me. I'd lost sight of Derrick, though I could hear him snarling and howling. Ines—thank god for vampires—got to Sarah first, her scythe at the ready.

In a completely detached manner, as though this bored her to pieces, Ines jumped on Sarah's back. With a single thrust, she pierced Sarah through the heart. Scythe forgotten, Ines grasped Sarah's head in both hands, and she twisted. Bones cracked as Sarah's head swiveled all the way around. I clenched my sword to keep from vomiting. I'd seen violence, participated in raids, killed when necessary, but Ines's cool, easy brutality scared me. *She's not human*, I reminded myself, *not even animal.* But Sarah grasped at Ines, throwing her off.

Sarah straightened herself, stretching her neck to both sides before turning her head back the right way. I could only watch in horror. I stood there, blades in hand, useless. Scared. A flame ignited at Sarah's feet, roaring up to immolate her. I smiled at Rachel, and she only nodded at me, running to blow up more skeletons. Christi had encircled us in chalk and began chanting. I could see the sweat on her brow, the flagging of her shoulders. *Come on, darling, just a bit more.*

The flames smoldered, and I no longer saw a body. I started to sag in relief, until a wolf erupted from the flames. A flayed wolf.

Sarah's wolf no longer had a pelt. Instead, I could see the red of every muscle, the pull of every wiry white tendon. Guilt flooded my senses. I did this to her. Alice wanted to find me so badly that she'd bound Sarah like this. The O'Shea pack was willing to create this abomination, to maim her and kill her. The wolf charged me, and I braced myself for the attack. Before Sarah's wolf hit me, a gray wolf knocked both of them to the ground. The wolves tussled, teeth, claws, and fur flying.

"Derrick!" I cried out, but it was too late.

Derrick's wolf lunged down, ripping out the reanimated wolf's jugular with its teeth. The skeletons began to retreat, and I rushed to Christi's side as she collapsed in exhaustion. My pulse pounded in my ears as Derrick transformed to a wolf man. Sarah's wolf lay bleeding on the ground while the wolf man howled, long and mournful. Then, with a wrenching, wet sound, the wolf man pulled the flayed wolf's head from its body.

Christi got sick beside me. But the fight ended. The life that animated the skeletons burned out. They all paused, suspended for a moment, before the bones scattered to the ground. The skeletons stopped coming up from the ground or over the fence. None of us moved or breathed, afraid to break the spell. Not even the wind stirred, the air feeling heavy and dense around us. The wolf lay still, blood drenching the grass, and the undead Sarah was truly dead.

"We need to burn the body," Ines finally said.

I helped Christi up. This felt different from the last attack. When Christi banished the skeletons the first time, nothing remained. Bones littered the lawn and the house finally stopped smoldering, green flame extinguished and the house remarkably still standing. We cautiously approached the flayed wolf's body. Sarah's body. Derrick had transformed back to a man.

"Derrick—" I started, but he held up his hand, his face completely blank. He stalked past us and disappeared into the house.

Christi touched my arm, bringing my attention back to our task. "Let him go," she said softly.

We didn't voice the unspoken truth of the matter: Derrick just killed his wife. She might have been an animated corpse, and he might not have been his mate, but she was still his. I wasn't certain I could've done the same. I imagined Christi lying there, and I swallowed bile. I couldn't understand what he must be going through.

"Do you have enough energy to do this?" I asked her, my arm still at her elbow, steadying her. "I'm sure I can find some lighter fluid."

She shook her head, "I need to do this." She swallowed hard. "For Derrick."

She stepped away from me, and I felt the wind change. It flowed through her hair and a brilliant white light bathed her. The stars shone brighter, the night grew darker. I felt breathless. I knew she invoked some deity, but I couldn't hear it. She raised her arms to the sky, and she shone so brightly that I couldn't look at her. I wanted to look away, but she commanded my attention, all of our attentions. The illumination consumed her. It became unclear where Christi ended and where the light began. I shielded my eyes, kneeling in supplication. My powerful goddess. I felt the light lift before flashing out like a shockwave. The night grew quiet once more.

When I opened my eyes, Christi fell to her knees, and the ashes of Sarah's wolf scattered in the wind. It was like Sarah was never there. All traces of her gone. I went to my goddess, helped her up, and cradled her in my arms. I vowed to never let this happen to her. I would kill Alice before I let my mate be sacrificed because of me.

Chapter Forty-Two: Christi

I stood at a fork in an asphalt road, with desert sands all around me. The sun beat down, making the heat unbearable. I saw nothing on the horizon except for the two roads and the signpost. I was getting tired of ending up here. My body wouldn't move, too exhausted from the fight. I realized then that this was no ordinary vision.

Tired, I sat at the base of the signpost and waited for something to happen. Dust rolled in on one of the roads. Out of it walked a tall, athletic woman, with long brown hair in a ponytail. She wore a white tee shirt and faded blue jeans with hiking boots. When I had seen her last, she had been naked, fighting her husband. Her corpse had been dirty and bloody. This Sarah projected an easy confidence. I felt the tug of her dominance, but it was the gentle pull of a friendly hand to hold, the comforting weight of a shoulder to cry on. She waved and smiled at me, radiating warmth and calm.

As dust rolled in on the other road, I realized that Sarah wasn't waving to me. Sarah, the woman, now crouched down, arms open and waiting. Through the dust leapt a glorious gray wolf. The wolf had clear gray eyes with dark markings around them like she wore eyeliner. Her pelt had a base of white with a dark gray, almost black, at the ends. She was larger than Nate's wolf, but just as lithe and lean. I had never seen an animal run so fast. She barreled down the road.

Sarah, the woman, laughed as the wolf gained speed to reach the other road. As she sped past me, I saw the wolf's underbelly was snow white. Pristine and beautiful. I had seen this wolf too, but not whole and complete like this. I marveled as she ran past me. The wolf jumped into Sarah's arms and vanished into her heart. Wolf and woman joined, now complete. Sarah rose, gave me a wave, and walked back the way she had come.

"Rest now, little wolf," a woman's voice whispered on the wind. When I looked around, I stood on the road alone.

Chapter Forty-Three: Derrick

I washed the gore off my face and put on clean clothes. Even though I washed myself, I would never be clean. I still felt the blood on my skin, felt her throat in my teeth. I couldn't look at myself in the mirror. Squeezing my eyes tightly, I tried to erase the image of Sarah in my mind. It didn't matter. I could still see her with my eyes closed. I would get through this. I survived the cage. I survived my father. I survived the pack. I could survive this. *I had to.* I set my jaw and left the bathroom. My hands betrayed me, still shaking.

Christi was in the kitchen. She had made a pot of coffee with my coffee maker, and she held a mug in her hand. She handed it to me wordlessly. I took a sip, but it tasted like sand in my mouth. I wanted to spit it out, but Christi wrapped her arms around me.

"She's whole now, Derrick," she said through tears. "I think she'd want you to know that. Sarah and her wolf had been separated, but they are together now."

I thrust the coffee mug back into Christi's empty hands and vomited into her kitchen sink. She handed me back the mug as I straightened.

"I'll clean it," she said. "Don't worry about it now."

I grunted in acknowledgement. We stepped out of the house together, her hand on my arm. She wasn't even a wolf, yet she knew how much I needed the touch of pack right now.

ghost. I floated out of myself for a moment, weightless, breathless. Then I remembered that ghosts likely wouldn't feel pain. I slammed back into my body, and everything hurt again.

Christi stepped toward Marlowe, taking her hands. Marlowe turned beet red and her ears stood straight up. "Thank you," Christi said in relief.

"She's just doing her job," Ines scowled. She gave me a look like I should be agreeing with her, but I shrugged.

Christi glared at Ines before giving Marlowe a soft smile. "Don't listen to her. We are grateful, job or not."

Marlowe took her hands from Christi's before waving her off with one hand, ears fluttering. "No need to thank us, ma'am." Marlowe started to herd us toward the door, making shooing motions with her hands. "Now, let us handle this."

None of us slept. Someone made more coffee. Christi cleaned the sink. I think I made something for us to eat. Or maybe someone put a plate of food in my hands. It didn't matter. We ate for fuel. No one said anything for a long time. We all just sat helplessly in Christi's living room. My field trip to the Dahlia had done nothing to hammer in the reality of what we faced, but this did.

"This is it, isn't it?" Christi said, not really a question. "Goddess, I can't imagine that my father would go to these lengths just because someone paid him."

Nate rubbed her back. She and Nate huddled together on the leather sofa. Rachel sat on the floor hugging her knees with Ines laid out on the chaise. I stood. If I had to think, I would drive myself insane. I just pushed any thoughts and feelings deep down in the pit with all the other terrible things that have happened to me.

"This isn't going to stop. *She* isn't going to stop," Nate added.

This was his fault. I should have never found him. I could still be in Colorado, dick-deep in ass and tits. Instead, I was here, trying to erase all memory of the woman I loved. I tried to forget what her blood tasted like. I tried to unhear the sound of her head being removed from her body. I tried to think of my actions as an outside observer. Yes, I did it, I killed her. But I couldn't step too close to it, or I would experience it all over again.

It didn't help that my wolf wailed mournfully in my head and hadn't stopped since Sarah died.

"I was afraid you'd say that." Christi sighed heavily. "To the Wilderness it is, then."

"To the Wilderness," Ines repeated.

"It's a trap," I muttered. I expected no one to really listen to me, but Ines clocked me.

"Yes." She cocked her head. "I believe that's the point."

Rachel picked at something on the floor. "If she's willing to go to these lengths for an old boyfriend, I can't imagine she's a saint. The plan is a good one."

"Someone has to stop her," Christi said, leaning into Nate.

"It might as well be us," Ines added, flipping her hair back.

I grinned with all of my teeth. "Fuck taking her wolf away, I'm going to kill her. You all better stay out of my way."

Epilogue

Joseph Bianchi rarely felt out of his depth. He had been born with a natural and easy charm. The stars seemed to align for everything he did. He was smart, attractive, and most importantly, rich. Most people ate out of the palm of his hand. There were, of course, exceptions, but they were family, and family had a way of disappointing him.

The confrontation with his daughter hadn't gone well. Him, a necromancer? The nerve. Christiana always had an overactive imagination, and he'd been the target of it many times. But that was an old hurt. He knew that pain produced results. Nothing easy was worth having. He got what he wanted by clawing and fighting for it. The harder to obtain, the harder he worked to attain it.

Even this little *situation* with the werewolf was a minor setback. Prior to Nathan, all of Joe's shifter subjects had died. He had tried four different formulas to perfect this last one. That Nathan had survived the dose at all was a resounding success in Joe's eyes. Still, his shifter pets informed him that it hadn't worked. He'd lost two good pets to the werewolf on the night of the full moon. A shame—good help was hard to come by. He needed more subjects, and more money for supplies. One werewolf was never going to be enough for this project anyway.

The shifter in front of him didn't agree. As Joe watched

him, the shifter didn't even pretend to be human. The wolf moved with an animal grace, circling his prey. Joe realized quickly that *he* was the prey. But he could play these dominance games. He was smarter, better, than a mere *animal*.

"Our patron is not pleased, Joe," the shifter said, leaning against one of the benches in the empty warehouse. "Not pleased at all."

Joe cleared his throat. "It was one werewolf. The formula needs some refinement, Farolf." Joe shrugged easily. "That's all."

The shifter Farolf pulled on a set of black leather driving gloves. He strode over to Joe, paused before him. He gripped the soft parts of Joe's face, above the jaw but below the cheeks, and squeezed. Pain blinded Joe. The wolf's piercing blue eyes examined Joe before he thrust him aside. Joe's glasses fell to the ground. Through blurred vision, Joe watched as the wolf stepped on them with a *crunch*.

Joe massaged his face. No one had ever treated him this way before. It both stunned and angered him. Who did this *animal* think he was? Joe didn't even *work* for the animals. His patron was higher on the food chain.

"He wants results," Farolf said before clicking his tongue in disappointment, "which you promised him."

Joe was a tall man, but this wolf towered over him. Still, Joe stood to his full height and summoned all of his arrogance. "Negative results are still results. Like I said, the formula needs refinement."

"The formula that you let them steal?"

"It was only a small fraction of what we have in storage—"

Joe's face stung as Farolf smacked him hard. It knocked the wind right of him. But Joe laughed in shock just the same. "How dare you!"

Farolf smacked him again. This time, Joe bit his tongue, tasting the tang of iron in his mouth. He spat at the wolf. Flecks of red dotted Farolf's face. Impassively, he wiped each droplet of spittle with a gloved hand. He sneered at Joe.

"You seem to forget yourself, Joe." With a motion of Farolf's eyes, the shifter bodyguards that typically protected Joe turned on him. They gripped his arms, clawed his legs.

Joe laughed, still convinced that he held the upper hand. "You can't hurt me. Who else will finish the formula for *him*?"

Farolf smiled without teeth and laughed through his nose. "You think it's just you?" He eyed Joe, his voice dripped with condescension. "You humans are so stupid sometimes. You are not the only one who can make a potion, Joe." He flicked his head, and the bodyguards began dragging Joe to the medical exam chair.

Joe's heart sped, and he scrambled with his feet to keep them from pulling him backwards. "Wait, no! What about my children? My family? You said you wouldn't involve them!"

Farolf turned his back on Joe. He found the *Bestiary* in a drawer, unsurprised it was there. What a headache *that* had been. The bookstore collection had been no help, though he knew his patron would be able to find a use for the rest of the dusty books and moldy parchment. Farolf didn't particularly care what happened to the books. He'd tracked the *Bestiary* to the coven, and then to Joe. The stupid human really thought he was pulling the wool over their eyes. True wolves needn't hide under fleece.

"It's too late for that now, Joe," he called out in a bit of a singsong voice, taunting Joe. The bodyguards strapped Joe into the chair, despite his kicking and screaming. Farolf laughed to himself. Now that he'd found what he came here for, there was no reason to draw this out. His voice darkened. "*You* involved them. They *are* involved."

Farolf walked out of the warehouse accompanied by Joseph's screams. The rest of his shifters emptied the storerooms of Joe's formulation. Farolf's team would have to take the project over. He *hated* working management.

A bodyguard fell in line behind him. Bright sunlight blinded them in the parking lot. Farolf pulled his sunglasses out of the breast pocket of his suit. There were rust-colored dots on his jacket. He sighed in annoyance as he donned the black frames. He'd have to get it dry-cleaned now.

"What now?" Balto asked in sotto voce, limping behind him.

"Leave him here if he survives. If he doesn't, dump the body where it won't be found."

"And you, sir?"

Farolf sneered as he took off his leather driving gloves. He threw them to the ground. "I have a train to catch."

The End

Thank you for reading **Moon Dance**! If you enjoyed it, consider signing up for my newsletter for monthly updates and exclusive content. Keep reading for a sneak peek at the continuation of the series in The Blood Pack Book Two: **Silver Song**.

Excerpt from Silver Song
Christi

The drive to the train station was a somber affair, with only
Rachel able to chat as the car made its way through the
Grapevine and into the dusty Central Valley. We had
squeezed into Big Bertha, pushing the trash and clothes to
the floor so we could sit at the banquette. The van had a smell
to it that was too fresh to just be the smell of an old van. I hid
my nose in my arm and tried not to think about it.

Trains were the only mode of transportation to and from
the Wilderness, carrying mostly supplies and the occasional
first-class passengers. Bandits raided these trains frequently,
so most had plainclothes law enforcement posing as
passengers to protect the cargo. The passengers were never
that important to protect, not when medication, guns, and
clothing made more money. From my understanding, Nate
and Derrick's pack had lived in a similar area in Colorado,
only a few luxuries away from being the Wild West.

All I wanted was some food and a shower, but Ines
ordered us along. She only stopped when some women
waiting at a bus stop called to her. I tried to follow along in
my twelfth grade Spanish, but Rachel darted over to them.
After some excited gestures, Rachel ran back.

"They want the van," Rachel said to Derrick.

"I didn't know you were Mexican," he muttered, and she slapped his arm.

"I'm Filipina, you idiot. I *learned* Spanish. Now, focus. They want to buy Big Bertha."

Derrick tossed her the keys. "Give it to them," he said, resigned.

"Derrick," I cautioned, but he shrugged me off.

"I don't need it, okay?" he shouted. "They do, so give it to them."

This time, both Rachel and Ines spoke to the women at a rapid pace in barely accented Spanish. As they ran back to us, the woman waved and thanked us.

"Did we just doom them? You can't drive through the Wilderness."

Ines shook her head, but Rachel answered for her. "They're going to Texas, on pilgrimage to Our Lady."

My stomach dropped. That was almost worse. After the Reveal, many people believed it was the second coming. A Texas woman claimed her young daughter had been visited by an angel, impregnated by God, and given birth to the son of God. She hadn't even bothered in reading Revelations to perform her con correctly, but it didn't matter. The Kingdom was founded in Texas just the same. They'd brought up the child to believe he was going to be the Savior, and his mother was venerated as the Virgin Mother. Poor girl had probably been abused, but now in her early 20s, she was treated as a queen. The avatar of a goddess. The mother of a god.

Ines touched my hand. "Let them believe what they believe."

"I already gave them the car, so let it go," Derrick grumbled. Nate and I gave each other a look. He grunted and pushed past us. We had no choice but to follow him.

The parking lot spread out in front of us, so we made the walk in the heat to the station. The California desert surrounded us, providing little shade. The landscape was brown and dusty, the parking lot black and empty. The train station was the only bright building for miles. We just had to get there. A mass of people blocked the entrance to the station. They held handmade signs and shouted at stony gargoyle security guards in black uniforms.

"Go back to where you came from!"

"Stay in the Wilderness!"

"Magic is evil!"

"Repent, sinners!"

"The end is near!"

"Kill the creatures!"

I heard about protests, but living in a big city, I was mostly sheltered from them. Nate held on to me as we pushed through the throng. Ines hissed at a protester make way. He spat in her face, and another protester threw holy water on her. Derrick swiped at him, and they gave us a wider berth. I couldn't even see Rachel. I could only focus on what was in front of me as Nate pushed us through. Someone threw trash, rotten vegetables and slime. I froze. Nate held me in his arms, shielding me from the spray.

"Shifter scum!"

He ignored it, pushing me on. My muscles tightened, and I had to use much of my brainpower reminding them how to move. My heart beat faster as Nate produced our tickets and showed them to the security guard. The guard nodded and let us through.

Once we were separated from the protesters, I could finally breathe. Nate's sweater was ruined, mystery liquids seeping through it. He pulled it off hurriedly, like it was going to bite him if he didn't. I couldn't blame him. I desperately wanted to change, worried that the hate would sink into my clothes and eat away at me. After tossing his sweater in the trash, Nate came over and pulled me in his arms.

"Are you alright?" he asked seriously.

"I should be asking you," I responded shakily. I had never experienced something like this. The grim line of Nate's mouth told me he had. He just shook his head, jaw set. I hugged him tighter. Ines shook out water from her dress, wiping away the spit from her face with disgust. Derrick moved to help her, but she snapped her fangs at him. He backed away. Rachel finally popped through the line of protesters.

"Was someone going to help me through?" she

questioned. We looked at her blankly. She had moved through the crowd unscathed and unshaken. "What?"

"Let's go," Derrick said, turning to the station.

Rachel followed after him, continuing to ask, "What? What?"

Nate squeezed my hand to reassure me. I smiled at him. There was no backing out now.

The Woe Winchester Station was named after the vampire scientist who'd developed the vaccine. He had been a Quaker in life, hence the unfortunate name. He donated all of the proceeds from the vaccine patent to the building of the train station. Winchester had accumulated enough wealth throughout his afterlife that he didn't need it.

The station looked like an old botanical garden, green filigree encapsulating large windows. Two large glass domes topped the station on either end. Like most post-Reveal architecture, the train station catered to the many magical creatures who didn't particularly enjoy being indoors. I preferred it, enjoying the return to the Beaux Arts-style buildings. They were always so bright and airy. Where there wasn't glass, white walls stuck out against the brown landscape around it. Bright Edison light signage directed us through the station, reminiscent of the early 20th century. The lights had the eerie glow of magic, and the passengers that walked through the station were like us, elves, shifters, vampires.

We stopped in a nondescript lobby, painted a stark white with black trim. My heart raced, and it started to feel difficult to breathe, but Nate took my hand. I tried to ground myself with his touch. I wasn't alone in this. We would be together. But would that be enough? A gaunt, thin man stood behind what looked to be a check-in desk, like we were at a hotel or car rental. There was a simple black door next to him with a rounded top, but square bottom.

"Good afternoon, folks," he said in a ridiculously chipper manner. "My name is Quill. How may I be of service?"

Ines stepped forward and handed him her ticket. "We have first-class tickets for Seattle."

From there, her friends would pick us up, taking us the last leg to the Aviary.

"Wonderful! I'll get you on your way shortly. First, I'll need to confirm some information from you." His smile didn't waver.

"Yes?" Ines asked impatiently.

"Last name?"

"Urso," she replied, though she was trying to whisper. I never knew her last name. In fact, I had assumed that she didn't have one, so this was news to me.

"First name?"

"Ines."

"Race?"

"Vampire," she responded, her voice getting increasingly annoyed. Rachel rubbed her back to calm her, but Ines's jaw still clenched. The clerk wasn't checking information during this time, just smiling at us and asking his questions. There didn't seem to be any papers or a computer on the desk. He didn't even look at the ticket in his hand.

"Is he going to consult something?" Derrick asked in a whisper, leaning into us. I shrugged helplessly.

"Excellent. And what is the purpose of your trip to Seattle? Business, pleasure, or both?"

"Business," Ines said through gritted teeth. "Is that all?"

The man smiled at her blankly for a moment. We all started to look at each other, unsure if we should prompt him.

"Just a few more moments, please. Everything looks aboveboard on our end. Now, do you have anything to declare before entering?"

We allowed him to look through our packs and survey our persons for additional belongings. The coolers full of the cure were largely ignored. Only Rachel had a few supplies confiscated.

"Hey! Hey!" she shrieked at him when he handled a deadly-looking lead canister. "Careful with that!"

Quill only smiled at her and set it aside.

"Wonderful! Now, if you please, enter the doorway one at a time. Ms. Urso."

Ines stalked to the door, opened it, and slammed it

closed behind her.

"Mr. Williams."

Derrick nodded at him before saying, "Too late to back out now." He too walked through the door, followed by Rachel.

"Mr. Nwodo-Johnston."

Nate kissed me. "See you on the platform." He was more hesitant than Derrick or Ines, but stepped through the door and onto the train platform.

Quill smiled at me a moment. "Ms. Owens, I need some more information before your passage."

I panicked, my heart racing. I was alone now. I schooled my features and kept my voice calm. *You can be free, all you have to do is run.*

"What seems to be the problem?"

"Not a problem, but your information seems to be incorrect in your booking, and I need to properly process that information. This will only take a moment."

I searched my brain for what could possibly be the problem. Not coming up with anything, I focused on my breath. *One. Two. Three. Four.*

"What is the origin of your magic?"

My magic? I clenched my hands and released them. "It's familial. My grandmother taught me."

What if I couldn't explain what he needed to know? I felt the tears welling, and I hated myself for being unable to deal with this. I wouldn't be able to go with them. Worse, maybe

Nate would try to stay with me and he wouldn't get the answers he needed. I couldn't let that happen. If I could pace, I would have. Anything to keep from crying in front of this very nice clerk.

After a few moments, Quill smiled at me. "That's all we need. Ms. Owens, you are free to walk through."

I sighed in relief. "Thank you!"

I rushed through the door. It took a terrifying, dark moment to come out on the other side.

Portal magic, it figured.

Acknowledgements

This was not the book I intended out to write. I had not set out to write anything I thought people actually might read at all. That was because in late November 2023, I had called up my husband to tell him that I was going to hurt myself. This suicidal episode led me to quit my job as a medical writer and left me staring at the pieces of my life. What was I going to do now? Who was I now? A therapist suggested I start writing fiction again, just for the fun it. So, I did.

The novel I worked on, a fantasy romance murder mystery (say that three times fast) just wouldn't come together. I adored the world I built and the characters, but it just didn't sing. Inspired by the Nintendo Switch game *Wylde Flowers*, I decided I would write a fluffy little paranormal romance between a werewolf and a witch. It wasn't going to be that serious or even a full novel. It was a fun project just to get the juices flowing and thus began *Moon Dance*. The characters emerged from my head like Athena from Zeus, fully formed and covered in armor. Though much of who they are and what they do are because of my weird little brain, I have taken inspiration from reality where I could.

Christi's explanation about the cave paintings as well as some of her magic are grounded in anthropological theories laid out in Chris Gosden's *Magic: A History: From Alchemy to Witchcraft, from the Ice Age to the Present*. If you have any interest in magic from a historical or anthropological lens at all, it is well worth the read.

Nate's various attempted cures for lycanthropy also have historical basis. Medieval cures for lycanthropy were based on Victoria Blud's *Thereby Hangs a Tail: Creation and Procreation in Medieval Werewolf Romances* published in January 2022 as part of the *Medieval Feminist Forum: A Journal of Gender and Sexuality*. Some of the medical basis was inspired by Nadine Metzger's *Battling demons with medical authority: werewolves, physicians, and rationalization*, published in *Hist Psychiatry* in September 2013. Finally, the ancient Greek curative of bleeding, milk baths, and pumpkin was from direct text translations by Sententiae Antiquae as part of their werewolf week. We as a society also have to thank 1931's *Dracula* and 1941's *The Wolf Man* for the entrance of wolfsbane and silver bullets into the vampire and werewolf lore.

Now that I have thanked divine inspiration and the sacred texts, I can begin to thank the people responsible for making this novel a reality. First to my editor, Ana Hansen. I handed you a 100K word mess and you have helped me shape it into a beautiful debut. Thank you for letting me run with all my *what ifs?* and bearing with me when I said *I think this needs to be two novels*. I couldn't have gotten *Moon Dance* across the finish line without you and the novel is so much better thanks to your thoughtful and careful critique and feedback. Working with you has made me a better writer and

I get a little teary thinking about how much we accomplished with this. Here's to many more books to come!

To my beta pack: Joanna Laird, Ashley Lansdown, and Carrie Werth. Thank you for sharing your initial thoughts and early excitement about the book, and for your willingness to be my guinea pigs. What a way to connect with old friends! While not beta readers, I do have to give additional thanks to Casey Murphy and Deanna Roussin who both acted as cheerleaders and kept me going.

To my favorite coffeeshops in El Segundo and in Redmond: Blue Butterfly, SoulFood, and Five Stones, for keeping me caffeinated. To my psychiatrist and therapist for keeping me medicated. To all of my other specialists, thank your for keeping my body functional. Both coffee and meds help get me out of bed every morning so I can write.

To my eighth-grade teacher, who asked my mom every time they ran into each other if I was a writer or not: it took some time, but now I am!

This novel was written on the ancestral land of the Coast Salish peoples (in the Pacific Northwest) and Tongva people (in Los Angeles). I acknowledge their rights to this land as the original stewards and caretakers.

Finally, thank you to my family. To my parents and in-laws for their support, even if I might have to tell you to skip some pages or chapters or stories entirely. Sorry about that.

To my grandmother, from whom I inherited a love of romance novels. Mamma, this one has a discreet cover so you don't need use your fabric cover to hide what you're reading.

To my sister, whose own publishing journey lit a fire under my butt to just do it already, and my own littles, Oliver and Cameron. I'm so proud to be your aunt.

To Zoe, the world's laziest husky and my lovebug, who gives me a reason to go for a walk and see the sunshine every day. She reminds me when I've been sitting too long or when it's time for dinner. So much of Sadie comes shamelessly from Zoe.

Lastly, to Christian. This truly wouldn't have been possible without you. Thank you for making my dreams come true on a daily basis. You give me the inspiration I need to write love stories. That you look damn sexy doing it is just the cherry on top. Forever and always.

XO,
Kay

By Kay Zempel

Magic Revealed
The Blood Pack Books
Moon Dance

Dance Me to the End (Blog Serial)

The Towers
The Dark Beside You (Newsletter Exclusive)

About the Author

Kay Zempel writes paranormal romance, fantasy romance, and erotic fantasy. *Moon Dance* is her debut novel. Kay is a former academic, educator, and technical writer, but she remains a world-builder at heart. A Southern California native, she now lives in the Pacific Northwest with her dog and husband. They are living out their own happy ever after.